# Overtaken

Midnight Airos

By: Tiana Erin Williams

winkypublishing@yahoo.com

ISBN 978-0692718896

# TABLE OF CONTENTS

## INTRODUCTION

People Say that fate is set in stone; sealed in the cold surfaces of events and circumstances.  I believe that it is up to us to fulfill our destiny.  A destiny that benefits us and the lives of others.  Instead of a sealed fate, I believe fate is simply etched on the sandy shores of life.  When the waves of opposition arise, if allowed, fate rendered can be...Overtaken.

# CHAPTER 1

## MY STORY: SCARLET LANSING

My name is Scarlet Annalise Lansing. As a twenty-five year old literacy graduate student, my life surprisingly has been interesting. I was raised in the small town of Rainy Ridge, Kentucky never knowing my mother. She died when I was only a year old. My dad was all I had.

As I grew up, it was apparent to me that my father truly wanted a son. He always invited me to watch football games with him, bought clothes that were more masculine than feminine, and constantly tried to teach me self-defense techniques. Every time I looked into his eyes, I could sense his disappointment.

Don't get me wrong, my dad was great to me. He always told me that there would never be a boy good enough for me, and he never ceased to tell me that I was beautiful and smart like my late mother. I would be his little girl forever. Even though he loved me dearly, he still wanted a son.

There was a high school that my father had gone to in Los Angeles, California called Audren Academy. Audren was established in 1689 but it's reputation was still impressive. Before I was born, my dad had decided that I would also attend this high school.

There is something else about Audren Academy that may be of some interest to you. It is an all-boys academy. Don't worry; I am really a girl. You see, in my family, every child that has ever been born has been a boy. It has been that way for some time. The family name of Lansing began four hundred years ago with David Lansing, all boys, until I was born.

With only males in our family, each father would automatically enroll, their soon-to-be born sons to Audren Academy. When my dad found out my mother was pregnant, he followed suit to tradition. Before I was born I was enrolled; it was assumed that I would also be a male child.

All enrollments are final and one must remain at the academy through their senior year. However, with my father being such a compassionate man, he decided that once I was old enough, I could decide whether I wanted to attend or not. When questioned about attending Audren, I would always smile and tell him I wanted to attend. One summer, when I was twelve years old, he repeatedly told me, "Scarlet, do not do this because you think it is what I want. I want you to be happy."

I ignored his words. I wanted to please him and I believed attending the academy was the perfect way to do it. I am glad I did because he died 3 weeks later in a car accident. Yes, I was able to make my dad happy. It has been thirteen years, but I still miss him very much.

As an orphan, my aunt Danielle in Rainy Ridge took me in. As for my mother, I can barely remember her, but my dad talked about her all the time. He said she was a beautiful, kind, and sensitive woman that loved me more than life itself. He told me that she was the one that gave me my favorite locket. I wear it every day. Whenever it is opened it plays a beautiful tune. My dad told me it was the lullaby she used to sing to me called "Midnight Airos" which means "Midnight Flower".

When I was about six years old, I told my dad about the strange dreams I had. I was in a woman's arms as she sang the same lullaby played from my locket. I could never see the woman's face, but I knew that she was smiling. The dream would get more and more vivid every time I had it, but I still could not see her face. It feels almost like a memory instead of a dream. My father always told me it was my mother in the dream. Even though I knew he may have been right, it irritated me that I had no true memories of her.

In spite of the death of both of my parents, my life went as smooth as could be expected and I can say that I was able to maintain some form of contentment. Then, during my last year at Audren Academy, my life changed.

I, Scarlet, have a secret that I have concealed in my heart for years now. In my senior year of high school, twelve days before graduation, something happened that I have never shared with anyone. As I relive the memories, I realize that I will have to take my time telling you everything...exactly as it happened. As I unravel my story that has never been told, I give you my word, that after hearing it, life as you know it will never be the same.

# CHAPTER 2

## BORDOM

Today is Tuesday, the most boring day of the week. In a weird way, it's kind of depressing. I mean, it's just a school day. A long rainy day and nothing exciting is happening. Most people would say living in Los Angeles is something to be desired. Not me. Walking the beaches, listening to the screech of the seagulls fluttering about, and watching people swim and tan has been my life for the past four years. After a while, doing the same thing over and over again gets dull.

Everyone around here thinks I am the type of person that is content living a normal, structured life; and for a while that was true. I am normally a home-body, and I never really got into the dating scene. I hear all the time that I am "such a nice and pretty girl", but I never really go for anyone around here. All the dates I have ever been on were pretty boring and most of the time I went because I didn't want to hurt the guy's feelings.

I have always cared about my appearance though. Light brown hair and green eyes, most people say that it is a good combination. I keep up with the styles and trends, but I always believed in adding my own style to whatever I wear. I am notoriously known for being relatively short. At 5-feet 2-inches, I have been petite my whole life. No matter what I eat, I never gain weight.

But something just doesn't seem right. For the past few weeks, all I want is ADVENTURE! I don't mean like going to the jungle and fighting tigers, or almost drowning in quick sand. I mean something exciting. A once in a life time experience! Sadly, I know that will never happen...at least not in this life time.

Thank God, it's finally last period. The best part of the day, (besides lunch) but it is also the worst part. History class; my least favorite subject and the most boring teacher in all of Audren teaches it. Mrs. Burns. Just hearing her name makes me want to yawn. She has to be at least 80 years old. Her thin hair is stained grey, and her glasses look like they came straight from the 70's. She couldn't even hear a bull-horn blown two inches from her ear.

Right now, I probably should be listening to the lesson that is being taught, but I never do. When I actually *do* listen, she never stays on topic. She always starts rambling on about global warming or something (yawn).

Looking around the room, I can see no one else is paying attention to Mrs. Burns either. People are passing notes, shooting spit balls, and the all-time favorite...sleeping; the same scene every day. As I peer around the class room, all I can see are boys, boys, and more boys.

I looked out the window for a change in scenery. Outside, I could see nothing but traffic and numerous people walking the sidewalks in the rain. The sound of busy streets, honking horns and the roar of the rain filled the air. The dreary, gray overcast was thick and blanketing the sun. I could only imagine how cool the outside world was. All I have ever known was my sheltered world away from all society. The only thing I could rely on for a taste of the real world is music videos and reality shows. The kids here aren't exactly angels, but I wish I went to a public school.

Since my father died, my aunt Danielle has been my legal guardian. She loves me to death. But sometimes she can be a little over protective. She lives in my hometown of Rainy Ridge, Kentucky. She always calls, or direct messages me through texts or some other form of social media. She always wants to make sure everything is okay. Even though she lives miles away, every step I take she knows about it.

Living in these stuffy dormitories is not what I would call cool either. But I must admit I do get a little homesick. The only time Audren allows you to visit home is Christmas and Thanksgiving. But now, it's the end of the school year and we have a little less than two weeks before graduation. Right now, graduating is the only thing I can think about.

I glanced at the clock above the board. *Almost 3:00PM*, I thought. School will be over in a matter of seconds. I should at least listen to the conclusion of the lesson. I don't even know what Mrs. Burns is talking about?

"So that is why the ancient Mayans are still highly noted today. If you take a look at page 345, you can see the lovely jewelry of the women during-"... the bell rings. The sound was earsplitting. That had to be the most obnoxious, deafening school bell ever made, but it was the only thing that could save me from Mrs. Burns, so I was thankful. But, as usual she continued teaching. She didn't hear the bell.

I spoke up. "Ms. Burns, the bell just rang," I informed.

She lifted one palm to her ear. "What did you say dear?" she shouted in her shaky little voice.

"I said class is over!" I shouted matching her volume politely as possible.

"Oh, you young people these days are always mumbling. Okay, class; that concludes our lesson for today. I want you to take notes on section four for homework. We will go over them tomorrow and review for the exam tomorrow first thing!" said Mrs. Burns as she erased the board. She continued muttering something, but it was too low to hear.

The day was finally over! I wasted no time as I darted towards the door. I squeezed between many of my classmates and into the hall that was flooded with boys. I shoved my history book into my crowded bag as I made my way to my locker.

All I could think of was getting back to my dorm and away from the various shouts and ruckus. Then I remembered; the only thing waiting for me there was paper work, text books, and worst of all...late and still blank college applications. Exams were almost here and I hadn't hit the books in ages. I must admit, I specialize in procrastination but for some reason my grades are outstanding. My thoughts were interrupted.

Matt ran up to me from down the hall. "Hey, Scarlet! Dude, that science test was a killer!" he sighed. "I know I failed, but at least I'm pulling a D+ for the report cards!" His puppy dog brown eyes glowed as he spoke. Though Matt was only my friend, he is good looking. He has dirty blonde hair that hangs a bit below his eyebrows.

Ryan came behind him. Ryan was a lot taller than Matt and I. He stood about 6 feet, 2 inches. His hair was a deep chocolate brown that was just an inch longer than Matt's. His eyes were a dark blue. He was good looking as well. "Are you kidding me? That test was so easy; you couldn't fail it even if you wanted to. All you had to do was analyze the monocular nomenclature of the ectoplasm-"

I interrupted him placing one finger on his lips. "Ryan please quit with the smart people talk for once. We all know you get this stuff, okay?" I said with a hint of irritation. I pried the locker door open and grabbed some books stuffing them into my now, overflowing bag. I quickly applied my new, strawberry flavored lip gloss that Aunt Danielle sent me. I winked at my reflection in my locker mirror before closing the door.

"It's okay," I started, "I've just had a lot on my mind lately, with exams and stuff," I put my arms around both of them as we walked. "You know I love both of you guys," I gave them both a kiss on the cheek. They were my best friends at Audren.

Matt interrupted, "Jeez, Scarlet, why do girls primp all the time?" he said disapprovingly, he had eyed the many accessories in my locker.

"Seriously," Ryan agreed in the same tone. "You guys always look in the mirror putting on eyeliner, lip gloss, and only God knows what else. It's like you guys are putting on a new face" He then looked down, "It's kind of creepy," he murmured.

I raised one eyebrow at that last comment. "Because," I said as I ran my brush through my hair. "These uniforms do me no justice," I said with a smile. "We actually try to look good for you dumb boys," I teased.

"If guys are so dumb, why waste your time on us?" he snorted, examining a ribbon I had taken out of my hair.

"I don't know, I guess that's just the way it works", I said as I shrugged my shoulders playfully.

"Well, I guess I won't complain," said Matt as he zipped up his jacket. "If girls want to look hot for me, I won't stop them. I would never judge a girl in a mini skirt. Less is more right?"

"You're sick," I teased.

"How am I sick? I know Ryan was thinking the exact same thing—maybe worse," he laughed.

Ryan began to blush. "Shut up, Matt."

"Dude, you're not even denying it!" I shouted as Matt and I laughed harder than before.

Just then, Adam Rithwood came trotting up to me. He is the captain of the football team, and was pretty cute. He's Italian, so his hair is very dark. He has a buzzed haircut and his eyes are a piercing auburn. He's interested in me, but he is not really my type. He is rude, a huge bully, and a womanizing machine that runs on watch batteries. Fortunately for him, I am not the type of girl to be rude to anyone, so I went ahead and spoke to him.

"Hey Adam, what's up?

"Hey, Scar, you look pretty today," he said as he kissed my hand. His way to wet lips almost made me bring up my lunch.

"Um...thanks Adam," I forced hoping my disgust wasn't obvious.

Matt immediately jumped in on my behalf. "Listen Buddy, give it a rest! She is obviously not interested and she never will be, so just back off." He crossed his arms staring Adam dead in the eye. If only he knew exactly how feeble he sounded just then.

Adam began to laugh. "Look what we've got here; a boyfriend wanna-be. Alright man, you talk big, let's see what you're made of." he said as he grabbed Matt by the collar. I could see a conniving glimpse in his eyes.

Now Matt has plenty of will power, but in physical strength, well, let's just say he sort of lacks. Matt was a taller than me, but his lanky physique didn't look too intimidating. Adam was a big guy. His muscles bulged from his shirt without even flexing. The kind of guy you *never* want to look at wrong. I could tell this was getting bad. So much for getting back to the dorm room on time.

# CHAPTER 3

## HEARING VOICES

"Adam, please stop. It's not worth it, okay?" I said in an effort to protect Matt, though my tone of voice was more irksome than anything.

All Adam did was give me a look that said, "Okay, but next time will be different." He let go of Matt's collar roughly, causing him to fall to the ground.

Matt capered up almost instantly, smugly dusting himself off and fixing his collar.

"Well," Adam started, facing me now. "I guess I should tell you the real reason I came over here, Scarlet," he said as he held both of my hands in his, which were pretty clammy.

I avoided his eye contact and tried to think of a quick excuse so I could hopefully avoid whatever was coming next. "Can this wait, because exams are coming up and I really need to-"

"I have waited too long for this. I mean, you can agree that we are pretty good friends, right?" He said nodding in a hopeful voice raising his eyebrows.

I hesitated before releasing the words. "To be honest, not really," I tried to be as nice as I could.

"Well, forget I said that," he said as he shook his head. "I was just wondering if you want to...go out some time. Maybe like to the movies or to the eatery?"

I shot a glance at him then to Ryan and Matt. They were both mouthing the word no. "I don't think I have time to-"

"And there you have it Adam, *she* doesn't want to go out with *you*," Matt butted in once again with just as much feebleness as before.

Adam glared at me menacingly.

"Whatever," he said coldly as he walked away pushing his way through the crowd...literally.

"Jeez, Matt, do you *always* have to act so immature?" asked Ryan with a glare of disapproval. "It's embarrassing."

"Whatever. I was just trying to help Scarlet, while you stood there and did nothing," Matt protested. "Plus, that guy had it coming to him."

I sighed. "Well, all I know is, I gotta study for that history exam. I'll probably end up pulling another all-nighter again." I grimaced at the thought.

"Scarlet, you really need to start getting some rest. You've fallen asleep in almost every class since last Tuesday," said Ryan, being the most responsible one out of us all...as usual.

"Yeah, I know," I sighed. "But once exams are over, it will get a lot better," I assured.

"Well if you ask me, who needs school anyway? To me, it's just a big waste of time. I mean really, you tell me when I'm gonna need to know the formula to find the circumference of a circle," said Matt as he folded his arms.

"Well, personally, no one asked you. Don't fill Scarlet's head with stupid stuff like that. School is definitely important. Our parents don't send us here just to waste our time and their hard earned money," Ryan scolded.

"What do you know anyway, Ryan?" Matt snapped.

Ryan chuckled, "A lot more than you do," he said under his breath.

"Alright, alright, we get it," I said as I slung my book bag over my shoulder. "Maybe we should stop at the plaza today."

The plaza was our hangout in the very back of the school. As we walked over, I thought about how fortunate we are to have the plaza. It is our campus strip mall. It is the only place where students can buy clothes and supplies for school. We used to go there more in the beginning of the year but we hadn't gone since last semester. I figured we could all use a break. I pointed forwards. "Guys, let's go to the fountain."

My favorite spot, by far, was the Audren Academy Fountain. Made of pure marble, it sat in the center of the plaza. The fountain was built about 200 years ago. The school tradition was to make a wish twice a year. They say if you make a wish on this fountain, your wish will come true. There is one rule though; you can't ever tell a soul what you wished for.

"This will be one of the last times we will get to see this old thing," Matt said as he kicked its base lightly.

"Yeah, and soon we will all be going to different schools," said Ryan with a morose sigh. It was true. Soon I would be going back home in Kentucky for a few months with my aunt before starting college in the fall. Ryan will be returning home to Texas and go to school there. Even Matt will be going to a creative arts school in Ohio where his family lives.

One bad thing about Audren Academy is that all the kids come from all over the country to go to school here; then, when graduation comes around, friends separate.

Everyone was quiet for a moment. I could tell we were all thinking the same thing. None of us were pretty excited about leaving each other. I finally spoke up. "Well we still have cell phones, and we can still see and talk to each other through social media." I said coloring my tone with optimism.

"Yeah..." they both said dryly. We all knew it wouldn't be the same.

"Well, here we are at the fountain, all three of us for one of the very last times. So we have to promise each other that we will be best friends until the end...no matter how far away we are from each other. I'm confident that everything will be fine."

"I promise, Scarlet," said Ryan.

"Yeah, I promise, too," said Matt. "But I am gonna miss this place," he admitted with a sigh.

"Now we're all together," I said in a higher tone. I desperately needed to lighten the mood. "I don't want to focus on the future. What matters is that we are with each other now. We should just be happy and wish on the fountain like always." I stared at them silently.    Their faces seemed to lighten up just a little. I gave both of them a hug. The sad thing is that this will be one of the last times I will have to hug my two best friends.

Everyone grabbed a quarter and tossed it in. I was sure we all wished for the same thing: *for us all to stay together.*

I wished long and hard even though I knew just one little fountain can't stop us from moving on to different places in life. After a while, we were done. I looked at them, they looked at me. Leaving a friend is one of the worse things that can happen.

I felt a drop of rain on my head. It has been raining on and off all day...just another dreary thing to add to this Tuesday. I felt another drop. One after another I felt the rain against my warm skin.

"We should probably head back before our books get all wet," Ryan suggested lifting his gaze towards the sky.

We all agreed. Then suddenly, without warning, the rain crashed on the ground heavily. The mad dash to the dorm hall was silent. Many thoughts filled the air as the rain poured violently.

Finally we arrived at our dorm hall. Kids were running and playing as always. Our dorm advisor is never here, so our hall is always hectic. Looking at everyone, I realized that I will miss them all. I breathed in the warm air in the hallway. I was certainly glad to be back.

"Hey, Scarlet," it was Carter from a few doors down.

"Hey, what's up?" I asked as Ryan and Matt greeted him.

"This is your last chance to get pictures in the yearbook. Mr. Patel wants the senior classmen to have an extra page in the back. Can I get one of you all?" He asked pointing to his camera and looking at all three of us.

"Sure thing," Ryan agreed.

"Yeah, that seems cool," Matt said approvingly.

"Okay, just smile big," he said lifting the camera to his right eye. After focusing it, he instructed us to move in closer together. "Alright, on three," he said.

The flash almost blinded me. I was sure to smile that fake, all too wide smile that everyone does for yearbook photos. Yearbooks were meant to remind you of some of the best years of your life. It makes you remember all old friends, teachers, and sports. I think I looked pretty good for the photo; but I am pretty sure either Matt or Ryan photo bombed the shot with bunny ears behind my head.

"Okay, thanks guys," Carter said as he peered at the screen reviewing the photo. "Alright, looking good, guys." He gave a thumbs-up. "Well, thanks again. See you in stats tomorrow, Scarlet." He then disappeared into the mob of teenagers loitering in the halls.

"Dude, I think I accidently closed my eyes at the last second," said Matt in a pitiful tone.

"Don't worry about it.  He said it looked good," replied Ryan as he grabbed my book bag and his from the ground. "I'm just glad that I have an extra picture in the year book."

"I think I looked okay," I replied after thanking Ryan for picking up my bag. "That will be my eighth picture in the whole yearbook!"

"I don't care how many I have, just as long as some lovely ladies from Braddock take a gander at it," said Matt accompanied with a chuckle.

I had forgotten about last week's prom.  The all-boys academy and the all-girls academy of Braddock came.  The boys definitely took their chance to mingle with the girls they had been deprived of.  They will be combining again for the end of the year trip on the last day of school.

Suddenly, Ryan began to tell us a story of a girl he had met at prom.  My mind was still wandering on other things.  I was dreading all the homework that was waiting on me...unfinished.

As we continued to slowly walk to our room, it hit me, like a baseball bolting to my forehead. *Room 74.*

Room 74 was an old abandoned dorm that has been condemned since 1978.  Everyone says that Room 74 is haunted, and that some guy died in it back in the 60's.  I'm not very superstitious, but I will be the first to admit, that place gave me chills just by looking at it.

I see this room every single day, and every time I do, it gives me a very uneasy feeling.  My stomach would always fill with butterflies that tormented my mood every time.  As we made our way down the hall, I couldn't help but casually gaze upon it.  All I wanted to do was look away, but my eyes would not obey.  We were just about to pass it when I heard a low voice come from the room.

"Scarlet," the voice called.

I stopped dead in my tracks. A cold chill ran down my spine, which left my body immobilized. I shifted my gaze over to Matt and Ryan. They were both still talking as if they had not heard the voice at all. It seemed that I was the only one that had heard it.

"So then I was like, 'Well, I like you, too. Can I have your number? Then she was like, 'I have a boyfriend, I don't think he would like that,' and then I—Scarlet, are you even listening?" asked Ryan, noticing my inattentive gaze.

"Did you guys hear that?" I asked trying not to sound too frightened. I needed to know if I was actually hearing voices—that wouldn't be a good sign. I could feel my heart collapse. They both exchanged looks and then peered at me in bewilderment.

"Did you not just hear someone say my name from Room 74?" I asked them once more.

"Well I didn't hear anything." Replied Matt.

"Yeah, me neither. Are you okay Scar? You look like you just saw a ghost," said Ryan looking concerned.

I cringed. I gaped back at the door. "Uh...its nothing, I'm...I'm just tired I guess," I insisted without taking my eyes off the dorm.

But I wasn't tired at all. I just didn't want my friends to think I was crazy. I have to admit that a voice calling my name from a dorm room that has been abandoned for **years** is a little farfetched. But I knew what I heard was not my imagination. It was all too clear to be only in my mind. What I heard was real.

# CHAPTER 4

## CURIOSITY

I tried to forget about the incident that took place earlier. I tried so hard to focus on my worksheets, but that dorm was all I could think about. I had been studying for countless hours, but I haven't learned a thing. I looked at my cell phone to get the time. 2:09 AM; I glanced over at Matt and Ryan. They must have been asleep for a long time.

I stood to my feet and put away my books. I was still in my school uniform, but I didn't feel like changing. I sighed as I glimpsed at my still late blank college applications. I printed them months ago from the internet hoping that seeing the questions would motivate me to complete them. I picked up one sheet and held it up to the light emanating from my small side table lamp.

"How would you describe yourself as a student?"

It was a simple question, but I wasn't nearly in the mood. Without care, I flung the sheet of paper back on the bed. I decided to grab my laptop and place it on my folded legs as I sat lazily in the bed under the sheets.

I must admit that I am normally a social media junky. Just as I pulled up the internet, I remembered how late it actually was. No reason to be online at this hour. Still, I signed into my e-mail account, determined to use anything as an excuse for not studying.

I wasn't surprised to see a message from my aunt Danielle. It was sent only a few hours ago. I really did love talking to her. Although she is a little over protective. She is thirty-six and married, but doesn't have any kids. She was pregnant once, but she had a miscarriage. I have been with her since I was twelve. I am like a daughter to her.

I clicked on the mail with the subject entitled, "We miss you babe!"

Hey, Scarlet! We have missed you so much over here! Well, I just wanted to check on you since I haven't called in a while. How have you been? I know you are really busy now with studying and whatever. Your uncle Dan got himself hurt at the factory the other day. Nothing serious; he just sprained his ankle; that old klutz, ha. Anyway, how was prom? I just got your pictures in the mail, and your date was so handsome! You looked absolutely stunning in that blue dress! I told you that one would look great! Oh and how are those friends of yours, Matt and Ryan? By the way, I need you to review your list and pick your top three college choices by next week, we can still meet the deadline for fall admissions. I hope you are filling out some of those applications.

I love you.

-Danielle

It made me smile to see her obviously doing well. I couldn't say the same about her reference to college choices. I didn't think she realized that this kind of stuff takes time. But it was nice to hear from her at least.

Hey, it's great to hear from you. I'm doing just fine. You were right about me being so busy. I have exams this week and next week so I have been studying like crazy. Prom was fun, too. Conner, my "date", as you would say, was just a friend of mine from English. But yeah, it was fun. Matt and Ryan are the same as always. I think that final graduation might be getting to them though. I think we all don't want to leave each other. Oh! I almost forgot! The graduation ceremony is on the 5th and it starts at 7PM. Can't wait to see you guys again! By the way, tell Uncle Dan to be more careful...if he can...lol.

-Scarlet

I pushed my computer to the foot of the bed. I scanned my mind for anything to do, but I realized that there was nothing. I laid back on my bed and looked at the ceiling fan as it slowly circulated around and around.  I could hear the rain crashing on the roof outside.  The breeze from the window brushed against my cheeks with small drops, too.  As I stood up to close it, my mind reflected back to Room 74.  No matter how much I tried to think of other things, the thought kept returning to me.  I decided to turn on the small television set on the other end of the tiny room.  I grabbed the remote and turned on the TV.  Old music videos; Ryan was watching something on it earlier.  I turned to the next channel.  It was some unfamiliar movie.  I turned to the next channel.  An old sci-fi show or something; definitely not catching my interest.  Channel after channel, mindless shows, nothing kept my interest.

I was just about to give up on TV for the night until I turned the channel to what seemed to be an interview with a middle-aged man.  He was dressed in a black suit and a button down white shirt with no tie.  His face was hard, and I could not read his expression.  The woman interviewing him, a blonde, was welcoming back the show from a commercial break.  It appeared to be a talk show.  I wasn't familiar with it though.

"Alright, we are back with Troy Collins!"  The audience greeted him with a warm round of applause.

"Now before the break, you were telling us about your new book, *Seeing the Unseen.*"  The host was holding the book up for the camera.  "Now Troy, what does this book really talk about?  The name is enough to send a reader buying it without a second thought," she said while placing the book back on a side table next to her.

"Basically, in this book, I am talking about numerous ways to face things that you are unsure of.  More and more instances in America today have occurred with things we, as humans, just cannot explain.  In my book, I want to challenge you to seek out what you are questioning.  Things are happening all around us that many are oblivious to; some things are of course unseen."  He coughed for a few seconds before continuing.  "I have had my fair share of unnatural experiences in my life; I talk about them in the book. I don't want anyone to be afraid to scavenger into things that they don't understand." His voice was very gruff and difficult to understand. I could tell he had never done anything so public before.

"Wow, Troy, that is amazing," said the host as she casually took a sip of her drink in a pink mug. The audience began to applaud again. "So you all know what that means," she said with the camera closing up on her. Her wrinkles were more visible now and her blonde hair looked more unnatural than before. "If anyone here or watching at home has experienced something weird or unusual lately, don't be afraid; uncover a new adventure!" her voice rasped with the enthusiasm that was obviously untrue. "Okay, now we can accept callers that have any questions for Troy." She then speedily stated the telephone number. At the bottom of the screen was a warning that said, *previously recorded.*

I turned off the television. I grimaced. I knew the only way I could get this off my mind would be to go check it out. I wasn't going to tell Matt and Ryan what I was doing. They would think I was insane for sure. I glanced at them again. They were deep in sleep. I took this chance and grabbed a jacket from my side of the closet. I was sure to be as quiet and discrete as possible. I slid on some shoes and made my way to the door. I turned the knob slowly. Despite my efforts, it made a loud, obnoxious creek.

This made Matt stir. He stat up drowsily rubbing his eyes and yawned. He squinted in my direction.

"What's the matter, Scar? You look like you're going somewhere," his voice cracked.

I had to think fast. "I'm...uh...I'm gonna check on the chickens?" I cupped my forehead in my palm almost instantly. I couldn't believe what I had just said.

"Dude, we got chickens? Sweet," he said with a sleepy grin.

"Yeah, they are about to…uh…lay some eggs so…I gotta go get them." I said

He yawned again. "Whatever, just turn out that light on your way out, will ya?" With that, he laid back down and placed a pillow over his head. With a few more squirms, I heard his loud snore, which, at that time, seemed like music to my ears. I slowly turned off the lights, and stepped out the barely opened door. I could breathe again.

The hall was barely lit, making it difficult to navigate my footsteps. I started down the hall, slowly. My heart started to pound as I stepped closer and closer to room 74. I had barely made it half way there, when the urge to turn back bombarded me. But I was determined not to give in that easily. The silence of my surroundings wasn't comforting. The hall felt so…so cold. It seemed as though the floor boards squeak more eerily at night. But I could barely hear it over the beat of my racing heart.

I sped up my walk unwillingly. The air felt thin…it was harder to breathe. Chills ran through every vein in my body. Walking felt almost impossible as a flurry of emotions began to stir within me. But before I knew it, there it was. Room 74 was right in front of me. It looked twice as creepy in the dark. I knew I would have to open the door. Loathsomely, I slowly placed my hand on the cold, rusted door knob. I glanced behind me to make sure no one was there.

I shifted my gaze back to the door. I sucked in a deep breath, to circulate within my lungs. My only hope was for it to be locked. At least then I could say I tried. I slowly turned knob and pushed the door forwards.

With a click, the door unlatched. I felt a shiver round down my spine. When I opened the door, there was a blinding light coming from the inside. The light was white, but the shine was so bright that I could barely open my eyes. I stood there in amazement with my arms shielding most of the light from my now burning pupils. I knew this was something not of this world.

Then, a mysterious breeze drew me in the doorway gently. This just didn't seem right. I tried to back away and close the door, but the wind became stronger and repelled my efforts as if it had a mind of its own. I was using all my strength in an attempt to close the door back. The wind picked up in power. The pictures on the wall began to shake as if it were an earthquake. It became even more difficult for me to keep my eyes open.

I felt my feet slowly start to elevate off the ground. I quickly grabbed the door frame; but, half of my body was in the door already. I wanted to cry out, but I could not utter a sound. The breath had been removed from my lungs. My silent cries remained unheard. With one more gust of wind, the door frame, on which I was holding on to, broke away from the wall. In a matter of seconds, I was plummeted beyond the doorway.

# CHAPTER 5

## SOUL TIES

I woke up with excruciating pain on the back of my neck. I noticed it was especially warm. With a groan from the pain, I slowly opened my eyes. I was astonished at what I saw—almost forgetting the pain. Not long ago, I was in the dorm hall, but here I am now, on a beach. I looked around and saw sand and water. In the front of me, nothing. Behind me, nothing. I was the only one on the beach. I saw no one.

I closed my eyes tight and concluded that this was all a dream. I thought I could wake myself up. But I knew this was reality; the sound of the crashing waves and the smell of salt water were pretty convincing. The air of the day was fresh. My mind could never conjure up such a realistic illusion. I still did not want to admit it, but this was not a dream.

I have no idea where I am or how to get back. I don't even know how I got here. Thoughts such as, "Would I ever get back home? Would I ever see my friends again? Am I dead? Am I crazy?" scrolled relentlessly across my mind. Warm tears began to stream down my cheeks.

I lay on the sun kissed sand. The heat of the day lighted upon my small form. Just then, my heart pulsated violently causing me to sit up. As I wiped away beads of sweat, I noticed a figure in the distance. I blocked the sun with my hand and squinted to get a better look. It appeared to be a boy coming towards me. His speed was tremendously fast. I immediately stood up and could see the boy looked about my age. I wanted to run, but for some reason my body simply did not allow it.

In a matter of seconds, a boy was standing in front of me; he seemed to be in a rush. He was at least five inches taller than me. He had deep black hair with smoky, dark eyes. His face reminded me of an angel.

28

His expression was firm.

"Come with me," said the boy as he took my hand and began to run.

I pulled my hand away from him. "Who are you?" I demanded.

He rolled his eyes slightly at my resistance.

"I am sorry but your questions must wait. We need to hurry, Scarlet," he said taking my hand again.

I pulled my hand away once more, angry now. "How do you know my-"

Before I could finish, he dashed in front of me. He kneeled down on one knee with his back to me. Sparkles, that seemed to come out of the air, swirled around him. Then, the sparkles seemed to form two odd celestial shapes on his back. The sparkles turned into two wings. I had never seen such beautiful, majestic wings before. They were white like that of an angel and they shimmered in the sunlight.

"Get on if you wish to live," he said pointing to his back. His tone wasn't very inviting.

I stood there for a moment, awestruck as I peered upon this cosmic view. The marvelous shimmer of each wing was truly captivating.

I did as I was told. I had no clue where I was, so I figured I should start separating friends from enemies now. As soon as I mounted on, he darted off the ground. "Hold on tight!" he shouted above the breeze. His voice was arthritic, and, in a strange way, smooth.

I grabbed the large feathers tight as we zoomed into the air. I looked down to see that the ground was no longer visible. The wind blew against my face causing my hair to ripple against the breeze freely.

But within minutes, we started to go lower and lower to prepare for landing. We gently glided to the ground. We were in an open valley with the brownest, dead grass I had ever seen. I quickly got off of his back. I watched as the wings quickly disappeared into sporadic shimmers and sparkles.

Almost stumbling over my own feet, I wasted no time. He seemed to be recuperating from the landing, but I didn't care. "Okay, now give me some answers!" I demanded.

"Alright, what do you wish to know?" he said in a calm tone. My guess was that he tried to keep me calm as well.

"Well...everything! Like, for starters," I said holding up one finger. "Who are you?"

"Tamaku, Master of the Air and Airos Pipe," he murmured.

"Okay, then, Mr. Tamaku, where on earth am I?"

"Well, I wouldn't exactly call it earth. It's also a very long story, and I think it would be best if—"

"Tell me," I insisted disregarding his excuses.

"As you wish," he relinquished taking in a deep breath. "Right now you are in a realm called Audren."

I thought for a moment. "Wait, that's the name of my school, and it's not a different realm," I said in disbelief.

"Yes, I will get to that shortly, just bear with me," he said, annoyed. He seemed as though he was trying to deal with my utter rudeness. "As I was saying, you are in a completely different realm than the one you live in. Audren is almost like a different world, if that is easier for you to understand. It is full of people and creatures that surpass anything you have ever encountered, I'm sure. It may not seem like much now, but Audren was once a beautiful and prosperous place," he gazed around the valley pausing for a moment as if reflecting on something. "It was filled with joy, laughter, and many smiles. We even had a king named Taress Diomatrico. He was very kind and loved this land and its people. He was always willing to give his life and everything he owned for Audren." He looked like he was going to say more, but fell lost in his own thoughts.

"So what happened?" I asked registering his story. He seemed to come back to reality. He then casted his gaze in every direction. Without warning, he took my hand and led me under a tree nearby.

"I apologize," he started eyeing our surroundings once more. "It is not safe to talk about this out in the open." He started again, "You see, King Taress had an advisor. *His name is Taurid.*

"You see, everyone in Audren has a special power they contain, like my flying as you just witnessed. Some people even have more than one. The powers vary from person to person and in levels of strength. Taurid had immense powers, but kept a large portion of them hidden from the king. He did many evil practices to better his powers in secret. One of these practices was to grant himself immortality. These practices did, indeed, grant him his wishes.

"They say that in his 6$^{th}$ year of service, he stopped growing older. The king soon noticed this and the palace started getting suspicious. One day, the king confronted Taurid. To suppress suspicion from the public, Taurid viciously murdered the king to keep his secret. But once the king was dead, he took other precautions..." He paused for a moment. I waited attentively.

"He declared himself the dictator of the Audren realm. Now that is just the story that most people believe. No one really knows for sure what happened all those years ago."

31

"So you're saying it probably didn't happen that way?" I asked.

"Maybe, maybe not; I believe so, but I could never be sure. But now all of our people are forced to serve him and obey all his rules to the full extent. He has put us in such fear, that the mere mention of his name is bone chilling. He has killed so many people; men, women, and children alike. He has ruled for more than 400 years. Since I was not alive back then, I do not know all the details; all I have is legend. But, it is said, that he has not aged a day since then either. His appearance is of his early 30's. Many people have tried to revolt against him, but no one to this day has ever come close to defeating him," he clenched his fist in anger. The calmness of his voice had altered to lividness.

"How do I play a role in this?" I asked hoping that the answer would not be frightening to me. This Tamaku character was definitely a good story-teller. His tale put me on edge.

"Here is the part that may shock you," said Tamaku as he locked his eyes with my own.

I sighed, "I thought so."

"Well it's like this; about the same time Taurid took over, a boy that was about your age arrived here. He went by the name of David Lansing. He came through the portal just as you did," he informed.

*David Lansing...David Lansing...*That was my father's great, great, great, great, grandfather or something like that. David was said to be insane telling stories about a different world with highly developed society and weapons. I then put two and two together. He wasn't crazy at all.

He analyzed my expression. "So you have, indeed, heard of the man that started this cycle?" asked Tamaku.

"This is all too weird," I protested shaking my head. "You mean to tell me a family member, one of my ancestors came here?"

"Yes. The Lansing family is very special. You see, in every generation of your family there is one person with special powers just as the people here in Audren. David Lansing was the first to contain these special powers. He was the first to start this cycle. However, David, Aaron, and Mikhail Lansing have made it here too. Do you understand so far?" he asked.

My mind was spinning. This had to be true. Those were indeed the names of my ancestors.

"I think so."

"There is more you should know. Only the first born child in each generation receives the powers. We like to call these special people 'Varcia'. Normal humans cannot enter this realm. Only a Varcia may enter, for they have powers like Aurdrenians. I don't know why, but only people in the Lansing family can be a Varcia. No normal human can enter this realm due to lack of spirit energy. However, we do have Varcia for a very important purpose," his eyes penetrated mine.

"Varcia have abilities that surpass any Audrenian. For some reason, their powers are stronger, and their moves are quicker. That is why we need Varcia, for they are the only people that can finally free us from Taurid. That is why you are here. *You are the last Varcia,* you are the last of the Lansing family to ever be able to contain powers. This is why you are our last string of hope. If you do not defeat Taurid, then no one can." He still held the same, solemn gaze.

"No! This is all wrong. You guys must have gotten the wrong person," I stammered.

"Like I told you, no normal human is able to enter here. If you were the wrong person, you would not have been able to pass through the portal.  Only a Varcia can pass." His eyebrows knit together from my repetitive arguing.  He was getting aggravated, but I could care less.

"Well, I'm sorry, Mr. Tamaku, but I can't do this. I feel very sorry for you and all, but I doubt I will be much help to you anyway. So, please, just show me back to this portal, or whatever it is, so I can go back home.  Please; *I just want to go home.*"

"I am afraid it is not that simple," he admitted. "Once you enter Audren, you cannot leave before uncovering the powers hidden inside you, and at least attempt to defeat Taurid.  The portal will reappear in exactly twelve days from this very moment, at the beach you landed on.  If you do not uncover your powers by then, not only would you have no way to kill Taurid, but the stakes are higher now.  As the last Varcia, if you don't kill Taurid, you will not be able to go through the portal, and you will never be able to return home." He emphasized the word *never.*

"Can I do all of that in only twelve days?" I asked incredulously.

Tamaku gave a warm smile breaking my serious yet irritated aura. "That is why I am here.  When the first Varcia arrived here, he was assigned a high power level Audrenian.  The person that he was assigned helped him until the end.  This person was his guardian. No Varcia could ever even have a chance of defeating Taurid without any help.  I will help you defeat Taurid, for it is my will and my duty to teach you everything you need to know." He paused.

"Scarlet, I am your guardian."

I thought for a moment. "So is that how you already knew my name?"

"Yes. Scarlet, I have known you for a while. That is my duty as a guardian...to watch over you."

"Then why am I just now getting here instead of before?"

"That part was out of my hands. You see, my duty is to guard you while you are in Audren. As a guardian, I cannot ensure your way here. You had to find your way here on your own. Not every Varcia has actually made it to the Audren realm. With you being the last Varcia, much pressure has been bestowed upon me to protect you."

"But I didn't make it here completely on my own," I admitted. "I heard a voice call me so…so I sort of followed it. This portal I entered through…it was in my school," then it came to me. There was a reason why my school was called Audren Academy.

"Yes, it is located in Audren Academy, but Taurid wanted the portal to be difficult to find. Taurid knows that Varcians have the ability to defeat him. That's why you have to help us, Scarlet. You are our last hope for survival."

I could see this civilization was very desperate for help. Everything was happening way too fast. As soon as I had arrived here, I was being told that I had to protect a whole race of people, I had special powers, and I had to defeat an evil dictator. I have no idea what to do. I wanted to help, but I was still very afraid. This boy named Tamaku was supposed to help me, and he seemed nice but could I really trust him? He said I was the last Varcia. The last person to save these people called the Audrenians, and I only had twelve days to do it. Was that even enough time? I couldn't even finish my science project on the asteroid belt in twelve days. He said I had to at least attempt to defeat Taurid, and to do that, I needed to uncover my powers—whatever they were. Am I even a match for him? But, as I thought about it, that was my only way home, and I wasn't about to let fear get in the way of that.

I took a deep breath. "I don't really understand everything yet, but if you are still willing to help me, I will try to rid this land of this Taurid. But I am kind of shaken by this, I mean, I'm only a normal high school student. I didn't even know I had powers up till now," I enlightened him. I could feel the quivering in my voice as I spoke.

Tamaku took both of my hands and gazed into my eyes. His dark gaze felt as though they were piercing into my soul—in a good way.

"Scarlet, I understand how you feel, and I also know this is very difficult for you to just jump into. But, I promise you that I will always protect you. I have known you for a long time, but you don't know me yet. I want you to get the chance to know me. I will gladly lay down my life for you without a second thought. It is my solemn duty to my people. Taurid must be stopped once and for all. I know you can do it. You have more strength then you realize. Just trust in me, and everything will become clearer...I promise."

I could tell he was sincere. He, beyond a shadow of a doubt, meant all that he was speaking, and I knew I could trust him. I did sort of want to help. All my life I had ran away from my problems or just ignored them. The loss of my father was the hardest, but I chose to ignore it. The fact that I am an orphan continues to haunt me, but I pretend it doesn't bother me. This was the first time someone—actually a lot of people—depended on me. I have always complained about being so sheltered. I knew I needed to embrace this journey ahead of me. It took me by storm, but I had to work with the small sailboat I had.

"So will you trust me?" His eyes sparkled in the sun light. His face was unyielding as the wind lightly tossed his black hair.

"I don't know all the details yet, but I think I can trust you," I said barely audible. I knew I wasn't fully aware of what I was getting into, but I was the superhero in this, and the good guy always wins...right?

"I will not let you down," he promised with a smile lighting his face.

# CHAPTER 6

## GETTING SETTLED

"We should probably get to a different place. No location is really safe anymore," he said motioning for me to get on his back. The wings dazzlingly appeared again, and I quickly mounted on. He started to run, and in a matter of seconds, we were catapulted into the air once again. I looked to my left and my right to see clouds surrounding me in every direction. I seemed to have discounted the beauty of the sky on my first ride. The white clouds levitated in the sky quilting the cool air. The sun was in the distance glimmering in the vibrant blue sky. This brought the very first smile to my face since my arrival. It was probably the smallest smile I ever had, but a smile at least.

An erect thought struck my mind. I remembered that graduation was exactly twelve days away. There was no way I would make it in time for the ceremony and explain my whereabouts when I get home...if I get home. I would surely miss all my exams. I wasn't even certain they would let me walk in the ceremony. I even promised Aunt Danielle that I would choose my top three colleges. This was all a horrific mess! I noticed my grasp on his wings had become tighter. To my surprise, he didn't notice.

I perceived him beginning to decrease in speed. We were about to land. We slowly came to a halt on the ground. I climbed off of his back and looked around. There were small shacks and stores all around, but knitted tightly together; a cluttered mess. Everything appeared to be covered in dirt.

"I know it isn't much, but this is the city."

As I peered around, I could not find one person anywhere. "There is no one here," I stated. "Just like the beach that I arrived on." There were stores and houses, but I saw no one.

"That is because during this time, Taurid's men go around the land to recruit more servants. The people do not want to be seen for fear of them or their children being hauled off to the palace," he looked up to the sky. "But that is very minor compared to the other things that man has done," he looked back at me again. "The people usually come out around this time. Do you want to have a look around?" he asked.

Just then, people came out from every store and house. The once abandoned looking streets were now overflowing with people. There were hundreds varying in age. There were babies, kids, teens, and adults. After seeing the tattered clothes they were all wearing, I noticed Tamaku was dressed fairly well. He wore a white, button down shirt that had the sleeves rolled to about his elbows. He also wore a navy pair of pants. It looked much like a uniform. I then remembered I was still wearing my school uniform.

As I looked around, I noticed many people glaring at me with scoffs of disapproval. I was sure they could tell I was a stranger here. I didn't exactly look like all of them. They all had very dark hair and light bluish eyes. Their skin was a very fair tan color; not quite brown, but not white either. I noticed that some of them were coming towards me.

Just then people started to crowd around me. They were pulling and tugging on me shouting things like: "Is she the one?" "Is that the last Varcia?" "How can we be sure it is not one of Taurid's tricks?"

The people were swarming to the point it became difficult for me to breath. I tried to shout for Tamaku, but my head just kept being forced down with brute movement. I was finally able to lift my head for a brief moment. I shouted for Tamaku to help me.

He quickly jumped on top of a building with a double front flip. I wasn't sure how he could gain such altitude so effortlessly. He pulled out a mysterious looking silver object. Due to the people, I could not get a good look at it. At that moment, I heard I beautiful tune fill the air it was the most relaxing melody I had ever heard in my life. Then I noticed the tugs on my clothing became less and less. I fell to the ground on my knees gasping for air. I rubbed my sore arms. I noticed everyone was standing quietly, free of movement. *Had Tamaku done this*? I thought. I shot my gaze back at Tamaku to see him quickly put away the mysterious silver object.

Everyone was facing Tamaku now. I struggled to my feet, and watched as he jumped off the building. I was expecting him to fall; I was sure getting down would be much more difficult than getting up. But to my surprise—though it shouldn't have been—he flawlessly landed on the ground without even so much as making a sound.

"Now that you all have settled," Tamaku shouted vigorously. "I would like to show you the key to the survival of our civilization. Her name is Scarlet." He motioned for me to join him in the front of the crowd. I looked around to see grimaces still plastered on the faces of the people. I reluctantly made my way towards the front.

"The acumens have come to pass! She is the last Varcia!" He pointed at me with his palm smiling. I nervously waved at the crowd who didn't look too thrilled to see me.

"Master Tamaku!" shouted a rather chubby child. "That's no Varcia! It's a girl! Everyone knows a dumb old girl could never beat Taurid!"

"On the contrary," stated Tamaku. I could tell he was trying to tame his irritation. "The elders told us that if any human enters Audren, he is a true warrior. They also stated that the last Varcia would be a female. Have you forgotten that?"

"Have *you* forgotten that all the elders have died? How can you be sure that this is the last Varcia? She looks rather weak," said an elderly woman pompously.

"I believe she has more than enough power and with our encouragement and support, we can win this time for sure!" He was struggling now; the crowd was getting to him; I could tell. The crowd was full of scowling faces and pungent swear words.

"We have been defeated too many times to even consider fighting again! We are all going to die by Taurid, so why should we fight?" shouted a man causing more people to begin shouting in agreement.

"Believe me, this time is different," Tamaku roared over the crowd. "Brothers and sisters of Audren, she is not like the other Varcia. Trust my judgment! I am her guardian, have you all forgotten?" his tone was now melodic and soothing. He was desperately trying to convince them.

People began to shout more thunderously. Their commotion was earsplitting. In the distance, I saw the crowd begin to split down the middle for some reason. After a moment, I saw one girl pushing her way through the sea of people, ambling towards the front.

"Well I believe Tamaku," she said almost before she was completely standing with him.

"He cares more about Audren then any of you. If anything, we should all be thanking him for all that he has done for us. If it wasn't for him, this village wouldn't be here," she looked irritated.

"All of you, continue with your business; you have no reason for standing here." Every one cleared immediately muttering amongst themselves.

The girl looked like she was in her 20's. She had shoulder length brown hair and light blue colored eyes just like the other Audrenians. Her petite essence did not match her piercing stare or booming voice she had just displayed. Her face was stunning. Her skin was flawless and her neck was long. She was shorter than me; maybe by about an inch or two. Surprisingly, she shifted her gaze towards me. "So you're Scarlet?" she asked, more softly. Her voice was light this time.

I was still slightly nervous. "Um, yes."

She put her slim hand on my shoulder. "It's okay; you can relax for now. Don't mind those people either," she said pointing her thumb behind her. "They have just been through a lot, and it is hard to trust anyone these days. But where are my manners? My name is Toki; I am Tamaku's older sister. I am pleased to meet our future hero," she said to me in a warm tone.

"The pleasure is mine, Miss Toki, ma'am," I said as I greeted her with a bow. I could feel the quiver in my speech.

She chuckled. "Don't worry, Scarlet; you don't have to be so nervous. You can just call me Toki; and **bowing**...really?" she chuckled again.

I tried to loosen up by flashing a smile.

"You know," started Toki as she inched toward Tamaku. "My brother has been waiting for the day you showed up here for so long. He must be so excited, aren't you Tamaku?" He looked embarrassed but said nothing.

"Well now that I'm here, I really think I should get started, considering I have such a limited amount of time here," I said to Toki.

"Don't be so hasty, Scarlet. Though you are only here for twelve days, you still must take your time in everything you wish to successfully accomplish," said Toki.

Tamaku walked closer to me. "What she has said is very true. You must take your time. You have just gotten here. I thought I should show you around the village and teach you how things work around here. First, I would like to show you my home."

I agreed. Toki followed close behind. The whole way she was singing a very familiar tune. It actually sounded much like the Midnight Airos lullaby that my locket played. Though her voice was not graceful, something about it soothed me.

It was a very long walk to Tamaku's house. We arrived at a small grass hut that was neighbored by no one.

"Here it is," he said motioning toward the hut. "I have lived here my whole life. I know it isn't much, but it's better than nothing," said Tamaku with a sigh. He opened the door for Toki and me to enter.

The hut was about the size of an average living room. The bare windows carved out on the wall created an airy effect. The hut was nearly empty except for a chair, a bed, and a small side table. I missed home already.

He showed me in. "This is where you will sleep, Scarlet," he said pointing to the only bed in the small hut.

"But where will you sleep?"

"On the floor of course. It is the least I could do for you. You, very well, deserve a warm bed to rest in. If that means I must sleep on the ground, then so be it."

"This is to be expected from Tamaku. He was always one to put others before himself," Toki whispered to me.

Tamaku was gaping at us trying to decipher what she was whispering.

Toki walked up to Tamaku and playfully slapped his head. "Stop staring at Scarlet like that!" she joked.

Tamaku blushed in embarrassment. "What? No I wasn't! Stop messing around, Toki!"

Toki giggled. "Oops, I'm sorry. I'll stop. But you look so cute when you blush!" she teased. She pinched one of his cheeks playfully.

I continued to scan the hut. It looked like it hadn't been cleaned in years. I spotted a picture on the drawer beside the bed.

Toki and Tamaku were still having wholesome brother-sister bickering, so I decided to get a better look at the picture. I wiped away the dust and saw a family photo. There was a very tall man, a woman, and two kids; a girl and a boy. The girl looked older than the boy. The boy looked a lot like a younger version of Tamaku. They all were smiling, and it looked like they were standing in front of this very hut. Suddenly I felt a hand on my shoulder. I immediately drew back from surprise.

"I see you saw that old thing. That is a picture of my family. In those days, I was probably the happiest child in Audren. I had my two heroes; my mother and father." He then lifted the photo from my grasp gently, he smiled vaguely. It looked more like a sad smile. A smile you would have as if you were remembering something that you lost or missed. "They were great people... Sometimes I can barely remember what they looked like. I guess that's why I keep this old photo around. I never want to forget their faces." A tear leaked from his eye, but he wiped it away on contact.

The picture was of Tamaku and his family? I was wondering why he lived here alone. Something must have happened to his parents. I knew that Taurid guy had something to do with it. I refrained from asking. It didn't seem like something he would suddenly want to talk about it. But I could relate to him. Both of my parents were already dead. I knew the pain all too well.

"But that was a long time ago," Tamaku finally said while he attempted to change the subject. "We shouldn't stand around aimlessly. We should be helping Scarlet get used to this place. It just gets a lot harder from here."

"Yes, you're right," insisted Toki. "Speaking of Scarlet, I actually have something for her that may be useful," she said with a smile that lighted her heart shaped face.

Toki daintily crouched down to take out a long, black box from under Tamaku's bed. She held it out to me with a large grin.

43

"Um, thank you, but what is it?"

She gave another warm smile. "Open it and find out, silly."

The box was heavier than I expected. I sat down on the bed and placed it on my lap. There was a rope tied around it. It took me a couple of tries to unwind it, but I soon became successful. I looked up at Toki and Tamaku before removing the lid. They both gave me nods of permission and encouragement. I turned my gaze back to the box. I slowly lifted the lid.

I felt my eyes widen at the sight. There was a sword. It was absolutely enchanting. It appeared to be pure silver with four emerald studs in the handle. I glided my hand across it feeling the deep craftsmanship of the relic.

"Are you seriously letting *me* have this?"

"Yes; it was the first Varcia's," she said. "Every Varcia must have a Raico. I am surprised Tamaku has not told you. This weapon is the only thing that can release high level powers. You can also use it as a sword, of course."

"So this thing is called a Raico?" I asked rhetorically. "That's a weird name." I examined the blade. It looked worthy of royalty.

This was all for real. I could not back out of this even if I wanted to. I had just received a sword that everyone expects me to smite evil with. Instead of placing it back in the box, I decided to latch it to my waste with the sheath that was in the box.

"Do you like it?" asked Toki.

"Yes, thank you very much. I'll keep it safe," I promised.

"I'm glad. Now we can show you around the village," said Toki as she opened the door.

Tamaku suggested that he stay behind and Toki and I go alone. It was obvious that he was still pretty beat up about his parents.

As we walked, I noticed many strange things I seemed to have overlooked on the way to the hut. I noticed none of the trees had leaves on them but it appeared to be the middle of summer. I also noticed there wasn't a single blade of green grass in sight. Instead it was all brown and dead. I finally decided to ask Toki.

"It has not rained in Audren since Taurid took over. That is why it is very difficult to find food. This place has been unfertile for ages. I've never even seen rain before." she informed as sorrow engulfed her tone.

"Tamaku and I grew up here," she continued. "We do not really know freedom. When we lived with our parents, we thought we knew the meaning, but we didn't." Her tone was more formal now. She no longer looked at me but straight ahead.

"Everyone currently living here is the same. Though we have never experienced freedom, it is the only thing we desire. This is why we need someone to help escape the fear of and waking up every day, just to remain in hiding. The life we live is enough to drive a person mad even when you are used to it.

"When Tamaku and I were young, Taurid killed our parent's right in front of us. Since then, I have taken care of Tamaku myself. I know that Tamaku still feels bad about it; every day the memories haunt him. He has never really been the same. All these years I have tried so hard to make life easy for him, but I have never had powers like other Audrenians.

I never really could protect him the way I wanted to. I always told him that we would meet our parents once again. But soon after their death, I was sent to work for Taurid. I was only thirteen; Tamaku was eight. Luckily for me, I do get to leave the palace everyday once my work is completed. But now that he is

45

older, he lives on his own.  Now, our dad was the head council man for the UAA, or the Underground Audren Association," said Toki.

"What's that?" I asked.

"A council that provides help for the Audrenians who need it more so then others.  The members are often assigned jobs to help the village.  Our father was a great man.  He led and helped all the people in our village.  Everyone loved him.  They believed he could win Audren's freedom without a Varcia.  Once he died, I guess everyone just lost hope for a better tomorrow.  Tamaku took that job recently, but for some reason the people reject him." she formed a frown on her face.  "He has great ideas, but no one seems to care.

He tries so hard to get the villagers to believe again.  It upsets me to know that he cares so much for people that hate him."  Her tone softened, "But that's just the way Tamaku is.  He truly has a heart of gold; always thinking of others, always helping those that persecute him.  I think that's what made raising him such pleasure.  He was always willing to help me out.  He still deserved much better.  I was happy when he found that old Airos Pipe that our father gave him."

"Is that the thing he used to calm the people down earlier?" I asked reflecting back.

"Yep; that's the one.  It was our fathers'.  The Airos Pipe is passed down from father to Son in our family.  After our father died, our grandfather taught him how to play it.  Since then, he has played the Airos Pipe almost every night.  It's his prized possession and the one thing that makes him feel at peace.  Sometimes I blame myself for him being so sad a lot of the time.  Though he is sweet, he is angry deep inside.  He doesn't show it.  But I know one of these days, he will go off, and I don't blame him.  People have taken advantage of Tamaku for far too long.  He is only seventeen but the people treat him like an adult with so much hate.  All he wants to do is bring joy back to this place."

I was in awe. I would have never guessed Tamaku's life was so dreary. It kind of makes me feel bad for him.

She continued, "I think it's good that you're here. Tamaku needs someone around his age to talk to. He really is a nice guy. He may seem a little strict at first, but I think you'll like him. I can tell that you're a nice girl and so pretty, too," she complimented with a motherly look in her eyes.

I smiled at this. "Thanks, and I can tell Tamaku is nice. But I must admit, I really want to go home."

"I know, but don't worry; you only have to stay here for twelve days. I know this must be terrible for you to be in such a strange place and not know anyone. Don't worry; if you ever need someone to talk to, I'm here." She then fell silent. "Tamaku told me that you will be graduating soon."

"Tamaku told you that?"

"Yes; Tamaku has to know a lot about your life. He has been watching over you for 7 years now. He was only ten when he started. That job was assigned to him by the elders when they were still living. You know he's your guardian right?"

"Yes, he told me, I just didn't think he would care enough to tell anyone."

"Tamaku cares about you very much. It is his job to watch over you, but he loves his work. It still puzzles me that he was given that job in the first place; at such a young age, too. Our father was a great hero of Audren, and some say that he is our father's spitting image. Our dad was the only one that continuously strived for our realm to become independent again. He always told Tamaku to stand up for what he believed in no matter how others may react. Even though Tamaku has the same will as our father, he never did earn the same respect."

She fell silent again. My guess is that she was thinking—maybe worrying about something. But soon, she turned to look at me again with a smile. "Well anyway," she finally said. "I just figured you should know a little more about us. We just have had a lot of rough times in our life. I mean, growing up without a mother or father can definitely take its toll on anyone...especially in such a dangerous place like this." She paused as we walked. "But I like you Scarlet. I just know we are going to be good friends." She gave me a warm smile.

"Yeah," I said with a smile. It has been a long time since I've talked to another girl so I wasn't really sure how to connect with her the way I wanted to. She was nice, so it was easy to just listen. I'd rather listen than talk anyway.

It is funny how life works. Once you feel as though you finally understand things, something changes. It's weird how I have been living all this time thinking that there was only one world. I have had a guardian watching over me from a completely different world. What other things have I been totally oblivious too?

The rest of the walk was silent.

We finally arrived to town. People were walking around just like in a normal town. We arrived to a busy market place. There were food stands, but there was barely any food there. The shelves were all nearly empty. I could see what Toki was talking about before. She began to tell me that this market place was the only place for food and tools in all of Audren.

As we were walking, I listened to all the rustle and bustle of the town. I noticed two older women quarrelling over bread, lanky cows trotting behind their masters, and children running to and fro. In the middle of all this stimulation, I saw the cutest little girl walking all by herself. She had to be about two or three. The little girl looked up at me with sparkly blue eyes. This made me begin to smile, but then a woman stomped up to me with a frown on her rigid lips.

48

"Get away from my baby," the woman said, fuming as she snatched the girl in her arms.

"I...I just saw her alone so I was going to-"

"Leave her alone, she was just trying to help," interjected Toki, challenging the woman.

The woman glared at Toki, then looked back at me. She stormed away quickly disappearing into the crowd.

"Why did she do that? All I did was try to help," I said sheepishly.

Toki exhaled noisily. "Like I said before, a lot of the people here are more protective than they should be. In this world it's always better to be safe than sorry. It's really hard to trust anyone these days. It may come across as rudeness, but you must understand our circumstances. There are many Audrenians that are loyal to Taurid and are under cover. It is never one hundred percent safe anywhere. It is almost impossible to tell whether someone is on Taurid's side or not. I know for a fact that there are many undercover workers for Taurid in this very market. They seem inevitable to avoid." She then looked up.

"Wait here while I go see if I can buy a watermelon for supper tonight."

I obeyed. I stared at her small form until I could no longer see any trace of her. I then transferred my gaze at a small bird on the top of a clothes line. Its feathers were a beautiful shade of blue and purple. But its body looked very weak and malnourished. It was amazing how anything could survive here.

Time seemed to crawl past slowly as I waited for Toki to return. As I stood, I felt a sudden thump on my back. I turned around to see a woman with a hood over her head, and a long robe that covered her entire body. She was very young...and beautiful; yet, her face seemed extremely familiar to me. It felt as if I had seen her before. I was so in fixated on her face I almost forgot to apologize for bumping into her—even though it technically was her fault. I started to apologize until I noticed she was staring at me awkwardly. She placed her hand on my cheek, gliding her fingertips from my temples to my lower jaw. This disturbed me greatly, but my body was frozen stiff. She continued to gaze into my eyes as if she was reflecting on something. A smile formed on her face. Not particularly smiling at me, but smiling to herself. She looked at me in awe. Her eyes began to shimmer from dampness.

I was confused.

Then a tear rolled down her cheek, and she began to hug me. "I guess it would be foolish for me to expect you to remember after all this time," she whispered. After looking at me for another long moment, she turned and walked down the corner. I was still at first. I then began to run after her pushing through the people. What was she talking about?

I could still see her, but she was quickly leaving my sight. I called for her to wait but she did not slow down. I turned the same corner she did to try and catch up. It was hard with so many people around. I tried to push my way through the crowd. It seemed as though "excuse me" meant nothing to anyone here. When I finally turned I found a dead end, but the woman was nowhere to be seen. This was where she went. I am sure of it because I watched her. There was no way she could have just disappeared...right? I was startled by Toki's voice from behind. She began to ask me why I had not stayed put. I told her what happened with the woman, but she did not seem surprised.

"You must understand, Scarlet that this world is nothing like yours. Things may seem strange here to you at first, but you will get the swing of things. You must have already concluded that there are people after you," she sighed. "That woman must have been some lunatic or something...I wouldn't be worried about it."

"But she seemed like she knew me from somewhere. I even think I might have known her, too." I watched as I saw her expression grow entangled in confusion.

"...That is strange." She looked down with her eyebrows wrinkled. She blinked twice.

"Well, like I said, things are very different here. It is still very early in your journey so I don't want you to worry about it, okay?" she said in her smooth, optimistic tone she always seemed to use.

"Okay," I agreed.

Toki showed me many more places in Audren, but I was not able to focus whatsoever. All I could think of was that peculiar woman. She knew me somehow. It was written all over her face that she knew me. For some reason, I think I may know her. Even her voice seemed to ring a bell in the back banks of my memory.

During the tour, however, I did get a good look at the place as a whole. Audrenian people did not look much different than the people from home, although there was an eerie feel to them. At the same time, the place was quite modern as well. The people were mostly to themselves seeming as though they had important business to attend to. Not all of them were so cold though. I did get a few smiles from city natives. I was supposed to be the one to help them all but they did not seem to care much. But I could understand that they have been hurt so many times, as Toki would say. I still did not fully take in what was happening to me. I was no longer Scarlet Lansing, but the last Varcia. I still hated every bit of this. I couldn't wait till I could go home.

By the time we got back, it was already nightfall. The day had completely vanished. I was kind of disappointed that I didn't get to start my training. Toki went to her own home while Tamaku and I went into his hut. I wished I could have stayed with Toki a bit longer.

"You must get enough rest for your training tomorrow. You will need every ounce of energy you have," said Tamaku. "Sleep well, Scarlet."

"Don't worry I will be ready for training." I smiled falsely. I then pulled the rough, itchy bed sheets over my shoulders. This was nothing like my dorm at the Academy. Here, I could feel the chill of the night pass right through the thin sheets. My body shivered and my teeth chattered. The mattress was lumpy and comfort was unattainable. The light of the moon shined through the large, open window. The moon looked just like the one back home…maybe even the same one. The glare of the light made my craving for home almost unbearable.

Hours crept past as I lay awake, thinking over my journey so far. This was all happening so rapidly. I sat up on the bed and glided my fingers through my hair. Just a little bit earlier today I was defending Matt from Adam. I was still leading a normal life. I said I wanted an adventure, but now all I want to do is return home. I began to think that maybe this was a lesson or something. Like, be careful what you wish for.

I collapsed back down on the bed. Maybe I was supposed to gain a new appreciation for the life I had. If that was true, it was definitely working. My thoughts were interrupted. I noticed Tamaku get up. I quickly pretended to be asleep as he took a short glimpse at me. I heard the hut door open then close. I opened one eye to see the hut empty. *Where is he off to this time of night?* I thought.

I peered out the window above the bed. There in the moonlight, I saw Tamaku sitting on a rock. He had something silver in his hand. I just knew it was the same object from before. I didn't know if it would be considered eavesdropping, but decided I would go get a better look. I could hear the same sound of beautiful music that I heard before.

I eased out of the door; unnoticed I hoped. The chill was worse than before. I could see Tamaku in the distance. I spotted a tree nearby. I quietly made my way to the tree, being careful with every step. After what seemed to be a lifetime, I finally made it behind the tree that was located only a few yards in back of him. I crouched down behind the thick tree, moving my head slightly so I could watch. I could see what he was holding clearly now. It appeared to be some kind of pipe or flute. He put the tip of the instrument to his lips. Then, a beautiful tune I had never before heard filled the air. This melody was warm and inviting. This sounded like a flute, but at the same time nothing like a flute.

Then I suddenly remembered something. Back when Tamaku and I first met, he told me his name was Tamaku, Master of the Air and Airos Pipe. Toki had also mentioned it today. *The Airos Pipe*. The music ceased with a chilling halt. All that could be heard were distant cicadas and light blowing of the wind.

"I know you are there," said Tamaku.

This startled me a bit. I immediately turned with my back against the bark. I was facing the opposite direction. I felt a cold sweat form on my forehead. My heart also began to race. How did he see me if he hadn't turned around the whole time? I thought I had been inaudible as I made my way outside of the hut.

He was silent. Should I get up? I was pretty sure he was waiting for me to do so. I slowly, reluctantly, stood to my feet.

# CHAPTER 7

## MIDNIGHT AIROS

Every step I took was slower than the one before it. Now I wasn't as careful with my walk, but I was still a little nervous. As I approached him, he still was facing forwards. I wasn't sure what to expect. When I finally stood in front of him, he seemed somewhat surprised.

"Oh, Scarlet, I thought you were Toki. Sometimes she sneaks around here at night to check on me. What are you doing up? Was my music too loud? I can stop if-"

"Oh, no, I am just a very light sleeper; but that tune, it…it was absolutely beautiful. I remember you telling me you were a master of the Airos Pipe, but I never expected that. The tune you played in town to calm the people down earlier was fantastic, as well. Tell me, what was that you just played?" I asked as I sat on the rock beside him, staring off into the woods that bordered a few feet away.

He gave a small, silent chuckle. "It's called Dance of Midnight. That was a song that my grandfather taught me. It was a special melody that was said to have the power to make a flower called the Midnight Airos grow in a place you would least expect. However, that is just an old legend—everyone knows that. But when he told me that story, I was very young. I believed it with all my heart.

You see, in Audren, a Midnight Airos is a sign of happiness and relief. It was a flower grown by the first King of Audren. When he saw how much affluence it brought, he made it so that it would flourish throughout Audren. He had his servants plant them everywhere for the people to enjoy. The flower was also supposed to mean that whatever struggle you were going through was over. It was said that only when there is good in the future ahead, the flower would bloom.

So I learned to play that song in hopes to one day find a Midnight Airos. I thought that if I found one, this Taurid mess would finally be cleared up. I played and played but nothing ever happened. Every day I would look to see if I could find a Midnight Airos. I finally gave up when my grandfather was murdered. It was one of Taurid's men," he looked as if he would burst into tears but did not. "

I was almost speechless. I had heard of the Midnight Airos before. It was in the lullaby she used to sing me.

"My grandfather refused to let my grandmother go to Taurid to serve him. He said that he would gladly die for her protection, she pleaded and pleaded with him to back down and save himself but he did not. So then and there he was killed. They took my grandmother without respecting his wishes. I never saw her again after that. We hope that she is still alive somewhere, but I know she is not. My grandfather had so much hope in a better Audren, kind of like my dad. I loved him to life, but everyone said he was nothing but a fool."

"Why would they say such terrible things?" I questioned, facing him now. "Just because he had hope they called him a fool?"

"I don't know. But, even I feel silly for believing I could find a Midnight Airos. I know a mere flower could never really bring happiness; but, flowers are not our priority right now. We just have to focus on getting you as strong as we can."

I said nothing to this. I stared back ahead. I was too deep in my own thoughts. I could not contemplate the events he just described. I keep hearing more and more terrible things done by Taurid. This was no man. He was a monster. Too many lives have been taken. Too many parents have been taken away from their children. Something had to be done and soon.

I felt my cheeks go red as tears began to stream from my eyes. Tamaku stepped off the rock and started towards me. My heart began to race as he slowly wrapped his arms around me. My grief had just turned to confusion. Why was I so worked up about this? All he was doing was hugging me. It felt good, but at the same time it was awkward. I just met the guy and he is already getting that close? My body felt cold and stiff. I pulled away quickly.

He looked at me with morose eyes.

I could tell I hurt his feelings.

"Sorry for that," he began. "I was just—"

I didn't say a word. With that I walked—practically ran back into the hut.

Tamaku stayed out there for I while. I was sure he was waiting till I fell asleep to come back in. I still laid awake thinking about that hug or embrace or whatever you would like to call it. I actually liked it. Then again I didn't like it. To shift my mood, I tried thinking about what Tamaku had said about his grandfather. It was amazing how these constant deaths are just everyday life in Audren. I knew I could find a Midnight Airos, or I would at least try. He thinks his grandfather's death was in vain. I disagree. His grandfather died to protect someone he loved. Even though the person he loved still got hauled away. To me, he died a hero.

## CHAPTER 8

## DARK DREAMS AND ABUNDANT APOLOGIES

All there was around me was white vacancy. There was nothing in my presence; just white nothingness. In the abyss, all I could see was a small boy with his back to me; he wore a white night gown. In front of him, there was a small pond of clear, colorless water. He just sat there. He wouldn't turn around to face me.

Then, I saw myself. I was wearing an all-black gown. It had no form, no decoration. My hair covered my face. As I walked towards the boy, the all-white world was slowly being drenched in darkness. The darkness was coming from me. The darkness followed my every foot step.

Soon, the vacancy was filled with the darkness that radiated from me. The clear water turned black. The boy then turned to look at me. He had opaque wings and hair as white as snow. He had searing blue eyes that looked almost unnatural.

There was a black crow that then sat upon my shoulder. It made a loud, bloodcurdling screech. Then, one after another, I was surrounded by crows. I stood right over the boy with my sword uncovered and raised high. I then formed a very chilling smile. Without warning, I swung my sword downwards. Again and again, I slashed the small boy. Before I could see the destruction I caused, I awakened.

I had awoken in a cold sweat and tears in my eyes. As I peered around the room, all I could see was the light of the midnight moon. The room was still but my heart was quite the contrary. I just had a dream...no, more like nightmare. I felt icy shivers run down my spine as I lay there motionlessly. My back was cold with the dampness of my own perspiration.

It seemed so real. Though I know I would never do this, I still can't help but be nervous. The images I saw made me feel like bawling. I had never seen such a terrible thing happen to anyone...I would never do that...*never*.

My body feels weak. My skin feels moist, and I feel nauseous. Why did I dream that? As soon as I fell asleep again, it was time to awaken.

"C'mon Scarlet, today is a big day for you," Tamaku said as he shook me lightly.

I figured I would just forget about that dream. Dreams don't really mean anything, right? I figured if I begged relentlessly for more time to sleep, he would be gracious; but my attempt failed. After what seemed to be an hour of coaxing, I finally gave in. When I sat up I noticed I still had my school uniform on. I wondered if I could ever get a shower while I was here. I know it has only been a day, but my body feels so sore.

"You are probably wondering when you will bathe again, aren't you?" said Tamaku as he smiled in my direction.

"Uh, yeah," I admitted. I didn't want to sound rude.

He chuckled. "Don't worry, in this realm, it may seem like everything is filthy, but if you pay very close attention, you will notice that none of the people are dirty at all. You see, in this realm, no living thing gets soiled. You will remain the same as you came."

I then looked down examining myself; it was true. I didn't even smell bad. I heard the hut door open. I looked up to see Toki with some containers in her hands smiling. This was definitely a good sign.

"Anyone up for breakfast?" she asked with a wide smile.

I saw the containers were filled with eggs, toast, and waffles. I was pretty taken aback to see the same type of food in Audren that was in my world. My stomach began to growl. Then I remembered my last meal was lunch at school. I was starving.

"Toki," I started. I could almost feel my mouth begin to water. "That looks-"

"Where did you get all of that?" Tamaku asked abruptly.

"Where do you think? The only people that have food," she replied rolling her eyes playfully.

"You mean that Taurid guy?" I asked eyeing the containers.

"Yeah, I was assigned to clean up in the kitchen this morning, so I just took the leftovers.

I figured you guys would be hungry," she said seeming proud. "I didn't really get a chance to buy the watermelon that—"

"Are you out of your mind, Toki?" shouted Tamaku. "If they find out you will surely be imprisoned, or...or worse!"

I was still confused.

"Relax, relax; they won't find out. I promise. Instead of scolding your *older* sister—might I add—you should be thanking me.

"Thank you for what? For never being smart about anything?" he said, clearly fuming.

The incandescent smile faded from her face. She looked at him with shimmering eyes. Toki shed a tear. She looked at Tamaku then glanced at me. She placed the food on the ground and started out the door with her head down quickly. Tamaku cringed at his apparent mistake. He quickly grabbed her by the arm, halting her from leaving.

"Look, Toki, I didn't mean that. You *are* smart, not to mention beautiful, and the best big sister a guy could ask for. That's why I can't risk losing you to them. You know what could happen.

We already lost...*them*. If I lose you, I would have no one left. I mean, I know that you are pretty good with the people at the palace, but you can't be so reckless when we have such a powerful dictator."

"I know. I know...I just wanted to be of some use to you. We all know how rare it is to get decent food around here. Half of the deaths are from starvation or the lack the right nutrients. All the stores are nearly empty and the prices are just so high," she clasped her forehead with her eyebrows lifted.

"I just wanted to make you happy. It's been a long time since I've seen you smile."

"I know, but never say that you are not useful."

"But I'm not useful, Tamaku. I don't have any powers—"

"It doesn't matter Toki! If you did not take care of me when Mother and Father died, I wouldn't even be standing here today." He wrapped his arms around her. "I owe you everything," he whispered.

I didn't know what to do. This seemed like a really personal moment. After a few moments of stillness, I finally spoke. "Well, I think we should eat the food; if we tried to return it that would be way too risky."

"Yes, I agree with Scarlet," Tamaku said glancing at me then back to Toki.

The food looked old and almost rotten. If I wasn't so hungry, I probably wouldn't have eaten any bit of it. I did not complain aloud. I simply ate as much I could stomach. As quickly as we started eating, it was gone. It tasted horrible, but it did fill me up at least. Tamaku and Toki both seemed to like it though.

"Well I had better get back to work. You and Scarlet need to start training," she said as she shoved one arm into a thin sweater. "I'll catch up with you guys later."

She proceeded out the door and waved. I had hoped that I could spend time with Toki again. She was way more fun than Tamaku. I guess guardians had to be all business.

After Toki left, Tamaku and I headed off to an old battle ground Tamaku had told me about on the way. When we arrived I saw how wide and open the space was. The wind blew lightly, causing my loosely held back hair to tassel. The slight breeze reminded me of the academy. It was on days like this, when Matt, Ryan, and I would take walks. We occasionally just took some chill time with all three of us. On those walks, we would often talk about normal teenager stuff. We could always let off steam during our walks. I don't know why, but it seemed like whenever we walked, it was easier to talk about our feelings.

I really miss those guys...

It was finally time to get this show on the road. I reached for my Raico but another hand beat me to it.

"Not yet," said Tamaku. "Your Raico must not be drawn until you find out what powers you actually possess."

"Will that take long?"

"Normally, yes, but I have devised a plan to simplify the procedures. Normally, in order to find your powers, it takes weeks. Unfortunately, we do not have that much time. Now, by being a Varcia, you possess certain abilities. We like to call it *element manipulation*. There are four different elements that are possible to manipulate. There is water, lightning, earth, and fire. These types of powers require your Raico by your side. With these powers, you can use the elements around you."

"So how am I gonna find those powers?"

"You see, in all humans and Audrenians there is a thing called *spirit energy*."

"Oh, yeah, I remember you mentioning that yesterday. You said that's why normal humans can't come to this realm; because they don't have enough or something."

He smiled, "So you were listening. Well, spirit energy is your drive to accomplish something. Spirit energy is the source of any power you can possess. Basically, if you don't have enough spirit energy riled up, you cannot perform certain techniques. You must keep your spirit energy strong at all times. Which means you must always keep your will to fight back. In other words, never give up. There is always a way out of something no matter how slim the chances are of you making it through. In order for your spirit energy to be strong as well, you must always keep your thoughts pure. Spirit energy is not visible, but it can be felt. So for this, all you need to do is get your spirit energy as strong as you can. As you progress in skill your spirit energy will grow as well. That is what we will work on today. So for now, just try to bring out your spirit energy."

"So, for this all I need to do is think happy thoughts?"

"You got it!" he said. "Just think about...uh, what makes you the happiest? You don't have to do this every time you use spirit energy, but assuming that this is your first time attempting it, you must complete this exercise in order to trigger your spirit energy. "

What really made me happy? I thought and thought. Then it came to me. I thought of Matt and Ryan. Those two were the best friends I had ever had. I could still remember the first time I met both of them. It was in the ninth grade on the first day of school. They were already friends then. They had been friends since the first grade. It was lunch time, but I had forgotten my lunch. I sat there at a lunch table all by myself. Everyone there was staring and whispering about me because I was the only girl. I said nothing to anyone and no one said anything to me.

I sat down at an empty lunch table. The other kids here didn't look too inviting. I sat down quietly and held my face in my hands. *Maybe coming to this high school was a bad idea after all*, I thought.

Then, I saw two boys making their way in my direction. I quickly glanced around to make sure it was me that they were actually approaching. My thoughts were verified as they both sat across from me. They both appeared to be freshmen, just like me. One was on the short side and had dark, blonde hair. The other was a lot taller, with brown hair that reached to the middle of his eyes. I couldn't help but notice they were really cute; especially the dark haired one.

"Dude, you are so hot. Are you sure you're a boy?" asked the blonde.

"Matt, were you paying attention at all in class today? Mrs. Trenton said that we were gonna have a girl this year for the first time in school history! Listen more Matt," scolded the other.

I giggled.

"See, Ryan!" said Matt. "He even laughs like a girl. That *has* to be a girl!"

"Did you hear anything I just said?!" Ryan shouted.

I finally spoke up. "Well, I am a girl. My name is Scarlet, Scarlet Lansing. I am pleased to meet you both." I tried to sound as polite as possible. I didn't want to ruin the chance of gaining friends.

"Wow, so you are a girl. Jeez, you sound all fancy, too." said Matt as he started poking my arm repeatedly. "Wow, you even feel like a girl!

"Excuse him," Ryan insisted as he scooted Matt over. "He isn't too bright. He acts more like a second grader than a ninth grader. He's Matt and I'm Ryan." He then lifted his gaze directly into my eyes. "We just came over because we noticed that you were all alone. Anyway, nice to meet you, but I gotta ask. Why are you not eating anything?—it is lunch time after all."

"I had packed a lunch, but I forgot it in my dorm," I replied.

"No worries! You can share lunch with me, Scarlet!" said Matt as he smiled wide. "My mom gives me way too much money a month anyway."

"Yeah you can share with me, too," Ryan said, more calmly, as he split his ham sandwich in two.

"So I guess we should sit with Scarlet every day at lunch now!" Exclaimed Matt in a way too hyper manner. As he looked at Ryan for approval—not that he needed it.

"I just remembered something! Wait, your last name is Lansing, right?" Asked Ryan.

"Yeah, why?"

He fished a crumpled piece of paper from his pocket. After a moment of gazing at it, he stood up. "I knew it!" he shouted. "It's the dorm room assignments," he pointed out. "You are me and Matt's roommate; Room 71, right? Look here!" he pointed to my name on the paper.

"You mean, I get to hang with Scarlet after school, too?!"

"Yup!" said Ryan. "This will actually be a pretty good year."

~~~*~~~

We three have been friends ever since. I remembered all sorts of hilarious times we spent together. But the day we met is my best memory.

64

Thirty minutes of my thinking had passed, but nothing happened. I decided to ask Tamaku why I was not getting any progress.

"It depends," he said. "What did you think about?"

"I thought about my friends back at school. But I do miss them very much."

He deliberated for a moment. "Perhaps you missing them is exactly what's holding you back. Try to concentrate on seeing them instead of memories. If you can't do that, then you may have to think of something else."

I tried what Tamaku told me, but nothing was working. He said I would be able to tell when my spirit energy is active. It sort of discouraged me that nothing was working in my favor. I thought of lots of things that made me happy. Like my favorite season, my favorite place to go, the time I got second place in the school talent show, but every single one of my attempts drastically failed. I looked over at Tamaku. I could tell he was getting restless standing there waiting on me. He smiled at me but I know he was just trying to be nice. Then it came to me.

"Tamaku you said spirit energy is your drive to do something, right?"

"Well, yeah. Why do you ask?"

I didn't answer him. I finally found a way for me to get this!

## CHAPTER 9

### SHEER WILL POWER

I closed my eyes tightly. Maybe happiness isn't what triggers *my* spirit energy. Maybe pure determination would be the key. There was one thing that I was most determined to do. That was to return home. If I used that, then maybe I could trigger my powers. I had been concentrating for a while now, but I would not give in.

Just when I wanted to give up, I felt some kind of pressure on my body. Was this what Tamaku was talking about? This must be what my spirit energy feels like. I think he noticed what was happening, too. When he saw me, the look on his face was priceless. It made me so happy to please him so much. He gave me a hug. "Scarlet, you got it! I never thought your spirit energy would glean so quickly." He spoke as if he thought I would never do it; but I was still happy.

"All I did was think about what I wanted most and it all kind of worked out on its own. I think I just had to figure out my power my own way. Thank you for the help you gave me Tamaku." I gave him a smile.

He chuckled. "Yeah, maybe you are right. But the training does not stop here. In addition to practicing gleaning your spirit energy at will, we must find your manipulation power. This will not be as easy. So I decided that I will start to teach you sword combat first. I hope you are prepared."

"Sword combat?" I echoed.

"Yes, you must learn the basics of using your Raico in hand-to-hand combat. Before any powers can be used, you must know how to wield your sword."

"Oh, I see. This should be easy."

"Ah, that is where you are wrong. Sword fighting is very important, and one slip of your hand could cost you your life. That is why I must teach you all there is to know first."

He then pulled out a dented, ragged sword from his side. He motioned for me to do the same.

I pulled out my glimmering Raico. As I did, my arm was forced down with a slight jerk. The sword was a lot heavier than it seemed. But I knew his sword was no match for my gleaming weapon. "Okay," I said, "What do I do?"

"We will simply start off with blocking. When I swing my sword you must block my attack using your sword. When in battle, your most important skill is defense. If you cannot block properly, you will not walk away from any battle alive. Even if your movements are quicker than your opponents, if you lack in defense, *you will lose.*"

This blocking lesson went on for quite a while. To my surprise, it was shockingly simple. His attacks were light and controlled. Though I was not nearly a match for his true strength my skills were forming well. A few times his speed would pick up in order to catch me off guard but my progress stayed consistent. My time in Fencing Club in my sophomore year had really paid off (surprise, surprise).

"Wow, you're doing very well; I'm impressed," he said nodding approvingly. "Now we shall move on to attacking. Defense is important, but you will never win a battle without attacking either. So I will try to block while you attempt to make a small cut on my body."

I nodded agreeing to the challenge. The sword's weight took a toll on my weary biceps but I did continue. So far, Tamaku had successfully blocked all my attacks. I had swung my sword in every direction but all failed. This went on for quite some time and I was growing tiresome of my repertory failures. My arms were still very much in pain. Even though this was a very unpleasant training I knew in the back of my mind that it was essential. "Time out," I said panting. Though I was tired, I had a trick up my sleeve...

"Sure thing, I apologize if I am-"

With no warning I swung my sword in his direction. With a swift swipe, I had completed my task! A small cut appeared on his right cheek. A smile formed on his lips as he wiped the trickle of blood away.

"You cheater!" he said with a chuckle.

"No, this is where *you* are mistaken. A warrior must always have more wit than her opponent!" I protested proudly. I emphasized the word "her".

"Well said Miss Lansing; well said. But your Raico training does not stop here. There is one more thing you must complete. Now, you must battle with me."

"Already?" I asked. "But I barely completed the other tasks."

"Actually, I think you did very well for your first time with your Raico. I do not expect you to win this battle, but you must learn the structure of a real fight. We will just see how far you get."

My whole body was aching now. The continuous strain on my muscles was getting worse. However, I was pretty excited for a real battle. "Okay, but this time, don't hold back so much."

He nodded in agreement. We both assumed our positions with swords in hand. Without warning, he swung his sword in my direction. I felt my eyes widen as I tried to hold my sword up in defense. My block had succeeded! Now I could tell Tamaku was getting a little more serious. He gripped his sword tighter. I tried to match his determination, but before I had time, his sword had made its way towards my upper body. I flinched, but made my sword collide with his. In an effort to attack, I swung my sword aimlessly.

To my surprise, he did, in fact, take a small blow to the chest. I had indeed made an attack! The element of surprise adorned his face. With that, he became even more determined to make a hit.

I never knew that the heat of battle could be so enjoyable! I eyed my prey once more to see him bent over panting for air. I now proceeded to attack! As I came closer, he still did not move. *This is way too easy,* I thought. With my sword in place, a surprise came to me. My attack was immediately blocked with a sword. I was unable to leave my spot.

"'A warrior must always have more wit than *his* opponent'," he echoed with a chuckle. "You were so confident, you could not see the diversion! Enemies will pull stunts like that all the time, but every time, you must see through it! But no worries, we will practice every day, and based on your progress thus far, it will be easier than I expected. But the next task will be by far, harder."

"I think I'm prepared for anything." I responded with an ostentatious edge. I was clearly a natural at this sword combat.

For the next bit of training, we had to go to a different location. Tamaku blind folded me so I could not know where he was leading me. This had me a little worried, but I did say before that I was prepared for anything. I knew we were going through the town. But at this time it was not as loud as normal since people don't come out this early. I remembered this from yesterday.

We had been walking for a while now. At this point, I had no idea where we were. All I knew was that it was extremely hot. "Tamaku, what time is it?"

"Judging by the sun's position right now…" he paused. "It is about 2:30. But don't worry. I promise we will fly back once training is over."

# CHAPTER 10

## I AM MY HERO

We at long last came to a stop. I was sweating on every inch of my body.

"Now, your next power to learn is element manipulation. In other words, element control. With this, all we need to do is find out what your element is."

"That seems simple enough, but can I open my eyes now?"

"Oh! Yes, I'm sorry. I almost forgot. But when you do, don't get scared by what you see, okay?"

"Well, it depends, what is it?"

Tamaku began to laugh. "I guess it depends on how you look at it.

I did not like the sound of this one bit. He was laughing, but I didn't know why. It didn't seem humorous. Then he took off the blind fold.

My eyes opened slowly adjusting to the light and heat of the day. There, right in front of me, was a cliff. I took a class on Geography Concepts last year, and just by looking at this cliff, I could tell it had to be at least 3000 feet down. I looked at Tamaku in utter disbelief. He just gave me a rather cute smirk. It caught me off guard for a moment. Until now, I hadn't really noticed *how* nice looking Tamaku was. I noticed his perfectly chiseled jaw line, and toned physique. His deep, black hair was layered so perfectly, reaching to the middle of his ears. His almost pitch black eyes were indeed something to gawk at (considering every other Audrenian I had seen had blue eyes). They seemed to pierce, even from a distance. But I soon came back to my senses, shaking my head briefly, remembering the cliff.

"Please don't tell me my training has anything to do with this death trap." I felt my lips quiver at the words.

"'Death trap'? You are being a little overly dramatic, don't ya think? Plus, you told me earlier that you were ready for anything."

"I told you I was prepared for anything, but I didn't say I was prepared to die!"

He chuckled a bit. "Relax, relax, I haven't even told you what we're doing yet."

"Okay," I sighed, somewhat relieved. "Let's hear it"

"Well, unfortunately for you, I think you had the right idea from the start."

I cupped my forehead with my palm. *I should have seen this coming.* "Do you mean...?"

"Yes. *You will be jumping off the edge of this cliff.*" He seemed almost happy as he motioned toward the high altitude feature.

For all the terrible statements to ever have been made, that was by far the worst. I looked at the cliff and gulped. I felt a bead of sweat role down my forehead. I then looked at Tamaku. "Are you insane?"

"More or less," he grinned, shrugging one shoulder. "But just finding your element type is not what this exercise is all about. Being a Varcia, you must have faith in your own abilities. There will not always be someone there to save you. In the end, you must believe that you are your ultimate hero each and every time."

I thought for a moment. "Okay, I guess I can understand that, but I don't see how any of this will help me find my element type."

"You see, to find your element, you must be faced with sudden danger—like this cliff. If you were suspended hundreds of feet in the air with no way to save yourself, your power element will come to your rescue. This exercise will not teach you how to control your powers, but it will unleash them."

"Are you sure my element will save me?" I trusted Tamaku, but I was still frightened. I mean, most people would call jumping off of a cliff suicide!

"Well, there is still the possibility of your power lying dormant, you plummeting to your death, and-"

"Tamaku!" I shouted.

"Relax, relax; I'm only joking," he said, putting his hands above his head as if he was surrendering. "You can get pretty worked up, can't you?" he chuckled.

"Please don't kid around like that. I'm scared enough as it is."

"Okay, but before we start, you must know something." He locked eyes with mine, intensifying the moment. "In this task, if something were to go wrong I cannot help you."

Now I was confused. "What? You said earlier you would always-"

"Yes, I know; but the whole point of this is sudden danger. Like I told you before, there will not always be someone to protect you each and every time danger is afoot. Do not be confused; I will try to be there for you as much as I can, but I can't promise that you won't get hurt or worse. Now with this, sudden danger is the key. If you knew you had someone to save you right now, it wouldn't be that dangerous, now would it?"

I shook my head.

"That's why I cannot help. If I did, I would be doing *you* a disservice."

I stood there in silence. Was this worth my life? Out of nowhere, the memory of Tamaku holding me when I cried in his arms last night came to me. I don't know why, but this memory gave me a large quantity of courage. It was almost like I instantly became a different person. Without thinking about it, I turned to Tamaku. I told him that I would do it.

"Alright, now there are a couple things you must do to make this work. You must keep your focus the whole time. Focus on only Scarlet, only yourself, and your own abilities. Remember; keep your spirit energy at maximum. This is how I can guarantee your safety."

"Okay," I said, still nervous, as I stepped to the edge of the cliff. My heart started to pound so hard I thought it would burst out of my chest and splatter on the ground. The rest of my body felt numb and cold. I looked back at Tamaku. He just nodded his head. I turned back to my task. My toes were touching the very edge of the rock. I closed my eyes. "Here goes," I whispered to myself.

All I did was lean forward, and before I knew it, I was plunging into the bottomless drop. I wanted to scream, but I did not utter a sound. I knew if I did, I would never be able to gain back the focus I needed to survive this. The breeze of the air whipped across my cheeks as I fell. Tamaku told me to just focus on myself and my own abilities. I just kept telling myself, time and time again, that I could do this. I did not need a hero. I was my hero.

# Chapter 11

## LOCKET RELATIONS

I started to feel an almost electrical surge run through my veins. I felt like I should be in pain, but my body was not hurting. Then I noticed that wind was no longer running through my hair. There was no gust against my cheeks. I felt still. I slowly opened my eyes. I was no longer falling in midair. I was actually suspended in the air itself. I looked down to my feet. I screeched in shock.

There I stood on a sheet of actual electricity; more like a lightning bolt. I was standing on it like a platform, yet I was not getting shocked by it. I looked up in the sky. No sign of any bad weather, just a clear, blue sky. *How would lightning be down here out of nowhere?* I thought. Then, I finally put two and two together and came to a conclusion. *Lightning was my element.* I had done it after all!

I looked around me and noticed that I was down very low. I had no idea how to get back to Tamaku at the top. Then I figured if I concentrated once more and rile up more spirit energy, I could get my lighting to shoot me up to the top; that seemed like a smart plan. Spirit energy got me this far.

I really had no clue how to use this power yet, but I just tried to be practical with my thinking. I put my plan into action, but nothing happened. I was wondering what I was doing wrong. I was riling up spirit energy just as before. Then, at random, the memory of my father giving me a beautiful ribbon to put in my hair for the first day of 1st grade came to my mind. The ribbon was my favorite color; scarlet (go figure). It had real pearls stitched in the silky material. It was the most feminine object my dad had ever bought me. It made me so happy when he gave it to me. It made me feel special. This memory brought a smile to my face.

I felt moisture seeping into my tennis shoes. I looked at my feet to see water and lighting creating a platform for me. Was this possible, two elements at the same time? I didn't know if this was good or bad. Before I could continue to debate with myself, I started to dart up into the air. I heard my screams echo in the air in repulse. I fell flat on my back side with a thump.

I looked down to see the water shooting up with the lightning spiraling around it. I was going at extreme speed. Up and up I went, getting closer to the edge. When I finally got close to the top, just in time, I jumped from my electric water platform. Once my feet came in contact with the ground, both elements disappeared into thin air. I saw Tamaku in the distance. He seemed almost bored as he sat on the ground, examining his finger nails. He did have confidence in me after all.

Though he was far away, I could see the brightness of his eyes radiating. He shouted something to me, but I couldn't quite make it out. However, I did hear four words. *You are truly amazing.* They weren't particularly special words coming from just anyone. But for some odd reason, when Tamaku said them, it sent my heart on an invigorating high. Forget cloud 9; I was on cloud 20.

He came running to me. I kneeled down on the ground in efforts to catch my breath. The jump I made off my element platform wasn't exactly a small task. Before I could say a word, Tamaku embraced me tightly. When he stopped, he gazed into my eyes, but said nothing. He had a small smile on his face. He looked as if he was about to burst into laughter.

"Tamaku, are you alright?" I said softly. I could not understand why he did not say anything.

"Yes, I'm fine," he insisted. "Scarlet, you did a spectacular job. I mean, I knew you could do it all along. But you did notice, right?" He began to laugh.

"Notice what?" I could almost feel the vacant look on my face.

"Scarlet, you used *two* different elements. Not only that, but with element manipulation, you have to use elements *around* you. For example: say your element type was fire. If you were in battle and you were in a damp cave, you could not use fire. But you used lightning and water and none of them are in this area! Somehow you activated both basically out of nowhere. Only extremely high leveled Audrenians can do that!"

*What I did was really that special?* I thought.

"It would take an extremely skilled warrior to pull this off. However you did all of this in a matter of seconds! The Audren realm has only seen such skill a few times before. The most known is the first Varcia, but it even took him days. As far as the lightning... that ability is extremely rare. I don't think I can stress this enough," he shook his head as if my success was mind boggling. "Do you see the magnitude of what you just did?"

I blushed a bit. No one has ever given me so many compliments at one time.

"Thank you, but doing well is my job now. I have to be as strong as I can."

He chuckled; not out of humor just in agreement. "That's true—but there is one thing I must ask though." His smile faded.

"Um, yes, anything."

"That locket around your neck," he said, gesturing towards the item. "I noticed it a while ago. Where did you get it?"

The question caught me off guard. It was a completely random. This was the first time anyone asked me about my locket before. I was slightly surprised that he took notice.

"My mother gave it to me. I was too little to remember. She died so long ago. To tell the truth, I never really knew her—but you probably already knew that. My father told me she gave it to me so

76

that I would never forget her.  Whenever I open it, it plays a lullaby that she used to sing to me." I opened it so he could hear the song. I thought he may like it, but the look on his face disturbed me. "Is there something wrong?"

"Scarlet, t—this song is an ancient Audrenian folk song.  It was sung to the children long, long ago.  This song has not been sung for over five centuries.  No human should know this song. Most Audrenians don't even know it.

"That can't be right, because how would my mother-"

"I do not know.  This is what is troubling me.  The title of the song is-"

"The Midnight Airos," we both said in unison.

"So you know it as well?  Just to be sure, play it once more," Tamaku instructed.

I obeyed.  I had never known the lyrics to the song.  Tamaku, to my surprise, began to sing.

*"With one true love and one true lover*

*The Midnight Airos will finally bloom*

*Staring into the bright eyes of a beautiful child*

*The Midnight Airos will arise very soon*

*With no one to water or care*

*With no one to plant it or see it grow*

*The Midnight Airos will always bloom when there is good*

*When there is joy, when there is hope*

*That is when the Airos appears*

*The Midnight Airos is only a flower,*

77

*And in the midst of evil will die*

*But the love for my child will never wither*

*Not now, not ever; nowhere in the quickly approaching future*

*The Midnight Airos will bring good intentions*

*For once you have one, your troubles will be over"*

All his notes matched perfectly with the song. It was no doubt that he had in fact known this song. His voice was so beautiful. It seemed like he was a former choir member from heaven.

"Yes, there is no mistaking it," he said. "This is the song. However, there is absolutely no way this song entered the human world, let alone anything regarding the Midnight Airos flower." He thought for a moment. Suddenly an astonished look formed on his face. "Unless..."

"Unless she was an Audrenian," I finished. "Maybe she lived here once." I somewhat considered the thought.

"No, no," Tamaku said shaking his head from side to side, as if to force the thought out of his mind. "There is no way. Only guardians of Varcia can enter the human world. Even if she was a guardian, the spirit energy would be so low she could not stay for long. She could not live among humans let alone have a family." He looked as if he was going to say something else but stopped himself. "Listen," he continued. "I do have a reason for asking about your locket in the first place."

"Okay, what is it?" I asked

"Maybe it would make more sense if I showed you." He said.

He reached toward my locket. I normally would never let anyone touch my locket, but I made an exception. He placed two fingers on the cold, silver surface. At the exact moment he came in physical contact with the locket, it began to glow in a marvelous gold color. He immediately ceased his touch—like if you just touched a hot stove, but immediately pull away discovering its scalding heat. I looked at my locket. I held it in my palm but nothing happened. Something disturbed me. On the locket, carved in its surface, was a large "A" in cursive script. This was never here before. I looked up at Tamaku in hopes to get some answers.

"It is just as I thought," he said, still gazing at the locket. "This is a relic from the Audren realm. You can always tell by the "A" on the object."

"But I have had this locket all my life and I never noticed an "A" on it until now," I protested.

"That is because it was not visible to your eyes. It has been in the human world for too long. But when a true Audrenian, such as myself, touches it, it will regain its true form."

"But that glow, what was that?"

"I'm not quite sure, but it seems to be powerful. I suggest that you do not remove this locket from your neck. It seems to have some sort of connection to you." His eyes were narrowed, creating two slits instead of open eyes. He appeared to be thinking rigorously—like he was trying to figure out something very difficult.

"That's fine; I have never taken this locket off before in my whole life."

"Okay, but it's getting late. We should begin to head back to my home."

As usual, I mounted on his back once more to fly home. I loved riding on Tamaku's back. I didn't know why, but it seemed to put me at peace, serenity. I actually really started to like Tamaku. He was sweet and gentle all the time—he was becoming very easy to be around. I had only seen him angry once. That was only because he wanted to protect his beloved sister, Toki. I have only known him for two days, but it feels like I have known him all my life now.

He says he has known me almost all my life since he is my guardian. He probably knows everything about me. It is sort of sad because I hardly know anything about him. I cannot help wondering what it will be like when this is all over. Will I still know Tamaku? Just everything about him intrigues me. I want to know how he has been hurt so much but can still be so gentle. He has told me years and years of history, almost as if he lived through it. He only looks about seventeen years like me. He said that Midnight Airos song had not been sung for ages; yet, he knew all the words to it. One of these days I will muster up the courage to ask him all these things. Until then, I am going to enjoy the ride.

~~~*~~~

After a while of flying we finally made it back to Tamaku's hut. Just like before, I slept on his bed and he slept on the floor. As usual, I couldn't fall asleep. It appeared as though our training lasted the whole day. However, I did come across a problem. I still did not know how to use my powers. I did not fret over this though. I knew Tamaku would help me tomorrow.

I turned over in the bed to get more comfortable. I waited as Tamaku finally blew out the lanterns that were granting unwanted light. I gave a sigh, fidgeting again, struggling for comfort. But again, it seemed unattainable. I still wasn't tired. I had too much to think about. Today was definitely more efficient than yesterday.

All of a sudden, I heard a noise. I looked over at Tamaku, but he was still sleeping soundly. I was about to conclude that it was all my imagination until I heard another noise.

"Knock it off, Tamaku," I said softly, yet irritably.

"Scarlet," said a voice.

It sounded like a girl.

I sat up to see Toki at the foot of the bed. I almost screamed from surprise, but I clasped my hand over my mouth.

"Sorry; didn't mean to scare you," she whispered.

Before I responded, I glanced back at Tamaku to make sure he was still sleeping.

"Not to be rude, but what are you doing here?"

She smiled and quietly made her way closer to me.

I inched over to give her room to sit down.

"I just wanted to talk to you," she said exposing her teeth in a wide smile. It didn't seem as if she wanted casual conversation.

I smiled. "Okay, what happened?"

"Okay, you caught me," she giggled. "Well…" she kept smiling.

"Well?" I probed. I was actually very interested in what she was going to say next.

"I…I'm free!" she said a little too loudly.

She and I glanced at Tamaku to make sure it did not awaken him.

"Wait, what?"

"I'm free! For some reason, Taurid let me go free today! A member of his court guards came to me today! I no longer have to work! Isn't this great?!"

I smiled wide. "Toki, that's wonderful!" I exclaimed in a whisper as I brought her into a hug.

"I'm so excited! I know I probably should have waited until the morning to stop by, but I just had to tell someone! Scarlet, I'm so happy you were the first to hear the news!"

"Me, too, Toki. But don't you think it's kind of odd that they just let you go like this? Do you think there's a catch to all this?"

She was silent for a moment. "I don't think so. Taurid is the type of person to punish immediately. I'm just glad I don't have to step foot in the palace again."

"Yeah, you're probably right. I just hope nothing bad happens to you. Based on what I hear about this man, he can be very sly."

"Well, let's not think like that," she seemed to be very bent on optimistic thoughts. That's what I really liked about Toki. I just hoped she was right. I have a really bad feeling about this sudden release; but, I wasn't going to say anything else about it.

"So how are you, Scarlet? Are you still dying to go home?"

"Well, not really. I am actually starting to like it here. Today, I found my two elements!"

"Did you just say *two* elements? That's absolutely amazing!"

I giggled. "Yeah, that's what Tamaku said." I smiled as I mentioned Tamaku.

Toki didn't miss it. "Whoa, you seem really fond of Tamaku," she said as she nudged my shoulder, teasing.

I laughed a little. "It's not even like that, okay?"

"Sure thing, Miss Varcia," she chortled. "But I am very glad that you and Tamaku are getting along. Sometimes Tamaku can be really annoying—trust me, I grew up with the kid," she joked. "He hasn't done anything weird with training, has he?"

82

"No; not really. Unless you consider having me jumping off a cliff weird," I said sarcastically.

"He did what?!" she almost shouted.

"Toki!" I scolded in a quiet voice.

We shot our gazes to Tamaku. He began to squirm around. He began to mumble a little. I couldn't make it out. He must have been dreaming.

We stared until he was still again.

"Sorry," Toki said softly. "But why did he make you jump off—better yet, why are you still alive?"

"It's not as bad as it sounds. I just wanted to see how you would react," I laughed. "He had me jump so I could find my element types. It was supposed to be sudden danger or something."

"Well, I was going to kick his butt, but since you don't seem to mind, I'll spare him," she chuckled. "By the way, what are your powers?"

"Water and lightning," I replied proudly.

"Nice, Scarlet. Lighting is extremely rare."

"Thanks. I also learned sword combat today, too. I even placed a small cut on Tamaku," I said.

"Wow, Tamaku's got some competition, huh?"

"Barely," I chuckled. "But he did teach me a lot. I now understand spirit energy. So basically, today went well."

"Tamaku must be happy. He really has a knack for teaching others." She peered out the window and at the moon. "I should probably go now," she said as she silently stood to her feet. "It was really great talking to you, Scarlet. Oh, and sorry about barging in like this." She said sweetly.

"It was great talking to you, too. I couldn't sleep anyway."

She then waved goodbye and slipped out.

I lay back and pulled the sheets over my shoulders. I wanted her to come back. I was even more awake than I was before. At this rate, I might not get even an hour of sleep. It really was cool talking to a girl. Guys don't always have the best attention spans. Plus, I could relate better to her.

But after a long while, my eyes began to get heavy. Just when I was falling into an unconscious stupor, I heard a noise outside the hut. I quickly sat up and looked at Tamaku. Then, again, I heard another noise. This time it sounded like a man shouting. I peered outside the window above the bed to get a look at the commotion. The image I saw was very frightening. There, right outside the hut, was Toki. There were two other men with her as well. They were standing above her, kicking her like a useless can on a sidewalk. She was covered with bruises and cuts—I could see that from a distance.

"This will teach you, useless piece of garbage," said one.

"You can't just go stealing things that don't belong to you." He stomped his foot on her face, then kicked her in the ribs. "It's a shame it had to come to this; you had such a pretty little face. Now, no one will ever recognize you."

"I wouldn't be surprised if you died here," said the other with a chuckle.

I couldn't believe what was happening. I immediately grabbed my Raico sword from the bedside. It felt even heavier than before. But I eased out the door so I wouldn't wake Tamaku. I knew I had to do this on my own. If he woke up, he would try to help me.

He said earlier that I need to trust my own powers. I still didn't know exactly what to do, but I at least had to try.

The men did not see me when I walked out the door. The two men were tall and looked about thirty or so. Their hair was greasy, pulled back, and their armor was tattered and slightly rusted with age. However, my presence did not go unnoticed for long.

"Hey, little lady. What's a pretty girl like you, waltzing out here with a sword like that for?" asked one, trying to sound what seemed to be melodic.

He pointed to my sword. I did not answer him. I infixed my eyes on Toki. Now that I was closer to her, I noticed how hurt she really was. From the distance, her cuts looked minor. Now I can see the deep gashes in her face. The most serious wound was on her stomach. The sight of the wound was gruesome, causing me to feel light headed. Blood flowed from her wounds creating a pool surrounding her. Both of her eyes were sealed shut. She tried a desperate attempt to say my name.

"Scar—Scar," she barely uttered a sound before getting kicked in the back from one of the men.

"Toki!" I shouted concerned.

This made me very angry. I clenched my sword so tightly due to the rage, I could feel the moistness of my own blood on my palm. I turned to the men. "You guys are disgusting! Why would you do this to her?"

"Did you hear that, Kale? She says we're disgusting," mocked one.

They both started to laugh darkly.

"Listen, kid," started the other man. "She stole from Taurid. She deserves to shed every drop of blood in her body. So it would be better for you if you just minded your own business and go back to sleep like a good girl or you can end up just like your friend here. Personally, I don't want to hurt you, but if you get in our way, we have no choice."

"But you are treating her like an animal!" I protested.

My mind kept telling me to be quiet and go back in the hut. My heart was telling me to fight and save Toki before it was too late.

"She is an animal. All you Audrenian scum are just dumb animals. If you weren't so stupid, you would have taken my advice and left while you had a chance. Now it's too late; there is no running away," one said.

The other man stepped closer to me and lifted my chin with his grungy finger. "See what happens when you try to be the big hero, sweetheart? It never works, but sadly, you won't be living long enough to learn your lesson," he whispered with a conniving smile.

I winced, pulling away from him quickly. I got in my battle stance with my Raico at ready. My hands, however, were shaking from fright.

The first man pulled out an ordinary sword from its sheath. He gave a horrible laugh and without warning, charged towards me with the deadly intent to kill.

My mind began to race. I did not know how to use my powers or wield a sword that well. I thought franticly, but there was no time to think. He was inches away. I dodged the swipe of his blade, but barely. He swung once more at me. I jumped back just in time. I knew I could not keep this up for long. Soon, my speed would decrease and I would surely get killed. I could never defeat him by only dodging. I had to look for an opening so I could attack him.

I still looked for openings while I was dodging him. *If only I could hit him once*, I thought. I looked at my surroundings to see what I could use to my advantage. I finally saw a rock. I figured if I threw it in his path he would trip and fall. Then that way, I could make my move. I pursued my plan. As he was getting ready for his next attack, I picked up the large rock with my free hand. I looked back to see him close behind me. When I threw the rock, he quickly avoided it like it was child's play. My one and only plan had failed…

The man was coming faster than before. I tried to back away again, but I backed into a wall. I was cornered and had nowhere to run.

The man began to laugh. "I've got to say this was a rather boring fight. I thought I would have a little more fun. It turns out you are just another defenseless weakling. Finish her off, Marshal," he commanded the other man.

The second man came up to me and pulled out his sword. He held it up high. He was ready to slice me in half. I shut my eyes and put my hands over my face. It would all be over soon. I know it's pretty corny, but I really did think I saw my life flash before my eyes. Then I heard a surprising clang of two swords. How was I still alive?

I had dropped my sword down on the ground. I opened my eyes slowly. Then, in front of me was the all too familiar shape of Tamaku. He had jumped right in with his sword in hand. While blocking the other man's sword, he looked back at me over his shoulder. "Scarlet, go get Toki and get out of here!"

I stood there in shock. My mouth grew dry and my throat tightened.

"Scarlet, go now!"

I hesitated, but obeyed him, running to Toki. She was unconscious. I was a little afraid to even look at her. There was so much blood. I looked at her face. She was so hurt; I could barely recognize her face just as the man said. I had just met this strong and beautiful Toki the other day. Who would have thought something like this would happen in only two days. I guess that goes to show...*anything* can happen to *anyone.*

I remember how emotional Tamaku got when he said Toki was the only family he had left after his parents died. Toki took care of him his whole life. If Toki died, he would have no one left. That is why he was so nervous when he found out she stole that food from the palace. He loves his sister so much—that was evident. That was one of the reasons why I admired Tamaku. I could not let him down. He is always helping me. It is time for me to return the favor.

Without giving it anymore thought I put her on my back. I headed for the woods just a few paces from the action. Before completely departing, I looked back at Tamaku. Fortunately, he had already taken care of the first man and was working on the second. Tamaku glanced at me. My guess was that he wanted to see where I was heading so he could meet up with me later. I was just about to go when I saw Tamaku take a huge blow in the arm. I cringed. The cut looked extremely deep. "Tamaku," I said, barely audible.

He looked at me. "Just take her away from here, I'll be just fine. I will meet with you in fifteen minutes," he promised, wincing from the pain on his arm

My body would not move. I watched as he struggled. "I can't leave you!" I pleaded.

"Yes, you can; I believe in your strength. That's why I am putting my sister's life in your hands."

My vision was getting clouded from tears still chambered in my eye sockets. I had not known why, but I really wanted Tamaku with me. It almost killed me to leave knowing he was in harm's way. I had to be strong. I ran into the moon lit forest, running into branches with Toki in my arms. *Please come back to me Tamaku, I* thought with tears streaming down my cheeks. I had almost forgotten it was cold outside. I felt almost numb. I pressed on.

# CHAPTER 12

## PULSATION

I had been walking through the woods for about ten minutes. I was exhausted. My legs ached and my feet were stinging from the many scrapes and cuts from walking barefoot. As I looked around, it was the same as before when I was walking to town the other day. Every plant was brown and dead. Even in this forest, no tree contained leaves or a sense of life.

I found the perfect spot to wait for Tamaku. It was a small area with no trees and only grass. I slowly put her down on the ground. I felt a chilled draft on my back where Toki was. My back was drenched with her blood. When I looked at her, she was very pale in the face. With that wound on her stomach, she had lost a tremendous amount of blood; I knew that for a fact.

I took her hand and placed it in mine. She was very cold. This worried me. I had to be calm—it was no time for hysterics— checked her arm for a pulse.

It was slow but steady.

I had to stop the bleeding. I took out my Raico and cut off a piece of my shirt from my sleeve. I bandaged the wound on her stomach. It didn't do much, but it helped. The bleeding slowed down, but it was still seeping through the cloth.

I found a large boulder to sit on. It had been about 30 minutes of me sitting here. Where is Tamaku? I pulled my legs to my chest and wrapped my arms around them. I laid my head on my knees. I wanted to cry. I really was scared to be on my own. Terrible thoughts entered my head. Things like, if Tamaku was killed or so badly injured, he couldn't make it here. What If he lost his way and couldn't find us, or Toki ended up dying? I tried to rid myself of these thoughts but every time they got stronger. My grim thoughts were interrupted. I heard a faint cough from Toki.

I immediately attended to her. "Toki, can you hear me?" I said softly. I didn't want to speak too loudly; but, I didn't know if she could sense that I was with her. She opened her mouth to try to say something. She could not speak.

"Toki, don't push yourself," I said running my fingertips from her temples to her jaw. "Don't worry, Tamaku will be here soon," I assured, though I wasn't sure if I was assuring myself instead.

She cleared her throat. "I...won't...make it Scarlet." She began to cough uncontrollably.

"Don't say that, Toki. You will make it. Your wounds will be healed soon. Tamaku will know what to do."

She opened her eyes slightly. "Scarlet, you are such a beautiful girl. Tamaku has been watching over you for a long time. You were all he ever talked about. He is very fond of you." She coughed and closed her eyes again. She gave a faint smile but it faded away quickly.

"Hey...hey, Toki?" I said while shaking her shoulder lightly.

She said nothing and did not move.

*Oh no*, I thought. I started to shake her more roughly. "Toki," I said with urgency in my tone. There was still no response.

I put my ear close to her heart. It was beating ridiculously slower than before. I was just glad it was beating at all. She was only unconscious. But I feared that her words of not making it might indeed be truth.

As I sat next to her, I thought of Tamaku again. This absence of his arrival began to worry me.

"Scarlet?" Toki panted.

I sat up and drew closer to her swiftly. "Yes?"

She continued to pant and gasp. "I can't breathe."

I looked at her and noticed a huge gash in her chest. Based on her breathing, I had come to a conclusion that one of her lungs was punctured. "Toki, don't talk, it will only make it worse." That was about all I could tell her. I honestly had no idea how to help her. I just wanted Tamaku to hurry up. I started to sweat from intense pressure. My heart felt as if it was timed and would blow at any moment.

I heard someone or something step on a stick in the bushes. I looked to my left to see the bush rumble. Someone was here.

# CHAPTER 13

## EARTH BOUND

"Come out!" I demanded. "I know you are there." I shouted, but I received no answer. I looked back at Toki and noticed she was breathing normally again. I stood up. "If you will not show yourself, that is fine with me. Please, just leave us alone, this is not the time to be playing games," I pleaded. I was scared enough as it was. If I had just let Tamaku fight those guys in the first place, we wouldn't even be in this mess.

Then, Tamaku stepped out from the bushes. He started to walk towards me. I do not know what came over me, but I ran as fast as I could to him. I knew it was a stupid thing to do at a time like this, but there was an over whelming sense of joy within me. When I got to him, I held him tight. Tears flowed from my eyes. "I thought I would never see you again." I laid my head on his chest. His skin was warm, comforting.

"Don't worry. I'm here now."

"Tamaku, Toki isn't doing too well."

"Oh, no." He immediately broke away from the hug without a second thought. He ran over to Toki. He put his hand on her forehead and bit his lower lip. "She is so cold," he said. He placed the back of his hand on her cheek.

She began to wake up. "Tamaku," she said, giving a weak smile. She chuckled a little.

"Look at the trouble you've gotten yourself into. I knew something terrible like this would happen," he complained jokingly, but he knew what he was saying was true.

"You sound more and more like father every day. You even have the same handsome face" She coughed. "You were only six

93

back when they died. You cried for so long. You would always ask me when they would come back home. I used to always say-"

"You would always say, that one day, we would meet them when we find them," Tamaku interrupted.

"We would find them in heaven," they said together.

Toki continued. "You still waited every day at the front door, night and day awaiting their return. I would always warn you about catching a cold. You never listened. It seemed like you always had a stuffy nose from sitting in that cold weather."

They both giggled.

"From the day they died I made a commitment. I was completely dedicated to taking care of my brother." A tear rolled down her cheek. "I know that is what they would have wanted. I also knew that one day I would have to let you be independent. I knew the time came when you became Scarlet's guardian. You were so responsible. Taking care of you was my main purpose in life. But now...I'm going to go meet Mother and Father. I'm just glad I got to see the last Varcia."

"Toki, do not speak such things. You will live! I swear it! Toki, you have saved me so many times. Now it's my turn...but I am only as strong as you are. You must believe, too. Stay strong for me, stay strong for yourself." I could hear his voice cracking with tears. "Just hold on," he pleaded, kissing her small, thin hand. His eyes poured with tears now.

He laid his head on her bloody torso. All the pain from so many years escaped in tears.

"Tamaku, do not mourn over my death," her voice was raspy now. You shall meet me once again. Mother and Father will be there as well. Where we will be is much better than this evil place. There, no tear will ever fall from our eyes. Then we will all be together again. We…will finally be a…" she fell silent. The grip she had on Tamaku's hand had loosened.

She was gone.

I wish I could relate to him. I, too, had lost my parents, but I still had other people around me. He had no one. My pain was immense, but his I will never truly understand. I wanted to comfort him but I did not know how. I gazed into his watery, dark eyes. This gaze I could not hold for the misery that dwelled within his eyes was overriding. This caused me to cry as well.

He gave Toki a kiss on the forehead. He gazed, still with sad eyes as he smoothed her hair. His gaze immediately transferred from her to me. He was silent but his eyes seemed to say it all. They seemed to question the agonizing pain we had just encountered. I came closer to him and sat at his right side. I cupped his hand in mine. "I'm so sorry, Tamaku," I whispered.

The sun began to rise. It appears that this mayhem had lasted all night. I looked at his barely lit face. His damp eyes were shimmering in the light. I wrapped my arms around him. He did not move for a while. He was cold, still. He reminded me of a lifeless statue. Then without taking his eyes off of his sister, he wrapped his arms around me. There we sat as the sun rose. The silence was killing me, but I did not loosen my grip. I felt moisture on my arms from his tears trickling from his deep eyes. Then without warning, he stood to his feet. There was something eerie about him at that moment.

"I will avenge my sister's death," he said in a low, soft voice. "No more Audrenian blood shall be spilled by their hands. Taurid's empire will fall. We will both defeat him once and for all. Everyone's suffering will no longer be in vain…including my own."

I could feel the hatred in his tone. It was hatred that had been passed down from so many generations of abuse and torment. Now the suffering stops. I couldn't even stop those weak henchmen earlier. I bit my lip and clenched my jaw. I was fighting back tears now...I needed no weakness to interfere. At this point, I won't stand a chance with Taurid. It has already been three days and what have I really accomplished? I must get stronger...for everyone.

# CHAPTER 14

## SERENITY

Tamaku gave me a clean shirt to put on. It was almost my size. It felt awkward when he didn't speak. I wasn't sure if it was okay to speak yet. I wasn't sure if his silence was mute grieving or if there was simply nothing more to say.

Tamaku and I buried Toki. We dug a small hole and marked her grave with a cross made from sticks. We buried her at her favorite place. It was the only place in all of Audren with a live plants and grass. A meadow, which Tamaku says she always took him to after their studies. It was called the Meadow of Serenity. He told me that flowers were her favorite thing. Her favorite flower of course was the Midnight Airos. She had never actually seen one.

Tamaku said he would one day find a Midnight Airos and mark her grave with it. He also said he would give her a proper funeral when all this madness was over.

On the ride home he let me ride on his back because my legs were in so much pain. He didn't even fly. He walked.

"Why did my sister have to die?" He asked suddenly breaking the silence. I had almost grown accustom to the silence.

"Tamaku please stop." I knew where this was going. I wasn't prepared to hear him start to blame himself for things that were clearly out of his hands.

"No, I just can't seem to understand," he said in a rushed tone.

"I wish I had all the answers, Tamaku," I said with a sigh.

"Do you think it's something I did?" he almost whispered

"Tamaku please stop this foolishness. It will only make things harder. Yes, it was very tragic, but you and I both know that there was nothing we could do. If anything, be happy for her. She is in a much better place. Get over it," but not a full second after, I cringed at my harsh, heartless tone just then realizing what I had done.

Tamaku stopped and let me. The rage in his eyes was disturbing. I had never seen this side of Tamaku before. His glare was cutting as his smoky eyes penetrated.

"Don't you think I know all of that?" He shouted, almost roared. He was fuming, his fists were so tightly balled.

"Tamaku," I began apologetically, contritely.

"No! I don't want to hear it! You will never understand." He began to cry. "You will always have someone to come home to. All I have is an empty hut. I loved her and you tell me to just get over her?"

"Tamaku I-"

"Shut your mouth! You don't have anything to say!" he said with a staggering effect.

I stammered as I began to leak tears. I quickly got to my aching feet and began to run. I didn't know where I was running to, but anywhere was better than with him.

After running for about a minute, I had to slow down, now my legs were aching. As I slowed down, I noticed I was in another forest. I had no clue where I was, but I kept going anyway, never setting my gaze behind. As I slowed down more to walk, I tripped over a rock. I fell face down on the ground. I had no energy to get up. My legs hurt too much. I just rolled over on my back and looked at the sky as the sun's heat radiated upon my tapered form. I looked down at my locket and clenched it in my fist.

Why did I have to come here? My urge to return home was atrocious. If only I had just ignored stupid Room 74. Why was I so enthralled with it anyway? I had thought Matt was naive for believing my chicken story, but no, I had to go talk to a room.

It reminded me slightly of a horror movie. We all know how it feels when there is that one stupid woman that was moving right toward the killer. Everyone in the theater says, "Don't go in there!" and "He's right there!" Despite everyone's warning, she mindlessly falls right into the trap that seemed so excruciatingly obvious. Then what happens? She dies.

If only I had the audience that warned me to stay away from the obviously unsafe dorm room. Wasn't hearing voices calling my name enough to keep me away? No; of course not. The old saying popped into my head: *Curiosity killed the cat.* I never even noticed how true that saying was until this very moment.

Suddenly...

"Scarlet," said a voice that sounded like a young woman.

I sat up and looked in every direction but saw no one. I just figured it was just my imagination. It wouldn't have been the first time my mind trailed off. This thought did not last long.

"Scarlet," said the voice again.

I knew this was not my imagination. "Who is there?" I demanded and stood to my feet. "Show yourself! I am not afraid to fight you!" I looked around but saw no trace of life anywhere. The truth is, I was afraid to fight this seemingly invisible opponent. I drew my Raico.

"Lower your sword. Do not be afraid, I am here to help," said the voice.

That's when I noticed how close the voice sounded. This meant it could not be in hiding.

"I can teach you how to work me," it said.

Then I thought about it. The thing I wanted to know how to work was my locket. Was my locket actually talking to me? No, that is impossible. It felt silly, but just to make sure, I held my locket up. The locket was glowing. "Are you the one talking to me?" I asked almost laughing, expecting no answer.

But I was wrong...

"No. It is not the locket itself. I am an energy being sealed within it. I am your guardian," it said.

"Wait, I thought Tamaku was my guardian."

"That he is, but only when you are in the human world, in hopes of you coming to the Audren realm. I am your guardian while you are in the Audren realm. My job is to assist you with your powers." Her voice was so velvety smooth. It sounded as beautiful as singing.

"So you can help me with my powers?" I asked still gripped that this was actually happening...I mean, I am talking to my locket.

"Yes, all you need to do is call my name and what power you would like to use and I will help you activate it."

"So what exactly is your name?"

"My name is Serenity," she affirmed.

"Wow that is a beautiful name."

"Yes, and with that name you shall be victorious among all evil forces."

"Serenity," I started. "May I please ask you a question?"

"Yes, my child."

"I have been in the Audren realm for 3 days now. Why is this the first time that you have ever spoken to me?"

"I have been lying dormant until about yesterday. Tamaku, your guardian, awakened me."

"Do you mean that time when he touched you and the locket glowed?" I recalled.

"Exactly."

"So you mean, this locket was really made in Audren?" I asked, dazed.

"Precisely. You do not understand how I was made in Audren, yet your mother gave this locket to you, do you?"

"Yeah, I don't understand," I divulged. "How did she get a hold of this locket if she was not an Audrenian? She couldn't have come here since she is not a Varcia like I am."

"I am your guardian, and I do know answers to many of your questions. Unfortunately, I cannot tell you everything you crave to know. Some secrets you must uncover for yourself. Fortunately, you do love adventure, do you not?"

I scrunched my eyebrows. "I do, but I just wish I knew more about all of this so I wouldn't be so confused. Everyone says I am the last Varcia, and the fate of Audren rests on my shoulders. I just don't understand it all. I mean, everything is so weird here. For starters, I am standing here talking to a locket...my guardian in the Audren Realm and the worst part is that Tamaku is very angry with me," I said desolate. I felt my face cringe on mentioning the quarrel though I guess it would be better to classify it as a situation gone completely wrong.

"Fret not, child," she reassured. "You shall understand everything that you cannot explain. Time is the ultimate answer to all questions. Time is what you need to understand all that you yourself question."

"I see what you mean." I didn't really know what she meant.

"Do not worry yourself. Everything will be as it is intended. I will leave you to think for now, if you need me just call my name. Try to find Tamaku as well. Remember, never be afraid." With that the light faded out on the locket.

I was afraid to face Tamaku again. He was so angry. But then Serenity's words rang in my ear. "Do not be afraid," I repeated aloud.

I then began to try to find my way out of the forest in hopes of finding Tamaku. I had gotten so deep in the forest that I did not know my way back to town. I had lost count of the times I passed a fallen tree. I had been walking in circles for what seemed to be hours now. I probably should have been vexed but when I thought about it, did I really even want to find Tamaku?

I took a rest by a tree. I had been up all night. My body ached and my head was throbbing. My eyes grew heavy. Fatigue was bombarding me unsparingly. I couldn't help but doze off in my resting spot.

Not long into my sleep, I heard music. It sounded like a flute but at the same time not a flute. It was also a very familiar sound. It finally hit me. It sounded just like the flute that Tamaku was playing the other night.

I stood to my grimy feet. I wondered if it was Tamaku playing. The sound was coming from my left. As I followed it, the music became louder and louder. I knew where exactly the music was coming from. As I moved away some bushes I was at a beautiful gurgling water fall with a stream. Here all the grass was actually green. The trees were filled with green leaves, and flowers adorned the vegetation. Some of the bushes hosted various fruits I had never seen before. Everything looked as alive as you could ever imagine.

I noticed that under the falls was a distorted figure.

"This is where the music is," I concluded.

I did not want to get too close. However I was curious; I peered into the falls and squinted my eyes. I still could not make out the figure. I was afraid to move closer to the eerie shadow.

Yet again, my adventurous spirit got the better of me. I eased my way silently through the bushes. I stepped on a small stepping stone in the stream to get a better look. As soon as my foot touched the stone the music stopped instantaneously. This caused my heart to pound heavily. My presence was definitely perceived. I felt butterflies battering inside my stomach.

I didn't want to speak but I realized it would probably be the best thing to do—it seemed almost inevitable. "Um...excuse me, I was just passing through and I heard your beautiful music. Then I just followed the tune," I shouted to the figure.

It did not speak or move. I still wasn't sure if this figure was a person or not. Its silence was not very inviting either. I felt beads of sweat glide down my forehead. "I am really sorry for disturbing you," I relinquished. "I will just leave now." I then began to back away before beginning to run away from the scenic waterfall. I was obviously not welcome.

"Wait," said the figure apathetically.

It sounded like the voice of a mere child. I turned around.

"You have entered my waterfall and attempted to leave without seeing my face?" the figure started. "Is that not why you stepped closer in the first place?" he was still behind the falls; I still could not cultivate a clue of this mysterious being that was speaking to me.

"Well yes, but I also stepped closer because the sound was so familiar. That instrument of yours did catch my attention," I said candidly.

"There used to be many Airos Pipe users many years ago. But now there are very few. The fact that you have heard such an instrument being played before is alarming," he said.

"A friend of mine uses the same instrument. I actually thought you may have been him, but I can see I was mistaken," I told him.

"Come closer," said the figure softly.

I obeyed but I was apprehensive.

There were stepping stones leading all the way to the waterfall. Every step that I took made my heart pound harder. My horror movie scenario was inching its way into my mind. I decided to ignore it.

Then there I stood right in front of the water fall with palms sweating, and legs shuddering. He did not move. From this close range, I could tell this boy was tremendously younger than me, he lacked in height.

He played a quick, upbeat tune. When it ended, the water that had been tumbling over the rocks stopped flowing. The figure was then unveiled. I almost screeched at the sight! It was him! It was the boy in my dream!—the dream in which I killed him. How could this be? The boy stood before me; he looked about 10 or 11 years old. He had beautiful, wavy, shoulder length, silver hair. It was definitely him.

He looked at me in bewilderment. He could tell I was disturbed by something. No, this couldn't be! Maybe I was just overreacting. Maybe this was all just a coincidence. Yeah, a coincidence that's all...yeah right.

His eyes were crystal blue. In his hand was a flute that was identical to Tamaku's Airos Pipe. The thing that surprised me the most was that the boy had shimmery, transparent, light blue wings that embellished his back. They resembled that of a dragonfly. Somehow I knew that they were not used for flying.

"My name is Omi. I am the last of the water flairs. This whole forest is mine and is my home. What is your name and where do you come from?" he was small but intimidating. His question seemed like a demand though I doubt he meant it that way.

I just decided I would ignore my uneasiness for the time being.

"My name is Scarlet Lansing. I'm not from around here...well, you probably knew that. I am visiting the city right outside of this forest."

"By your scent I can tell you come from the human world. I haven't seen a human around here before."

"Yes, but you said this forest is yours. Do you live here all by yourself?"

"Yes, this is the thirteenth year of me being by my lonesome. It gets lonely sometimes. That is why I play my Airos Pipe. Whenever I play music, I feel comfort."

I smiled at this.

"No one ever comes around here with the whole Taurid business that everyone is so fixated on. There have even been rumors that this forest is haunted by the spirits of those that Taurid killed." He shook his head peering down, "People will believe anything these days." He whipped his gaze back into my eyes so fast, I barely caught it. "What brings you this deep in the forest?"

Due to his speedy reflexes, my reply was slightly delayed. "To tell the truth, I am very much lost. I was wondering around to try to find the way back to town. I actually need to get back very soon but I'm afraid I am not familiar with this forest. If it isn't too much trouble, do you think you can you help me please?" I sounded as courteous as I could.

"This place has always been my home. I know every stone, plant, twist, and turn in this whole forest. You seem true in your story so I will help you, but the walk will be long and you might grow quite weary," he warned. It was amazing how his small, boyish pitch was at the same time sounding as a grown man with abundant wisdom.

"Oh that doesn't bother me. Thank you very much. Omi, right?"

He nodded. "Just follow me and make sure to keep up or you will lose your way. This forest is full of passages and tunnels that will lead you to unwanted places." He then began to walk on the stepping stones heading for shore ahead of me. I quickly skipped a few stones to catch up.

I walked closely behind him. "Omi, how come every plant in Audren is dead and brown, even in this forest but by this waterfall of yours, everything is green and alive?"

"Water is the source of all life—all creation knows that. I am a water flair. I was born at that water fall," he said pointing his thumb behind him. "Even my family lived there. I haven't ventured out in a very long time." He pulled out his flute and began to play another tune. At the end of the melody, the water began to tumble over the rocks once more. "Now we can be on our way."

I looked at him in amazement. With one small tune, he could stop water and make it flow again. "Wow, how did you do that?" I hadn't actually meant to say the words aloud.

"It is a simple water manipulation technique. My pipe is more than an instrument. It is a weapon," he said.

I could see he was a water manipulator from the start but his skill was amazing.  I still lingered on the fact that this boy did not act his age at all.  He was very mature...quite like an adult.

At that moment, I had a revelation.  The reason why Audrenians survived without water around is because their only sources were the water manipulators that were skilled enough to summon any kind of fresh water.

We were walking for a while, passing through the large forest stepping over rocks, sliding through tight spaces, and leaping over logs.  Then the thought of Tamaku crept into my mind.  Tamaku was so angry with me.  I accidently sighed aloud.

Omi didn't miss it.  "Is there something troubling you, Scarlet?  We have been going for a while now; we can take a rest if you like," he offered.

"No.  I'm fine.  We must continue.  I was just uh... thinking."

He studied my face for a moment, which made me a little uncomfortable.

"Your wish is to become stronger, is it not?" he murmured.

"Um, yes but how did you know that?" I said a bit tensely.

# CHAPTER 15

## NEW

"It's in your eyes. However, I must warn you, in this realm you will face many troubles. One thing you must remember is to never act on revenge or hate. Those two components will quickly lead to destruction."

I immediately thought of Tamaku again. He had the look of pure hatred when Toki died. The darkness in his eyes was immense. He wanted revenge on Taurid at all cost.

We continued through the forest.

"'Omi'," I breathed. "...That's a really cool name"

"Thank you. It was given to me by my mother. She was a very sweet-"

As we walked, Omi stopped, placing his arm in front of me. When I tried to ask him what the meaning of this sudden pause was, he only hushed me. He slowly peered around the forest as the sounds of cicadas buzzed through the air. He would not say a word. Was something wrong? Just then, Omi turned to look at me. His eyes felt as though they would cut right through me. He then whispered but I could not understand what he had said. I looked at him with confusion.

"Get down." He said in a vigorous tone.

I immediately obeyed. I dropped to my knees; but, before my mind could utter another thought, I heard a large, heart stopping roar. I looked up to see a beast standing in front of Omi. I could barely stand to look at the horrific sight. The beast resembled a lion but with a demonic twist. Its eyes were the color of dreadful flames. Its coat was the shade of coal and it stood to about 7 feet on all fours. The beast's teeth were the size of swords but looked twice as sharp. I had never set my eyes upon such a sight. I wanted to shriek from the horror, but my mouth could not enunciate a sound. My breath was gone along with my mobility. With another roar from the monster, my body felt numb as a whole.

"Get away!" commanded Omi.

The creature began to walk towards Omi. Omi then lifted one hand. The beast however did notice. It then casted its gaze to my frozen body.

"Don't you dare," said Omi as he lifted his other hand.

In a matter of seconds, two gusts of water shot from his palms and to the beast's enormous form. The impact forced it against a tree with a crash. A large cry flowed from the beast as it returned to its feet but then dropped back down like a tumbling tower—only three times as loud. It was still very much alive, but its mobility became questionable. I still dared not to move. Omi then pulled a sword from his side. His steps continued towards his target.

He seemed so relaxed, almost bored and uninterested. The sword was thin but long. As it glistened in the sunlight, the blade then disappeared with a gush inside the animal's body. It gave an agonizing screech but it only lasted a moment, for the beast then lay dead. Omi removed his sword and cleaned it on the grass. He then looked my way motioning for me to stand.

I was still very much shaken by the events that had just occurred; but, I obeyed nonetheless. My legs felt as brittle as limp tree branches, and my arms like noodles. With one foot in front of the other, I slowly began to walk as Omi had instructed.

"Scarlet, it is over...don't be afraid." He held out his hand for me to grasp.

I still could not understand how Omi could kill such a monster with that much composure and ease. I glanced at the creature. He was indeed dead but I still could not bear to look.

"Omi...how could you do that so well?" I asked taking his tiny hand.

"That kind of creature is very common in this forest. I have been fighting them from a young age and they are rather simple to defeat. I am surprised you did not run into one on the way to my water fall."

"You mean...there is a chance we may run into another one?"

He nodded. "But that is not of any importance. Now we must focus on getting out of this forest."

With a small time to rest, we were back on our feet. When I arrived here it was early morning and now it was getting dark. How far did I actually go in this forest?

"We cannot travel when it is night fall. There are too many dangers that lurk in this forest at night. I had hoped we would make it back before dusk, but we still have a little more to go. I guess we have no choice but to sleep outside. We will start again in the morning," he informed. He did, in fact, appear to know exactly what he was talking about.

I reluctantly agreed. I was still worried about another beast creeping by us in the night. As we sat around the camp fire that Omi had prepared, I stared at his fire lit face. He was playing his Airos Pipe again. He did play quite well. He acted so old but was so young. I suddenly could not keep my silence.

"Omi, may I ask you something? He looked up from his pipe, ceasing the music.

"Yes, what is it?" He looked indifferent.

"If you don't mind me asking, how old are you?"

"I am twenty-four," he said with his expression unchanged.

110

It could not be real. I knew he wasn't seven years older than me. "I know that you are not 24 years old. Twelve I could believe, but not 24. Don't worry, you can tell me the truth," I chuckled.

"I am. I have no reason to lie to you," he said in an apathetic tone once more.

I raised one eye brow. "Then how come-"

"How come I look so young?—is that what you were going to say?"

I looked down in shame. Was that a bad thing to ask?

"This is because this is not my true form," he continued.

"What do you mean? Is that even possible?"

"Normally it is not, however with the immense powers of Taurid, I can't be sure anymore."

"You mean he is the one that did this to you?"

"I will tell you the story" he said as he sat up a little. "There was a time when this whole forest was beautiful and abundant. Not one creature, plant or animal, went unattended. Some said it was the most beautiful place in the entire Audren realm. This forest belonged to us, the water flairs. We were the ones that gave it life. I was only eleven years old when Taurid and his men arrived. Taurid had one wish back then. He wanted to gain more power. The water flairs look very brittle and weak, but we are—well, were—a very powerful race. When he learned of this, he wanted our power for his own evil in which I do not know. He wanted to drain our spirit energy from our very bodies. In order to do so to any flair, you must separate their soul from their physical body. In other words you must kill them. I remember that night very clearly. It was the night of the Water Manipulation Festival...I was drawing water from the water fall to drink with my baby sister right before the festival started..."

~~~*~~~

I sighed as I filled the buckets with water. I was going to have to make several trips. Why would mother make me draw water when the party is about to start? She is always telling me to do things and take away my fun. The worst part is she made me take Sacrae along with me. Even now, all I can here is her whining about something, and I'm pretty sure she just used the bathroom in her pants because I smell something disgusting.

"Hey, Omi," said a musical voice. It startled me and I accidently dropped one of the buckets.

"What," I shouted as I turned around. Then I saw who it was. It was Mary-Alice, the cutest girl I knew. She was the only girl in our entire village that I could ever really talk to without sounding stupid. I don't like her or anything I just....well she is pretty. I just really liked her blonde hair that was neatly put into short pigtails. Her blue eyes were really cool too; but, I don't like her like that. Well...

"Oh, hey, Mary-Alice, what are you doing here?" I asked, trying my best to make the words come out right.

"Well, I just wanted to make sure you were coming tonight. I couldn't find you anywhere," she said. "I just heard from Jamison that you were out here."

I could feel myself sweating and my thoughts getting jumbled. I had to answer her. She was just looking at me. "Well, uh, I'm going, I just have to do that stuff. I mean, I want to go, I just am really busy. Wait, that's not what I meant, I-"

She began to laugh. "You're funny, Omi. I know what you mean." She began to smile sweetly at me. She casually looked down and caught a glimpse at my little sister.

"Oh, you brought Sacrae!" she then shifted her talk to her.

112

"Oh, look how adorable you are. Are you having fun with Omi?"

Sacrae laughed not even understanding a word that was said. Babies are so annoying. I don't know why people take the time to talk to them. They just laugh and stare.

"Sorry, she can't talk yet. You know, since she's a baby and stuff."

Mary-Alice laughed again as she picked up Sacra. "I know that, silly. Babies still need to be talked to. That's how they learn," she said as she lightly bounced Sacra in her arms. Mary-Alice still had that cute smile she always had. But I don't even like girls yet, so I don't like her; just so you know.

"Yea, I knew that. I just um...I just didn't say I knew," I knew I sounded like an idiot. She raised one eyebrow but kept a smile.

"Alright," she held out her word in a long skeptical way. "But I think we should go to the festival now. I can help you with some of those buckets," she said as she put down Sacra.

"Uh, no, that's okay. I mean I can do it by myself. Well, not that you're not strong enough 'cause you're a girl or anything but I just don't want you to have to help me,"

I was sweating like a pig! I only hoped she didn't notice. She was always smiling; it was so hard to tell what she was thinking. She giggled covering her mouth.

"I think I'm going to help," she said as she grabbed two buckets.

She directed her gaze to my sister.

"Do you want to help, too, Sacrae?" she asked playfully.

Sacrae giggled. Mary-Alice picked her up and held her in one arm, holding two buckets with the other. I saw them already walking towards the village.  I quickly took the last two buckets and followed.  I lagged behind due to the weight of the water, but it seemed like Mary-Alice handled it just fine.

"Catch up, slow poke," she called from ahead, and giggled.

I then attempted to pick up my speed but as I did, I tripped and fell flat on my face.  I started to get up but before I could she helped me to my feet.  I could feel my heart race.  She giggled again.

"You're so weird, Omi."

I didn't even endeavor saying anything.  I knew I would sound dumb.

"And that's why I like you," she then kissed my cheek and swiftly ran to the front again, grasping the buckets she was carrying.  I couldn't move.  I knew my face was entirely red, I did like her but I had no-.  My thoughts were interrupted by the sound of the emergency bugle.  Oh, no.  Something was going on.  Mary-Alice immediately shot her gaze back at me, realizing what was happening.

Running towards her I yelled.  "We have to get back to the village!" I grabbed my sister and took Mary-Alice's hand, as she dropped the buckets.  We began to run as quickly as we could.  We didn't stop.  I then saw the village in the distance but it seemed like there was too much light.  In a few seconds, I figured out that it was fire.

"Omi, they're here!" she said frantically.

Oh, no.  Why were they here?  As we got closer I saw terrible things.  So many of my friends were lying dead along with many members of my family.  Everyone was running and screaming about.  I figured we should go to my house to stay out of the streets but before I could utter another thought I felt Mary-Alice being taken from my hold.  I turned around to see a tall, scruffy man holding her by the neck.  She was gasping yet pleading with him to let her down. The man then ruthlessly choked her until it seemed as though her breath was gone. He then seemed to extract some sort of blue light from her body. *It was the water manipulation ability.* He then transferred the light into a container with more of this blue light. I felt a tear role down my cheek as I dashed away from the scene.

I couldn't believe that Mary-Alice had died right before my eyes. But I couldn't think about that. I had to get Sacrae out as soon as possible. I knew my house was too far away and I couldn't afford to run into any more trouble. Passing by burning huts and various frantic people, I made my way to the southern outskirts of the village. I figured we would have to go to town to flee from the chaos.

As minutes went by, I had finally made it outside the village. The air was no longer filled with the exhaust of smoke and the illumination of flames. I passed through some bushes. But in a matter of seconds my baby sister was wailing. Why was she crying? I put her down to examine her. I spotted a small cut on her chubby left leg. She continued to cry despite my efforts to calm her. She had to be quiet. It was a miracle that no one discovered us as we left the village. If she kept this up, someone would find us for sure.

Then, close behind, I heard footsteps coming quickly. I peered into the shadows and saw a distorted form in a slight distance. I immediately hid the best I could in a nearby bush thicket. However, Sacrae was still crying. I had placed my hand over her mouth to suppress the sound but I knew it was still very much audible. My heart was pumping so quickly and violently it felt painful. The footsteps grew louder, my sweating worsened. I pressed Sacrae against my chest to muffle the crying. But as I did, the bush I was hiding behind was lifted straight from its roots and exposed us to the open air. I shuttered as I saw Taurid standing over me in the flesh! How could this be? I had always thought that he sent his soldiers to do his dirty work. Never would I have expected him to be out on the grounds of slaughter. I could not move. His eyes were penetrating into mine causing my thoughts to jumble. He then took Sacra from my hands and held her roughly in the air by her arm. She was crying more than ever now; kicking and struggling to get free.

"I just knew that there some more water flairs scurrying about. I can smell your scent from a mile away." He then let out a terrible laugh. A laughed that felt as though it was intertwined with demonic forces. I could barely stay conscious from the overwhelming evil. The invisible waves of dark aura were rippling off of him and onto me. I felt dizzy.

"I suppose I should kill her," he said to himself audibly. I saw him reach for his sword that was on his waist. I instinctively shielded my eyes with my arms. All I heard was the sound of crying until it slowly died away. I knew what had happened.

"I will kill you as well, child," he said pointing his sword that was barely touching my neck. I then stood up and begged. "Please, spare me! I will do anything; please just do not kill me!" I could hear the despair in my voice.

He chuckled, "Alright, I won't kill you." He seemed false. I knew there had to be a catch to such an act of kindness.

"But...since you cheated death, I will set a curse upon you." He held his chin, thinking of a bad enough curse, I presumed. Finally he spoke. "You shall remain the same age you are now for all of eternity. You shall see everyone around you die and in your darkest hour, you will not be able to die like you will wish. You shall live on forever in the same appearance. The only thing that will age is your mind."

I could feel beads of sweat dripping from my forehead. After a few words I did not understand, I felt my eyes grow heavy. I fell to the ground but I did not feel the pain. All I felt were my eyes closing...

~~~*~~~

"So that is why you look like an eleven year old?" I said.

"Yes, I would continue to age but my appearance will never change." He wiped away his few tears. I began to apologize for causing him to tell such an obviously hurtful story.

"It's fine. I have gotten over that long ago." He stopped for a moment. "I look up to you, Scarlet. With you being the last Varcia, I know you will be the one to defeat that evil man."

I sighed. "That's just it. Everyone has such high hopes for me, the Last Varcia... I don't know if I can do it. I am just a normal teenager, not a warrior," I said slightly ashamed.

"I would not worry about that. You will find your strength, Scarlet. I can see it. That is why I must ask you something."

"What is it?"

"Taurid has taken many things from me. It would make me happy to fight him by your side because you want to defeat him for the right reasons. I promise I will not ask for much. I will carry my own weight. I have sensed that you are a water element type. I can also sense that your ability level is very low. That is why I am willing to help you with your water manipulation. I will teach you everything there is to know. So please, may I join your journey?"

"Of course, I would like nothing more. Thank you for your help as well! I could use some."

"The pleasure is mine," he said with a grin. It was the very first one I had seen him make.

"Thank you so much. I am more than ready to train! I just want to make it out of this forest before tomorrow night. I need to see how Tamaku is holding up...the last time I talked to him was not very pleasant."

Omi looked curious. "This Tamaku you speak of, is he your boyfriend?"

"Oh, no," I exclaimed as I shook my head. "He is just my guardian, but we have become very good friends." I amended with a smiled.

"You are very fond of him, aren't you?"

"Well," I began to blush. "He is a very sweet guy. He told me that it is his duty to put his life on the line for me. He also said it was his true heart's desire."

"That is one loyal guardian you have," he complimented.

"Yes but I am beginning to worry about him. He has so much hatred in his heart. It is also filled with revenge on Taurid."

"Do not worry. By the way you are describing him I can tell his intentions are not evil. His rage is for the right reasons."

This was a relief. Now I wish I could take back what happened. I was so quick to shut Tamaku up and I didn't listen to what he was trying to say. He had a right to yell at me like that. If he had done that to me, I would have gotten angry, too. But there is no use in dwelling on the past. What's done is done. Now...I need to focus on how to make things right.

# CHAPTER 16

## WATER CYCLONE 64

I soon lost track of the hours that crept by. Omi and I talked about many different things. I showed him my Raico and he was actually impressed by my sword handling. He told me that we would start training tomorrow after I found Tamaku. I just hoped that Tamaku would forgive me. I never really realized how much I thought about Tamaku. After Omi had gone to sleep, I was still deep in thought about how I would face Tamaku once more.

I glanced over at Omi. He was still fast asleep. He looked so peaceful. Omi was a cute kid…I mean adult, whichever. He seemed like such a nice guy. I couldn't wait to see all the cool new techniques that he would teach me tomorrow. I would finally be able to use Serenity. I was also glad that Omi would be joining me on my journey. But I still could not fathom the story he had told me about the destruction of his race. I began to wonder how many people had died from Taurid. Based on what I'm hearing, I'd think there weren't any more Audrenians to save.

That morning we immediately started on our way. It was a little chillier than normal. I was very hungry as well. The last time I had eaten was when Toki brought us breakfast. I didn't complain. I sucked in the cool air of dawn. As we walked, I did notice that Omi had not said a word since we set back out. "Are you okay, Omi?"

He did not answer.

"Omi," I said again as I lightly tapped his shoulder.

He seemed to snap out of his trance and looked up at me. He flashed a smile apologetically.

"Oh, yes I'm fine; I was just deep in thought."

"Oh, I am so sorry for disturbing you. You were just so quiet," I said apologetically.

"No worries; I just can't tell you how excited I am for the journey ahead. For me it is like a dream come true. Like you, I love adventure, it is just that all these years I had no one to venture with. Now I have you, Scarlet." He smiled once more flashing his white teeth though he tried to compose himself on the spot.

"I am glad that you are so excited," I laughed. "You know, I think we have a pretty good chance at defeating Taurid. To me, he is darkness and we are light, and you know what they say: even the smallest light shines in the darkness." I had remembered my science teacher, Mr. Kowalski, had told us that.

"Wow. You seem way more confident than you did last night. What is with the sudden change in your attitude?" he chuckled.

"I don't know. I have had mixed feelings this whole time I have been here; but, part of me says that I will be triumphant. The other part of me says that I don't have a chance. But I think I will focus on being more optimistic. You know, look at the cup half full instead of half empty," I said.

We continued to walk. As the day progressed, I could feel the heat of the afternoon beaming down on my head and shoulders. "Omi, are we almost there?" I asked trying not to sound too impatient.

"Yes, just a little further," he assured.

I wanted to see Tamaku. I could still only hope for the best. I don't know why I care so much. I didn't want to hurt him like that ever again though. I was sure Omi would like Tamaku. When I first met Omi, I have to admit I did have my suspicions from his dull, indifferent aura; but, I had no reason to be cautious of him. As far as I was concerned, he is just like everyone else in this realm...hurt.

Omi had begun to tell me that his legs were in pain, so I carried him on my back. I couldn't blame him. His small legs weren't as equipped as mine to travel the tough terrain. To my surprise, the sun was already beginning to set. This really got my spirits down. The whole day seemed like we were never getting closer to our destination. I anticipated being back by now. But as we continued, I began to notice some familiar dried plants.

"Scarlet, look ahead, we have arrived at long last."

His words were true. Here we were just outside of Tamaku's all-too-familiar hut. Now we just had to find Tamaku. I was helping Omi off of my back when someone called my name. I looked up to see Tamaku darting towards me. I didn't have time to breathe before I was in his arms.

"Tamaku," my voice muffled in his shoulder. "I am so sorry—"

"No, I am sorry. I let my anger get the better of me. Right when you left, I completely broke down. I knew I had hurt you but I just couldn't bring myself to chase after you. I wondered if I would ever see your face again. Scarlet, I'm sorry for snapping at you like that. I could have dealt with my feeling so much better. You were trying to help me but for some reason I couldn't see that," he said sadly

"Tamaku, I forgive you. I was dumb for not listening to—"

"No, no you weren't. You were just trying to help. I get that. You returned here, even after all the pain I put you through." His tone was repentant.

I broke away from his arms. "It's all over now. I never want to think about or talk about this again."

"Yes, then it is finished. Thank you." he seemed more relived then I was. I knew he wouldn't be mad forever, but I didn't expect this either.

I remembered Omi. I turned back at him. "Omi, this is my guardian that I spoke of." I turned back to Tamaku. "Tamaku, this is

Omi. He is a friend that I met; he is the one who helped me out of the forest in one piece. He will be joining us. He's gonna teach me water manipulation." I smiled but I hoped that Tamaku was open for another person with us.

After that introduction Tamaku and Omi talked for what seemed like hours—that was a relief. I would occasionally give a "cool" or "that's true" here and there in the conversation but half of the things they talked about were completely foreign to a human such as me. They took a liking to each other just as I thought. However, I didn't know it would be this instantaneous. I must admit that the whole time I couldn't keep my eyes off of Tamaku. His dark hair tumbled over his forehead perfectly, bringing out his dark eyes. He stood tall with perfect posture which is a rare sight for anyone. Every time he smiled, his bright and dazzling, white teeth glimmered. Every now and then, our eyes would meet and he would smile the same, perfect way. He was very nice to look at for any girl but that's not how I looked at him. Though he was laughing and smiling I could still see the same pain in his eyes that I saw when Toki passed away.

"Hey, guys, don't you think it is getting late?" I insisted. I had enough of just sitting there watching others have a conversation. The darkness was bringing a chill along with it. I was already rubbing my arms, attempting to warm myself with friction.

"Yes, you are right, it is already dark out. I also made some dinner if you are interested," said Tamaku as he gazed at the sky.

Of course I was. While they continued to talk in the hut, I ate some dinner. It was nothing big but it was something. I couldn't tell what it was exactly. It appeared to be a slab of meat but the texture of it felt more like dry paste. This may sound crazy, but it wasn't half bad. I didn't ask what it was—I honestly didn't want to know.

Not too long later, Omi was fast asleep on Tamaku's bed. Even though Omi was an adult, he still had the body of a child. He needed his rest. Tamaku was sitting down polishing his Airos Pipe.

I sat down next to him.

"Hey, did you know that Omi has an Airos Pipe, too?" said Tamaku without taking his eyes off his pipe. I knew his mind wasn't fully away from the incident. I could see why he didn't want to look me in the eye.

"Yes, he told me." I tried my best to make it less awkward. I didn't want us to always be this way.

"Did you also know that he is older than both of us?"

"Yeah, he's 24, right?" I said already knowing the answer.

"Yeah, something like that," he paused for a moment before continuing. "Omi is really nice. He said he is the last of his kind."

"Yeah, he's a water flair." I couldn't keep my eyes off of Tamaku. For some reason, I continued to study his pleasant features. After a moment of me staring, he then locked his eyes with mine. With anyone else, I would have looked away immediately but his gaze intrigued me. Looking at his handsome face made me more fascinated each time. We were both intrigued, I think. Our eyes were truly locked in place. A small smiled stealthily moved on his lips. This caused me to grin as well. He laughed a bit.

"What are you looking at me like that for?" he chuckled.

"Your face is just so...so..." I started to giggle.

"Oh my word!" he interjected playfully. "Are you, Miss, inferring that I am ugly?"

"You are actually disgustingly hideous," I teased as I widened my eyes.

123

He gave a humorous pout that was almost too cute to be true. He crossed his arms lifting his nose to the sky. We both began to laugh. But as it calmed, he faced me with a more serious facial expression. He cleared his throat casually. "But seriously, what about my face?" he still wore a smile.

I looked down anticipating a blush coming on. "Your face just interests me," I admitted, leaving out the fact that he was remarkably gorgeous.

He raised one eyebrow as his shimmering eyes peered into mine. "Interests you?" he echoed almost incredulous.

"Yeah."

He nervously smiled. "Is that good?" he said with a hint of worry.

"I would say so," I said shooting him a smirk. "You're cute," I added with just enough indifference to mask my embarrassment.

He chuckled as he scratched the crown of his head. "Thanks, but I am curious about something," he added.

"And what might that be?" I said, thankful that he changed the subject.

"In the human world...what was your favorite thing to do?" he asked, which somewhat surprised me. I liked to do lots of things. It was kind of hard to pick just one.

"I guess text messaging...it's the best way to talk without...well, talking."

His expression turned to confusion. "What is text messaging?" he asked saying the words as if they were in a foreign language. He still attempted to figure it out.

You have got to be kidding. "Well it's like writing someone a message, just on a cell phone," I explained.

"Cell phone?" he asked with another stack of perplexity.

"You don't know what a cell phone is either?" I asked with disbelief.

"No..."

I sighed. "Will, um...it's um..." it was more difficult to explain than I had expected. "It's like a little machine that you talk in if you aren't with someone."

It seemed like a light bulb in his head flickered on. "Wait a minute! I think I recall what you're describing. I have always been so confused about that tiny contraption I have seen humans talk into. Sometimes they would laugh at, and cry about it. I just didn't understand."

"Yeah, that's a cell phone except...when you use it, you can talk to a friend of family member; not the phone," I explained.

"So you can talk to them without actually being in front of them?" he sounded skeptical.

"That's right. But if you're my guardian and you watch over me, how come you don't know what any of this stuff is already?" I asked.

He lowered his gaze. "Well, even though I could see into your world, I couldn't hear what is going on. To tell the truth...I never really focused on that stuff...my mind was always on you." He gave a small crooked grin. His voice was velvety and captivating. I couldn't help but flash a small smile; but then I remembered that *everyone* at home thought I was cute.

"But I do know of one thing that you guys do in the human world," he amended.

"Shoot. You guys put these things in your ears that have wires coming out of them. I think it plays some kind of sound that makes people happy sometimes. I've seen you do it, too," he pointed out. He thought for a moment before speaking. "I think the thing is a called a smart-part" He sounded proud of himself but he was sadly wrong.

I suddenly remembered something. Surely I had at least one electronic device in my jacket pocket. I had forgotten all about my smartphone. But based on all the madness that had taken place, I wasn't certain that it was still there. Holding up one finger, I made my way to my jacket across the room that was draped over the one chair in the hut. As I reached it, I was thrilled to feel it's cold smooth surface and it was fully charged.

"Is this what you meant?" I asked Tamaku as his eyes were glued to my phone.

"Yes! You actually brought it?" He asked as he clutched it.

"Yes...but it was sort of an accident". I knew I had a few of my favorite songs downloaded for offline use. "Do you want to listen to it?"

"What kind of sounds come out of it?" he asked with his eyes still fixed on the trinket.

"It plays music of course."

"Wow, what kind?" he asked a little too eagerly for my taste.

"All kinds like...rock, rap, pop, hip hop, lots of kinds. I'm guessing you don't know what any of that is."

"Well, I'm curious about this 'rap' music. Can I hear it?" he asked.

I wasn't sure if he would like rap. I only had a few tracks of it so I let him choose. I watched his face as he listened. His mouth stayed wide open. He looked as if he processed every sound. About half way through that song, I paused it. "So...did you like it?" I cringed.

"It was hard to know what they were saying. They were talking too fast for me to understand but it was fun!" he smiled wide. He then narrowed his eyes in perplexity. "I have one question though."

"What?"

"What are '22s and 32s'?" he asked.

I chortled. "Um, they are just rims," I said. His face was still puzzled. "You know," I coaxed. "Like on cars?"

He kept the same face. Then his expression changed, jovial. "Wait, like the shiny things on the wheels?" He smiled.

I giggled at his rather adorable enthusiasm.

"Okay, now what does it mean to *hate on* someone?" he said the words stiffly, enunciating each syllable.

"It just means to be mean to someone or be jealous," I explained.

"Wow, the human world is so weird."

I then decided to scroll through my songs to find something of the Pop genre. I successfully found one of my favorites. I hit play to see Tamaku listen just as carefully as he did to the rap. I was unable to tell if he liked it or not. His expression seemed indifferent. When it was over, I asked him what he thought with my eyebrows raised.

He thought for a moment. "It was pretty good…but I liked the first one better." He still seemed pleased. He seemed eager for the next song. I figured I would end with one of my favorite rock songs.

As he listened, I notice him bob his head a little. His smile was wide as he caught on to the chorus and sang bits and pieces.

"This music you guys listen to is so interesting. There are so many different sounds playing at once."

"Well that's just a little taste of what the human world is like."

I turned off my smartphone as I put it away in my jacket, Tamaku continued about Omi. "Omi said that he has taken a real liking to you. He said that for some reason when he looked in your eyes, he saw hope or something. He also said that if Taurid gets defeated, the curse will be broken and his appearance would match his age. I wonder what he will look like."

"Yeah, I do, too. He is already a very cute kid," I added.

Tamaku chuckled at this. "Yeah, I guess I do have to admit."

I could tell it was awkward for him to say that, but it was humorous.

We both laughed.

"Hey, Tamaku," I said as the laughter calmed.

"Yeah?"

"Well, I saw your Airos Pipe do some cool stuff, but what else can it do?"

"That's a good question. But the fact is, the Airos Pipe can do more things than anyone can count. I would even say it could do just about anything. But you have to know the tune for every technique. I only know a few of them."

"Well how many do you know?" I asked, intrigued.

He thought for a moment, mouthing things to himself. "I know about seventeen of them."

I was a little let down that he knew so little. But I guess it was impressive to know so many tunes, and what tricks matched up with them. I was in band in seventh grade and I played the clarinet. I couldn't even play one song without the sheet music in front of me.

"Can you show me some?"

"Sure," he then glanced at Omi sleeping. "But we would have to go outside...it's a little chilly though."

"I don't mind," I chuckled. I found it silly that he would think I would pass up spending time with him for a little wind chill. Absurd really. Trying to appear natural, I could not stop involuntarily thinking of Tamaku. I couldn't talk myself out of the hypothesis of how I was slowly, yet surely, falling for him. My hypothesis has now become a very non-negotiable theory. But if my theory is no longer being tested or questioned, wouldn't that then make it a fact?

Tamaku was right about the chill. I didn't even notice my shivering until Tamaku placed my jacket over my shoulders. I didn't even see him grab it.

I slid my arms into each sleeve. I zipped it up to the very top. My little hooded jacket didn't seem to do much for warmth, but it was better than my bare skin.

He led us a few meters from the house and sat down. I kneeled down on my knees.

"Okay," he said, not seeming cold at all.

"Well," I prompted, still shivering.

"The first one I ever learned was the Tranquility Blanket. I used it the other day when the Towns people were almost smothering you."

"Oh! I remember that. Everyone immediately calmed down."

"Yes. The tune is made for when the enemies are outnumbering and causes them to be less brutal and more serene," he said. "Now this next one doesn't really have a name. One day I was just messing around playing random notes and this happened. It's honestly not even an attack."

He then played a really fast and scattered tune. It didn't sound like music at all. It was more like a two year old attempting to play the drums. But when it was over, two daisies appeared out of the hollow spaces in the pipe. I clapped my hands and laughed quietly.

He pulled one out and slipped it behind my ear. The other, he placed in my lap.

"That was sweet," I said, gaping at the flowers, touching the petals to make sure they were real. It reminded me of being at a magic show, and a magician making flowers appear.

"Want to see another one?" he asked, already knowing the answer.

He then showed me all types of techniques. One was called Freeze of Substance, which can make anything turn to ice. Another was called Color Blind, where your enemy will see all kinds of different colors that cloud their vision. There were so many, I can barely keep track. But I do know that I was smiling almost every second. I had almost forgotten about the cold how cold it was.

As we walked back in the hut, Tamaku looked over at Omi asleep on the bed. "So I guess we both have to sleep on the floor tonight."

"Yeah, I would wake him up but he is so darn cute when he is asleep." I giggled.

We had talked for a while longer but it soon became late. Tamaku set two blankets on the ground to sleep on. I took the spot at the foot of the bed. He wasn't too far away from me. He blew out the few lamps letting darkness flood the tiny hut. It was still and quiet.

Yet again, I lay awake thinking. This time, I was thinking of Tamaku. I like everything about him. He really cares about me...I almost wish I could stay here longer and spend more time with him. I know we didn't get off to the best start. I honestly didn't really like him too much at first. It wasn't until my training that I saw another side to him, that soft, caring, and compassionate side. When I saw him for the first time today, all I wanted to do was stay in his arms. I feel safe when I am with him. Then again, it makes me sad because I don't think he sees me the same way.

It would actually be pretty funny if he actually liked me, too. Not funny in a "ha, ha" way. Just in a weird way. But what if he really did and I never knew? What if it was so blatantly obvious that it was somehow undetectable? Is that even possible?

I feel like one of those women in a romantic movie. They are always so lost in their own thoughts; they can't tell that the guy they like feels the exact same way. It's funny because the whole time watching the movie, you can't understand why the woman can't see such obvious affection. But Tamaku hasn't done anything that categorizes as obvious affection for me. Or did he? Maybe those movies are actually how life works. Girls always say guys are oblivious, but maybe we are, too. Maybe we are even more clueless than we say the male race is. Maybe guys aren't clueless at all—okay, that is definitely a lie.

I suddenly remembered the little song my friends and I would sing when we were young. *Boys go to Jupiter to get more stupider, girls go to college to get more knowledge.* I laughed to myself. Back then, we thought that was cool and true to some extent. Enough rambling, and back to the big picture...does Tamaku have feelings for me? Even the slightest bit?

I know I shouldn't focus on this, but I can't stop thinking of him. Every time he looks into my eyes, I feel really good. I don't

131

know; I mean, it's probably not the smartest idea to fall for a guy that's doesn't even live in the same realm as you. Never thought I would have to say that, but then again, he's just so sweet... I was twirling one of the daisies in between my fingertips from before. I couldn't really see them in the darkness, but they still felt beautiful...which probably doesn't make sense... But nothing has really made a lot of sense in my life lately. Pigs that fly don't seem that unrealistic to me anymore. I am here lying in a hut in a different realm, with magical creatures and have powers myself. Who am I to doubt the existence of Alice in Wonderland?

I let out one final yawn. I had enough of random thoughts. I pulled up the rough sheets for a little bit of warmth and closed my eyes. I woke up the next morning before Tamaku and Omi. I like waking up early. It gives me time to gather my thoughts...or daydreams. I looked down and saw there was something strange. My wounds healed at an extremely quick pace. My feet were all cut and scratched yesterday, but now there wasn't a trace of any wounds. This place just gets weirder and weirder all the time.

After about an hour of random thoughts, Omi looked up at me with bright eyes. He waved and smiled sleepily.

"Good morning, Scarlet," he yawned as he stretched his arms.

"Good morning, Omi. Did you sleep well?"

"I sure did. But I couldn't help but hear you talking about my 'cuteness'," he said smiling but he made a face.

I started to giggle. "Oh, you heard that?" I smiled, more embarrassed than anything.

"Ha, ha, yeah, but I didn't really mind. The only thing I had a problem with was *Tamaku* agreeing," he over dramatically shivered. "It gives me chills," he joked.

I clenched my stomach in laughter. I didn't want to laugh too loud since Tamaku was still sleeping. "Yeah, that was pretty weird," I chuckled.

"But hey, if he thinks I'm cute, I won't judge him," he teased. We were both holding back laughter but we could both see it was pretty inevitable. "Just kidding," he finally said. "I think we all know who he has eyes for."

I stopped laughing. "What do you mean?"

"Oh, come on, it's so obvious," he said smiling more so at my ignorance. He continued to study my face that I knew was completely blank in thought. He snickered looking away.

"Humans..." he said to himself.

What was he talking about? I honestly didn't know who he was talking about. I only wished it was me.

He cleared his throat. I returned to reality only to be greeted by an awkward silence—I hated those.

"So how did you sleep?" he asked, breaking the almost indissoluble quietness.

"Fine, I guess. I never really sleep well. I'm always up thinking about other things."

"Hmm; like what?" He probed.

"Just things like my powers, Taurid, home-"

"What's the human world like?" he asked animatedly. He seemed very eager.

I thought for a moment. It was hard to explain for someone who had never been there. "Um, I guess it's like this world, but a lot different, too."

He cocked his head to the side, confused.

133

"Well, at least where I live, it's very...very...." I was really having difficulties explaining this. "Different," I concluded. "There are so many different things. There is war, technology, fun places to go, and lots of things to learn. There are many, many places in my world. Unlike here, there is more than just one civilization in my realm."

He seemed mesmerized as if he was trying to imagine it himself. "How many are there?" he asked.

"Way too many to count," I chuckled. I honestly didn't even know how many countries there were in the world.

"Wow," he said. "How do you fit all those people in your world? There must be tens of thousands!"

"Trust me, there are way more than that. Almost every different civilization looks different. There are people with fairer skin, like mine," I said holding out my arm.

"You mean there are people of *different* color skin? Like green and blue?" he asked, overflowing with excitement now. That boyish charm was showing.

"No, no; nothing like that. But there are people with brown skin, tan skin, reddish brown skin—the list can go on forever."

He was nodding slowly to himself. "Okay, I get it now...It's just like here. There are flairs, dwarfs, fawns-"

"You guys have those here?" I didn't think there were other creatures.

"Oh, yes," he nodded vigorously. "There are many talking beasts. There are Ski-lofts—they live deep in the thicket burrows. There are Mistuflorins—they live under ground. I guess this list goes on and on, too."

My mind was soaring. I had no idea of these different creatures. "How come I haven't seen any of these creatures? All the Audrenians I've seen looked like humans," I asked.

"You can't see them. It's because of your eyes or course."

My *eyes*? "What do you mean, Omi?"

"*I mean*, humans can't see them. Sure you have enough spirit energy to enter this realm, but you will never be able to see Audren in its entirety. You are still only human," he pointed out.

I guess that made sense. I did wish I could see these other creatures.

"But that's okay," he said with a grin. "At least you can see flairs," he joked.

"Ha, ha, yeah—that's a relief," I said. But I did mean it. I really was glad to know Omi. He was actually really cool.

"But I don't want to waste any more time. I think we should begin training now," he stood up fixing his clothes a little.

I agreed. With that, Omi and I left into the backyard. It was surprisingly a pretty large space. The cool wind of the morning was refreshing. The chirps and chatters of the birds filled the air reminding me of how early it really was.

I figured it would be a good idea to tell him about Serenity.

After my explanation, he examined the locket he looked in my eyes. "That is truly amazing. Well, I guess this Serenity will be a real help to you and I. This means I only have to show you the technique and how to position correctly. Then all you have to do is shout out the name of the attack and Serenity will take care of the rest. But there is one difficult part. You do know what spirit energy is, don't you?"

"Tamaku told me about it a little bit. He said that spirit energy is your drive to do something. I think it also means will power."

"Yes, that is true. Did he tell you anything about spirit energy balance?" he assessed.

"Spirit energy balance?" I repeated.

"Spirit energy balance is when you keep your thoughts intact and focused. In battle it is very difficult to maintain complete composer when there is the possibility you may not walk away alive. In other words, you must not let the enemy get to you in your mind. Do not be afraid of failure—it's just a way to learn. Doing these things will keep your spirit energy balanced and intact. You must keep balance during every single one of your moves. That is what you will be practicing today."

This worried me. I guess I thought I would be getting a free ride with Serenity, but I was sadly mistaken.

"First I will have to give you a technique. This one is very simple. It is called Water Sphere. It is when you use water to make small balls to launch at your enemy—really simple." His tone sounded as if this shouldn't be a problem for me.

He showed me what position I had to take on. I had to extend and put together both of my arms out forwards. My legs had to be completely lined up with my shoulders. It was pretty simple. Then came the hard part: spirit energy balancing. I still didn't completely understand how to do it. I just thought of Taurid to give me the drive I needed, then I just had to try and pair it up with focus and confidence on my goal. It didn't take me long to put these two together.

"Serenity, Water Sphere!" I shouted. It seemed as though I had failed but I decided to wait a little longer.

For a few seconds nothing happened. Then without warning four water spheres shot out from the palms of my hands. They were not very strong. Instead of actually launching, they kind of eased out in somewhat of a spherical shape. I watched as the water fell onto the barren ground. In only a few seconds, the water seeped into the thirsty dirt completely. It was mind blowing how water appeared out of my hands. I glanced back at Omi.

I decided to give this another try. I stood in my position again, repeating everything. Then, just as I was about to stop, my body was jerked backwards by a blast of water that shot out of my palms. My heart skipped a beat, maybe two; it wasn't from fear but the adrenaline.

"Scarlet, that was amazing! That was almost perfect and on your first try, too!" he exclaimed. He seemed thoroughly surprised.

"Yes, you used me perfectly." It was Serenity's voice. "That is all there is to it. It was not as difficult as you thought, now was it?"

I smiled. "No, it wasn't. But how did you know I was thinking that?"

"When I unveiled myself to you, we, at that moment, became one," she informed.

No wonder she understood me so well.

"That still was a very simple move," Omi interjected. "This may seem effortless, but with more moves comes more battle positions. Your spirit energy level and balance will have to be more exact. For these moves, perfection is the key. But not to worry; I believe you can do it easily, Scarlet," said Omi. "Now, it's time to get serious," his tone was low.

"This next move is a little bit more difficult," continued Omi. "It is called Water Cyclone. We will start with Water Cyclone 1. For this, your spirit energy is even more important than your positioning. Your spirit energy will need to be stronger this time. Your positioning must be somewhat perfect," he informed.

The position was exactly the same as the previous attack. I exhaled as I got prepared for the next position.

"Okay, now go for it!" shouted Omi throwing me a thumbs-up.

With one more glance in his direction, I got in the positioning. I was supposed to make my spirit energy stronger this time but I didn't exactly know how. If only spirit energy could be seen, then maybe I could do this easier. I also had to balance my spirit energy. This was way too complicated.

"Come on Scarlet! Let's get a move on!" shouted Omi as he clapped his hands together.

I wanted to, but I didn't want to mess up. *Okay, Scarlet*, I thought. *All you have to do is exactly what you did before.* I tried to build up my confidence. "Serenity, Water Cyclone 1, go!"

Nothing happened.

With a look of disappointment, Omi crossed his arms. "Your spirit energy is too low. Your balance is also way off. Scarlet, you must focus. Now try again, but this time, be more motivated." He stepped away, farther, and narrowed his eyes in my direction.

I got back in position. I kept trying to focus but something was distracting me. However, I didn't know what that something was. To top it all off, I was still a little confused about this spirit energy stuff. I didn't want to ask Omi to explain it again. He already looked irritated enough (I would have never guessed he was so impatient when it comes to battle). I guess what I did before was just a lucky shot. "Serenity, Water Cy-"

There, near some trees I saw that mysterious woman. The same woman that I bumped into at the market place a few days ago, I'm sure of it. She wore the same cloak that seemed to cover her whole body. Her rich, chocolate colored hair was wavy and long. She had the same stunning emerald eyes. She was standing in plain view. For some reason, no one else seemed to notice her. She was standing right beside Omi, practically one foot away from him.

*How does he not see her or sense her presence? Even an average human being could do that*, I thought. She was looking...no, glaring at me. Her gaze was cutting. I was actually getting very frightened. Why am I the only one that sees her?

Then the woman out stretched her arm towards my direction. I began to panic. She didn't look like a threat but she didn't look particularly on my side. I could feel beads of sweat starting. I wanted to get away but I was locked in her aloof stare. Then, a mysterious light came from the woman's hand.

"Scarlet, what are you staring at?" Omi asked following my gaze. He looked confused...he didn't see her.

I didn't answer. The woman then began to sing. She sang the song of the Midnight Airos. The light became brighter and brighter. For some reason I was no longer afraid. The song seemed to have put my soul at peace somehow. The mysterious beam of light from her hand was slowly traveling to me. I did not move out of its way. The light intrigued me deeply. I did not know what was coming over me but I also did not want it to stop. I felt as though I was in a trance of some sort. I could barely notice anything around me.

I reached my hand out towards the light. It touched my finger tip. It touched my hand, then my arm, then my chest, then my legs, then my feet. The light was running through my entire body. I was drenched with the light.

Then, without warning, a piercing pain penetrated my body. I wanted to yell out but my body just simply would not; I wanted to get away but my body still would not move. I knew Omi was shouting at me, but I could no longer hear him clearly. I felt like there was water in my ears blurring communication. The pain grew worse. I fell to my knees. I could not make a sound, though I needed help. Then, I do not know why, but for some reason I weakly whispered the words, "Serenity, Water Cyclone 64."

The light had immediately vanished. I felt a force being lifted, handing me over to the binds of reality. The woman was also nowhere to be seen. Before I could comprehend all of this, a gigantic whirlpool of water came from the sky. "Was this my doing?" I mouthed.

The water then crashed down to the ground with a roar. It soon had me suspended in its waves, but quickly under its surface. The water was very strong and heavy on my petite body. It swished me in every direction. I couldn't tell which direction the surface was. I tried so many times to lift my head above the water, only to find myself deeper in.

I was losing breath from the tiresome acts I was performing. I outstretched my hands sporadically in every direction. I then finally found a cool gust of air on the very tips of my fingers on my right. I made attempts to swim to the spot. I wasn't sure if it was still there. Who knew how many times I changed positions in the short seconds?

But then I found it. My head was above the rough waters still struggling to force me back in its clutches.

"Scarlet, take my hand!"

I turned to see Tamaku. He had some kind of spherical barrier that was keeping him safe from the water. Omi was already in the barrier as well, unconscious. I reached out for Tamaku, but the waves were too strong, pulling me back underwater.

"Serenity, do something!" my body was losing energy and fast. I gained only a gasp of air. I could not keep treading such rough water.

140

"Serenity, can't you reverse it?" I asked desperately, panting for air.

Still…no answer. I rushed through my mind thinking of ways to stop this. I had no idea and my muscles lost strength every second. I tried everything I could.

"Serenity, Water Cyclone 64, eliminate!" I felt my mouth fill with water. Still nothing, I tried something else.

"Serenity, Water Cyclone 64, reverse!"

Nothing happened. Then it came to me. I needed to stop being frantic and focus. I stopped moving. I closed my eyes.

"Serenity, Water Cyclone 64, withdraw."

# CHAPTER 17

## EVIL INTENT

"Scarlet, wake up," someone was shaking me.

My eyes remained closed. I cringed at the pain my body was now under.

"Scarlet, please," said the voice

I opened my eyes to see Tamaku and Omi standing over me anxiously. I was in Tamaku's bed. "What? Why am I in here? Where did that woman go?"

"What woman?" Omi asked, perplexed.

"Oh, yeah...you couldn't see her," I recalled. My eyes were closing again. I tried to sit up but I jerked back down from the sting. I winced from the pain on my body. "I feel like I got hit by a train," I murmured.

"You were acting very strange back there Scarlet. You just stopped and started spacing out. I would call your name but you wouldn't answer. Then you just collapsed and you were sweating relentlessly. When I went over to go help you up, this strange barrier of light formed around you, shocking me by the touch. That's when you did the Water Cyclone 64. I tried to stop you, but it was too late. The technique is very powerful. Somehow your breakdown seemed to have given you energy. If it had not been for Tamaku, you and I would have drowned in those terrible waves. Somehow, you seemed to have reversed the technique."

Omi seemed thankful, but the glare in his eyes was not pleasant.

"It was this strange woman that gave me the power," I explained weakly. "She was singing the Midnight Airos song. I think she was singing it to me. She was very beautiful, but there was something very bizarre about her as well.  But for some reason, I trusted her."

Tamaku and Omi exchanged looks, and then returned their gaze to me.

"Well more importantly, are you okay, Scarlet?" Tamaku finally asked.

"Yes; even though my body hurts I still have a lot of... energy."

"That is good to hear but you should probably get some rest for today," Omi suggested.

I have gotten so tired of going all these days without getting anything accomplished.  Everyone acts like I don't have a very limited time here.  "Omi, please let me train just a little bit more.  I have already been here for four days.  That means I only have eight more days left before I have to leave.  I can't keep blowing off training."  I made my voice as pleading as possible almost squeezing out a tear.

"You do have a point," he said stroking his chin thoughtfully.  It was silent for a moment.

"Alright we will practice a little more today"

"Thank you so much, Omi!" I sat up to hug him but was forced back down by the pain.  I still wanted to train so I had to pretend the pain was less then it truly was.  I forced myself up, fighting back a recoiling expression.

We went outside once more.  I gazed around to see everything just as it was before.  He was right about that technique being reversed somehow.

I was still in pain but I could ignore it.  For hours and hours Omi taught me numerous moves.  He seemed very surprised at my progress but I was even more staggered by my intense turnaround from before. I was getting these moves down effortlessly at an "exceptional" rate, as he would say. He seemed very happy but I was not. The whole time I had been having terrible thoughts.

The whole time I was with Omi, I thought of nothing but hurting him, maybe even killing him. Every time he talked to me I wanted to see blood. These thoughts were getting stronger and stronger with every second that floated by. I almost couldn't control myself. I wanted to hurt him, but I did not want to hurt him. I didn't know why I felt this way. Since that woman was here I have had nothing but evil thoughts. Was she the cause of all of this? I would bet anything it was the light that caused my pain earlier. Since then, I have also had massive strength. Omi even said my spirit energy has skyrocketed as well. It makes me think of that dream I had. The one where I killed the young boy that looked eerily similar to Omi.

I do not like this. Something might be wrong. I can almost feel the evil running through my veins. It's like...like I am infected with it. It is like a sickness that runs through the heart and mind. That's the only way I can describe it...

A while ago, I imagined Omi dying. It was like a movie that played in my head. I saw him gushing blood and slowly coming to a painful demise. The thought brought an involuntary smile to my face as the compulsive thoughts engulfed my mood. As much as I try to erase such an image, it keeps coming back to me.

Also, none of my thoughts are making sense anymore. Something is definitely wrong with me. How do I stop it? Even now as I look at Omi, I have nothing but murderous thoughts; more like intents. I already know that my power level has surpassed his—I doubt that he knew that. I can easily take him out. *What am I thinking?*

Maybe I should tell him and Tamaku that something is wrong with me. They would not believe me. They might think it is a defect from the getting hurt earlier. I had to keep my thoughts unannounced...and at bay. It's not like they could help anyway. Maybe if I don't look at Omi I can stop thinking such terrible things. That was the best plan I could come up with for the time being.

"Wow, Scarlet! I didn't learn Water Aricia until just a couple months ago. At this rate you could probably defeat me!"

He laughed at this but he did not know the reality to his statement.

"Let's stop," I said coldly.

His smile turned into bewilderment. "What? Why? You are doing so well and it is still early." He was smiling again, bigger. "You have already mastered Mist Cloke, Dance of the Water Mines, Repel Overcast, Whirl Pool-Whirl Wind, Water Sc-"

"I said I want to stop!" I shouted feeling the frost in my tone. My eyes narrowed on him, dissecting his reaction.

Omi's smile quickly faded. "I apologize...I didn't mean to be so disrespectful," he almost whispered. His gaze was cast downwards.

What have I done? "Omi, no, I'm sorry. I have a lot of things going through my mind right now." I closed my eyes massaging my temples with my fingers. "Please forgive me, I just...I just need some time to gather my thoughts."

"It is fine. We shall stop for today," he said monotonously. "You have accomplished a lot in such a short amount of time. I don't know how you got so powerful so quickly. But I shouldn't expect any less from the last Varcia," he smiled halfheartedly.

He seemed to have forgiven me very easily but I still felt guilty.

We both went into the hut. Tamaku had prepared a small dinner. When we came in, he gave a big warm smile. He gave me that look that I like again. But this time I could not enjoy it. I could not even look him in the eyes. Even with Tamaku, I had evil thoughts. I tried to conceal them the best I could, but based on their silence and stares, he and Omi both knew something was wrong: neither of them spoke a word about it.

<center>~~~Tamaku's View~~~</center>

Scarlet has definitely been acting strange. She will not even look at me. I wondered if she was angry with me or something. I talked to Omi about it after supper. He told me that she has gotten extremely powerful but it does not seem to be *her* power. Almost as if something else has come into her body controlling her like a puppet. He said that every move he taught her she conducted perfectly. He also mentioned that the aura of her spirit energy was different than before. He said this one was darker and of course more powerful. He said it was very unlikely and he didn't really believe so.

I did not think such a thing was possible either, but now I wonder. Scarlet began to act strange after that incident with some invisible woman earlier. She seemed so frightened about it, but Omi said that there was no woman. Maybe there was someone there. Maybe this woman is the one that did this to Scarlet. This must be Taurid's doing.

Omi also mentioned that she suddenly became very upset and shouted at him. I told him that Scarlet was never the type to raise her voice at someone.

I want to ask Scarlet what the problem is, but it might anger her. I want to help her in any way I can. I also know that if she wanted to talk about it she would come to me.

It is none of my business.

This will soon pass, I am sure. Scarlet is a sweet girl. She would never go and do harm to someone else for no reason. But if there is something evil controlling her... I have no choice but to intervene.

# CHAPTER 18

## CONSUME ME NOT

I can tell that Tamaku is worried...I hate it. I have to act as normal as possible. But every time I so much as look at him, I have the same wicked intents. I want the two of them to be safe but I do not know how long I can fight this. That woman was a helper for Taurid; I know that much.

I do not want Omi or especially Tamaku worrying too much. This Taurid is the real deal. Anyone that can somehow get into another's thoughts to control them is someone to be feared.

The next day, Omi offered to train with me but I decided to train alone. I wanted to further practice the skill he had already taught me. I practiced over 47 moves and preformed them even better than I did yesterday—apparently perfection can be surpassed. Right when I was about to go get Omi, I was interrupted.

"Scarlet," said Serenity. "Is there something wrong?"

Did she know about my thoughts?

"Your spirit energy is different from before. It is not as light and gentle as it was. Now it is different...it is almost full of darkness. I know this because whenever you use a power, for that moment our spiritual energy collides. My spirit energy is resenting yours making it difficult to work with you, but for some reason you are still very powerful even without me. It is almost like you don't need me at all. The woman that you mentioned before, I saw her as well."

"You mean, you saw the strange light and everything?"

"Yes, but when I saw her, I could sense that her intent was not evil. However, the power she gave you was not hers either. It was Taurid's." Her light, lovely, voice was concerned.

"You must be mistaken, there is no way the enemy would *give* me power," I said in disbelief —though I was perceiving the same idea.

"I know it doesn't seem very rational, but I am convinced that is the truth. That woman wanted to give you the power so you could become stronger. My guess is that Taurid knew nothing of this. But there is one thing I know for certain; you can fight this and you must. I know that the pureness of your heart will never be tainted by this evil. Just remember that good is always stronger than any evil force. Whenever these thoughts come to mind, just repel them with good... that much I know. There may be a way that you can purify the power so you can use it and drive only the evil out."

Her voice lowered. "There is one last thing that you should know. That woman-"

"Scarlet, come here for a second!" Omi shouted from the hut.

"Okay, in a minute!" I shouted back at him.

I turned back to the locket. "Okay, what is the thing I should know?" I asked.

"Never mind, I will let you figure that out for yourself."

"No, please! Just tell me quickly," I coaxed.

But with that, the glow upon the locket dimmed.

I sighed.

# CHAPTER 19

## TAURID

"We have found her, my lord," said a soldier.

"Unhand her!" commanded Taurid brutally.

The two soldiers unhanded the chained woman at once, letting her collapse to her knees, and eased out of the throne room without a second glance.

Taurid stood and circled around the woman. The clacking footsteps were steady and rang in the throne room.

"Now where did you wonder off to, Kiley?"

"I was just out for a walk in the woods," replied Kiley with her gaze cast downwards.

"Woman, why do you lie to the face of your master? Do you not know that I see all? I am already aware of where you were." The authority in his voice was dominating. He narrowed his eyes at Kiley.

She was not withered. "You speak as though you are God himself," she scolded with a tired, raspy voice. "You have no right to say those things! You are nothing but an evil, arrogant man!"

Taurid slapped her cheek without a second thought. He spat out a profanity with his fist tensed.

"Who are you to speak to me that way? I know that you gave that Varcia my power." He settled down a bit before continuing by drawing in a deep breath. "But what I am interested in knowing is how you got a hold of it."

She stayed silent.

He slapped her once more. This time, a trickle of blood streamed from her lip.

"What do you think you were doing giving her such immense power?" He asked.

"I gave it to her so that she could beat you with ease. You foolish man, I know that she will be victorious over you!"

"*You* are the fool!" he bellowed, creating a thunderous roar that filled the room. "That power that you gave her is of pure demonic essence. Now her thoughts shall be consumed with darkness. She will not be able to fight the evil for long, for the evil itself shall engulf her completely, taking over her mind and soul." He paused. His once tensed eyebrows loosened. The corners of his lips lifted, creating a dark smile. "But I am not angry with you for this act of treason. In a way, I am quite blissful, delighted even. Now I look forward to this brawl between the Varcia and me. She will finally be at my level...it has been a long time since I have had a good fight."

"Just wait Taurid. She will not let evil takeover her. Your days are numbered. This land will finally be ridden of this evil that you bestowed upon it. Then when you die, the Midnight Airos will finally appear!" She was shouting now, though it wasn't as loud as she meant it to be. Her dry, thirsty throat made it painful.

"Shut your mouth! I will not listen to such nonsense! If you continue, I will kill you here and now!"

Kiley fell silent for a moment. "I am not afraid of death, and I am certainly not afraid of you."

"Remember Kiley, there was a time where you said you loved me." He slide his icy finger under her chin. She could feel his wintry breath brushing against her face.

"Get your hands off of me!" she said as she shook him off. "That's when I was ignorant to the animal that you have always been. But I will never make that mistake again. You became intertwined with evil. I want nothing to do with you now!"

"Have you forgotten? I was the one who took you in when you had nowhere to go. When I became the emperor of this land I wanted you to be my queen. I wanted to rule with you for all eternity. I granted you immortality. I showered you in gifts and jewels! But you were never grateful."

"Can't you see? I didn't want all of that! All I wanted was a normal life. You never let me live my life the way I wanted. It was always about you, Taurid! You killed King Taress mercilessly just for the throne! You thirsted for blood and power. I wanted no part in your demonic rituals and your murderous pursuits! That's why I went to the human world. I was never going to return!"

Silence filled the thick, cold air.

"Then why did you?"

"I...I couldn't let Scarlet have any kind of connection to this place. She needed a normal life where she would be safe. I didn't want her to know anything of this realm. I was worried you would come for me. But now I deeply regret my actions. I wish I would had have stayed with her...she needed a mother in her life...but I wasn't there for her."

"Well, she is here now, and you will witness her death in a matter of days. Don't worry; I'll make her death quick and painless....maybe." A horrible smile creeped on his lips.

A tear rolled down Kiley's cheek. She stammered at his remark.

# CHAPTER 20

## FRIEND

"Yes, Omi, what did you need?"

"I just wanted you to know how impressed I am with you. I wanted to give you something that you could remember me by." He pulled out a blue and white bracelet. It was made of transparent beads that shimmered in the light. It was beautiful. "This belonged to my mother. She was very skilled in water manipulation as well. Now, I want you to have it."

"Omi, I couldn't possibly take that," I said shaking my head as I pushed his hand away.

"It is okay, Scarlet. I'm not sure what has been up with you lately, but I want you to know that Tamaku and I will always be your friends; *no matter what.*"

I took the bracelet but I still felt terrible. Those thoughts were coming in my head again! "Thank you very much, Omi. So do you want to train?" I forced a smile.

"That's the other thing I wanted to tell you," he chuckled. "I'm afraid I have taught you everything I know, and your skill is better than mine, too. You have become quite an expert! Tamaku will be helping you with sword fighting tomorrow. You will probably get that done quickly, too. But for now you should try and rest."

"Okay, I think I'm going to go outside." With a push on the door, I was invited with warm air. I sat down on the dirt ground. The thoughts were not going away. Normally, they stop when I'm not looking at anyone or talking. I decided to do what Serenity said. Fight evil with good. For some reason, I kept thinking of Tamaku. I guess Tamaku did make me happy. I never really thought badly of Tamaku...almost.

I looked at the bracelet Omi gave to me. It was very pretty. The colors seemed to glisten and glimmer in the light of the sun that balanced in the sky. Omi really considered me a good friend —now that made me feel good, at least. I considered Omi as a friend, too. I decided that I would get Omi a gift.

I heard the door open. I saw Tamaku walking out with headphones in his ears and my smartphone in his hand.

"Um, hi?" I said, more asking why he had my smartphone in the first place.

He chuckled. "Sorry, but I just can't seem to get enough of this rap music," he said taking a seat next to me.

"I'm surprised you could even turn it on," I said coldly. I wasn't feeling too hot about things. I wasn't really in a talking mood.

"Okay, I have another question; what is a 'club'," he asked robotically, sounding out every sound.

I couldn't help but giggle. "It's just a place where people go to dance and hangout and whatever. You know, meet other people."

"Oh," he said holding out the sound.

I was feeling a little better. We sat in silence as he listened to the music. I could hear a muffled version of the song from the loud volume. It really did make me miss home. Rap was Matt's favorite music, too. Come to think of it, this was his favorite song last year. He knew every word.

I turned my head to look at Tamaku. He was really getting into the music. He was bobbing his head and mouthing some of the lyrics.

I started to laugh a little. When I did, he looked at me with wide eyes, removing his headphones.

"What's so funny?" he asked, smiling himself.

I snickered. "It's nothing."

"Yeah, right; I think your laughing at me," he teased.

"Okay, you thought right," I laughed.

He chuckled. "I guess I am pretty clueless when it comes to the human world. It's just never really interested me before."

"Yeah, well the human world is a pretty interesting place. Something new is always happening."

"That seems nice. It's always the same thing here. Sometimes, it feels like I'm living the same day over and over again."

"Isn't that a bit extreme?" I asked.

"Probably, but this place is repetitive. I *still* don't really understand why Taurid wants this land anyway. It isn't any place I would want to take control over. Everywhere you look, there is dead grass, dead trees, dead crops....everything is just dead. The people here may as well be dead...they only live to wait for death."

I thought for a moment. What he was saying did make sense. What was the reason Taurid wanted this land anyway? Who would want control over a "dead" kingdom?

"Yeah, I agree. I guess it's just the fact that he has power that entices him to keep going. It's amazing what lengths people will go to just to get it. Then once they have it, they always want more.

"That's true; power does have a large effect on people. I never really knew the whole story behind his *whole* uprising."

I suddenly remembered how Tamaku told me the story when I first arrived here. Apparently Taurid murdered the former king for the throne four hundred years ago and hasn't aged a day.

"Well, I don't really care how he came to power, I just want him out."

Tamaku snickered. "That makes sense," he said. "But aside from that, how are you feeling? You haven't exactly been yourself lately," he noted.

I was hoping he wouldn't mention this. I didn't want to tell him. "I've been fine," I lied. "I guess this place has really dawned on me," I smiled falsely. I hoped he couldn't tell.

He didn't say anything for a very long time. "Well, I'm glad to hear that."

"You're not worrying about me, are you?" I asked.

"Should I?"

"No; you shouldn't. I just wanted to make sure you weren't stressing on my behalf. I know how good of a friend you are. I don't want you getting worked up over nothing."

He smiled at the friend comment. "Well, if you say it's nothing, then I believe you. Friends just have to look out for each other, right?"

We exchanged looks for a moment. More like stares for a long moment. Sometimes, I couldn't stop myself from gaping into his captivating pools of dark silky eyes. I really didn't know why he stared back. But I think stare isn't the right word...more like gazed. We didn't seem to mind gazing into each other's eyes at all—or at least I didn't.

The sun was setting, causing a beautiful orange, pinkish glow to loom on his blemish free skin. He really was beautiful. Not in a girly way, but in a mesmerizing, loss of words way. Sort of like the way you would feel if you got to stare at the Mona Lisa in person— like you got to hold it and everything. Due to the fact it is world renowned and very historical, you would feel lucky to be in its presence. It would just be a compelling, beautiful sight.

But for me, he could have been just average looking—I would still be just as fascinated. It wasn't just his appearance that captivated me. You know how everyone gives off a certain vibe or feeling? I guess it's kind of like that. I had always heard that the eyes were a way to see into a person's heart. I guess that's why I stare at his' so much.

Before she died, Toki told me that when she looks into Tamaku's eyes, she could see hope. But when I look into his eyes, I see someone that has a will and a sweetness that is sweeter than any honey ever produced. It is something I have always seen, but have never been able to put my finger on it. Just looking at him makes me almost forget all the problems I was having. But he didn't forget. I can also see worry in his eyes.

He then gave a crooked smile, still locking eyes with mine. I couldn't help but crack a smile out, too. With every second that glided past, our smiles grew larger and larger to the point where our teeth were exposed. We both began to laugh, looking away.

"Sorry," we both unintentionally said in unison. We then began to laugh again.

"Sorry," Tamaku said. "I guess your eyes were interesting this time."

"Is that a good thing?" I said.

"Nope," he said he said. "It's actually terrible."

We laughed again.

"But I do have just one more question," he said raising one finger.

"What?" I asked preparing for another rap question.

He seemed more hesitant—almost like he was still debating whether or to ask. "What do you think about me?" he forced.

I was taken aback by the sudden change in conversation. It wasn't every day that people would ask me something like that. I didn't know what to say. I could see his expression twist as my answer prolonged, but my thoughts were jumbling and my head was spinning.

"Not to sound generic or anything, but I think you're one of the best guys I've ever gotten a chance to know." I guess that was right. I surely wasn't going to mention that I was quickly falling for him. Ha...

He smiled. Not a happy smile, but not a sad one either. It was hard for me to read.

"Thanks," he finally said.

We sat silent for a moment. "So, um...what do you think about me?" I asked, slightly embarrassed.

He chuckled. I only hoped I wasn't blushing.

"I think you're a person that thinks about others and what they think too much. I think you try to please people, when in actuality...all they want to do is please you." He wasn't smiling anymore. He wasn't looking at me either.

What did he mean? I never thought I cared about what others think. But I guess I am a people pleaser at times. But who isn't? I won't talk to Omi and Tamaku about what's wrong due to the fact I may worry them. He was right on the nose with that.

"I'm not saying it's bad. But if something is wrong, don't try to keep others from worrying; just say so," he amended.

I thought for a moment. I was really speechless now. Had he figured it all out? What he was saying did make sense, but I wasn't prepared to start leaking out the truth just yet.

After dinner I went out to go look for a gift for Omi. For some reason, while I was searching, I had a couple of those compulsive thoughts but they were very easy to ignore. Maybe I had been overreacting about this whole thing. All I had to do was fight it and no one would get hurt. This brought a smile to my face. I could finally turn back to my old self. Tamaku and Omi would be happy.

I could not find a lot of things that I liked. I had been walking around for about 2 hours. The only things I found were a stone, a piece of a water crystal, and a Peacock's feather. They were nice but not what I was looking for. I figured what I had gathered would have to do. The chill of the night air was almost unbearable. I had on the same light jacket that I brought along, but it was still hardly enough protection from the cold. My cheeks and fingers were bitten by the low temperature. I rubbed my hands together for warmth.

I had begun to walk back to the hut. I was tired and all I wanted to do was sleep. I was very dissatisfied though. I wanted to get Omi the perfect gift. As I was walking I noticed something shine in the grass. I ran to see what the strange shine was. Then there it was; the perfect gift for Omi. It was a silver necklace with one charm on it. The charm was of a water flair carrying a sword. It was still covered with dirt. I wiped it away revealing that the little water flair had blue gems in its surface. I blew on it lightly to remove some of the impurities that had infiltrated in the cracks. It was absolutely gorgeous. Even in the darkness, it twinkled bright. I knew he would love it. I could almost feel it!

I started back home very happily. I couldn't even feel the cold weather anymore. I couldn't wait till morning so I could show Omi his gift. I put the necklace in my skirt pocket for safe keeping.

I still had a little ways to go before I would reach the hut. My feet were in pain but I had no regrets. I then heard some sort of crash coming from my right. I turned to look, though by the sound of it, I knew it was far from where I stood. It was still enough to make me want to seek it out. Someone might be in trouble. I decided to go check it out. I walked towards the sound I had heard. It was probably nothing but I wanted to make sure.

I had been walking for a while now. I honestly wasn't sure where I was going. It had been so long since the crash was heard, I didn't know if I was even going in the right direction. *Maybe it really was nothing*, I had begun to think.

It wasn't until I heard another crash that I changed my mind. I was indeed going the right way. I decided to stay on the mission I set for myself. I had made my way to an abandoned looking village. It looked like no one had stepped foot here in ages. However, I was sure this is where the sound came from. I had looked around the area for a while but nothing turned up. I started to turn back. It was late and it seemed like the crash was nothing to be concerned about.

"Help me," said a weak voice.

I turned around but I saw nothing. I looked all around. I began to think it was all in my imagination. I turned back and started on my way home again. Just as I began to take another step, I saw a girl lying on the ground just a few feet away from me.

The girl lifted her head slightly and looked in my eyes. She looked a little older than me. She looked very sick. Her face was ghost white; very different from the Audren people's darker skin. Her bones seemed to pop from her skin, her voice was barely audible.

I ran and crouched down in front of her. "What happened?"

"Help," she said.

It was obvious that she was in no condition to answer questions. What was she doing here in an abandoned village? Where did she come from? How would I help her? I decided to pick her up and hoist her on my back. I would bring her to the hut. Maybe Omi and Tamaku could help. But before I could rear another thought, I heard a cry of an infant; no, a child. I scanned the area to see one hut with light shining through the window. I knew that was the source of the crying.

I looked back down at the girl. She was in no condition to wait outside, but I could not have carried her in that hut if there were any real danger. I cupped my forehead. I had no choice but to take a risk. I set the girl down gently. I rustled off my jacket and placed it over her body. It wasn't much, but it was better than nothing.

The cries were louder now. Without another moment, I dashed for the hut. My legs were still sore from training which made it difficult to run quickly. I had barely made it when I heard the crying again. But all of a sudden, I didn't feel very heroic but rather frightened.

I clenched the handle to my Raico. This was going to be my first fight...my first *real* fight. The first fight where I actually had a chance of winning. With that, I swung open the hut door with my sword drawn. As I stepped in the doorway, I immediately noticed four children with red faces and tears streaming. They all looked at me but continued to whimper.

"Stand back," I commanded them. I immediately shifted my gaze to a tall man standing over a woman. The women lay motionless at his feet. The man wore a hood that shielded his face. I also spotted various drops of blood scattered...this wasn't good.

"Please, lady, please help us!" said one of the children.

The man started towards me. "What are you doing?" I asked.

"This is not any of your concerns. Leave now." His voice was literally like nails to a chalkboard to my ears. It was low and raspy.

I raised my sword. "No," I refused.

"You are picking a fight with me?" He snarled. "You obviously do not know who you are up against."

"I am not afraid of you." It was true. I knew I could easily take care of him, but I did not want to kill him.

He quickly whipped out a small dagger from his robe. I, too, was ready to attack with my Raico. He swung his small knife with speed, but my movements were quick as well! With time to spare, I dodged his attack with ease. With a flick of the wrist, I created a somewhat large gash on my opponent's arm. Not even close to my true intentions.

With no time to recuperate, his blade was inches away from my neck. With a burst of power, I blocked his attack. I was ready to counter him. I aimed for his head, but with one wrong move I missed my target. Instead, the hood that shielded him was now on the ground, knocking down various pots and relics as well.

The children's cries became louder. I shifted my sight to the man and shrieked at the sight. His face was terribly burned. The whole right side of his face, seemed to be completely scrambled.

"I am done playing around with you," he said, spitting out a thread of swears. With that, he charged towards me with brute force. The hut was such a tight space; I barely had room to dodge him. Then, I did all I could do. I blocked him with my sword, but he was just too strong. My arm was growing weary...I didn't know how long I could last.

I could feel the beads of sweat rolling down my forehead. But I just couldn't hold on. In an instant my Raico fell to the ground. I tried to scramble for my sword but I was caught by my long hair.

I struggled to break free from his grasp but instead he hoisted me in the air by my throat. I reached for his hands, attempting to pry them away from my neck. My lungs were struggling for air. I dug my fingernails into his skin. I could feel my fingernails infiltrating his hands, feeling the blood ooze. If only I could reach my sword. The Riaco looked so close in reach, yet so far.

He was threatening me to stop, but I did not. I continued as he began to squeeze tighter. My strength was decreasing due to the lack of oxygen. I could no longer struggle for my body was draining of energy rapidly. My vision became clouded and my head began to throb. I could no longer feel my numb limbs. I closed my eyes.

# CHAPTER 21

## CHILDREN OF THE ELEMENTS

"Stop it!" shouted a girl.

Just then, I was dropped to the ground roughly, feeling the skin on my knees scrape away. Immediately, I panted for air. I rubbed my neck in attempts to soothe it. I stood weakly to see what had happened. Then, before my eyes, I saw my enemy elapsed in flames on the ground. There stood a young girl. Was she the one responsible for this attack?

But before any more thought, I noticed the flames were spread throughout the hut. Soon, the gasses from the fire would fill the room. We needed to get out. The children were already coughing.

I quickly grabbed my Raico along with their tiny hands, "This way," I shouted. They obediently followed my lead. The smoke had already begun to affect my vision. "Hurry," I coaxed.

My eyes were watering now. My sight was almost unattainable. Everything seemed blurry. The only way I could navigate my steps was by the deep, orange color of the fire. My eyes were stinging to the point that I could not leave them open. I reached frantically in front of me in hopes to reach an exit. I could barely hear the children's coughs above my own. Then suddenly my trouble was over. I felt air that wasn't hot and thick. I felt cold air, sweet cold air.

Without a second thought, I dashed out of the opening into the breeze of the night. I released the children's hands, wiping my eyes and attempting to open them again. They did, in fact, open but the sting returned. Before long, it had dulled; not to any sense of comfort but it lessened. I looked back at the flame-covered hut. *We barely made it,* I thought.

I turned back to the children. They were staring at me with shimmering eyes.

"Hey, are you all okay?"

They all nodded with faces still stained with tears.

There were three kids. There was a girl (the one that saved me) that looked about ten years old. She only came up to my chest. She had sky blue eyes with rich caramel brown hair. Her front two teeth were missing as well. There were also two boys. They seemed to be identical twins that looked no older than 8. They both had matching stringy, sandy, brown hair and blue eyes. They were pretty cute kids.

"So does anyone care to tell me what happened?" I said examining them all. They didn't look as bad as I would have expected. One of the twins spoke up. "That man in there was a soldier of Taurid. Taurid has been after lightning users for a long time now. Our family was the only one in Audren that contained lightning element ability."

He sounded like an adult had been telling him that his whole life. I remember Tamaku saying lightning element manipulation was scarce but I didn't realize until now how scarce it was.

"So you are all lightning users then?"

The other twin spoke. "No, only our mother was, but she died a long time ago. None of us got the ability except our oldest sister Lawny. Taurid knows that only one of us has the power but he doesn't know who."

"So they attacked you to find out?"

"Yes. We told the man we weren't the ones, but he didn't believe us."

"Okay, well, where is your sister?"

The girl replied. "She was going to get help but never came back. She has been very sick lately," she admitted dolefully.

Then it clicked. That girl I saw up the road must have been their sister. "Wait, what does she look like?"

"Well," she began. "She has blue eyes and long silver hair. She doesn't look too good..."

"Come with me," I said. I had begun running back to the place where I had seen the girl. I headed to the place that I had laid her down and placed my jacket over her.

In a short time we had arrived. But there was one problem... The girl was nowhere to be found. My jacket sat alone on the dirt ground.

"Where had she gone to?" I thought.

"I'm so sorry, I...I seriously thought she was here," I said as I picked up the jacket.

"That's okay, lady," said one twin. "She hates us anyway."

"Oh, don't say that," I asseverated in a comforting tone.

"No she does," said the girl. "She hits us a lot; really hard."

"Yeah, and she yells at us a lot, too!" said another twin.

I tried to change the focus. I didn't want to stand there all night talking about a sister that wasn't even there. "Well, do you guys have a place to go?—like a family member's house?"

"That women that was dead in our house, was our aunt Tillie. She had come to watch after us when Lawny started to get sick. Now I guess we have no one." The girl looked downwards with a sigh.

I thought for a moment. I guess Tamaku wouldn't mind having a few extra people around the house. The poor kids had nowhere to go—he could understand that.

"Well, you can all stay with me if you want."

"Really?! Thanks, lady!" said a twin as he gave me thumbs up.

I chuckled. "You're welcome. By the way, you can call me Scarlet."

"Wait a minute, I think I know you," said the girl as she rubbed her chin.

"Yeah! She's that Last Varcia girl!" said a twin pointing at me a little overly excited.

"Well, yes, but I didn't know that people knew about me," I said modestly.

"Are you kidding? Everybody knows about the Last Varcia! You are like, well, famous!" she exclaimed.

I blushed a bit. "Well, I'm not that great. You were the one that set that guy on fire for me," I said.

"Oh, that was just a simple fire element technique. Well by the way, I'm Piper and these are my brothers Conch and Roke." She pointed to each of her brothers. At first I thought they looked exactly the same (I wasn't really paying much attention before), but now I could see that the one called Conch was a bit lankier. His hair was also a lot longer. His hair reached to his collar bone while his brother's ended at his earlobe. "Oh, and thanks for coming to our rescue like that," she said.

"Yeah!" exclaimed Conch. "You looked so cool!"

"Thanks. So you guys are all fire users?"

"Yep, all three of us! What's your element?" asked Roke having the other ones share his interest involuntarily.

"Water and Lightning," I replied.

They all exchanged looks. "Sweet!" they elated in unison.

"Wow, you have, like, two elements! That's awesome!" Roke broadcasted.

I was actually surprised that these kids were much like the kids in my world. Even down to their facial expressions, they seemed just like any normal kids. "Yea, well, I only know how to use my water ability."

"Oh, that's not good..." said Piper.

"Tell me about it," I griped. "Well I guess we should get going. The hut is kind of far from here and it's late."

"Okay, but first, tell us how you came to Audren, Last Varcia!" pleaded Piper in a rather annoying tone.

"Please call me Scarlet," I insisted with slight irritation.

"Okay, okay, whatever. Just tell us how you got here!" she pleaded.

"Alright, well it all started when I landed on a beach."

"Whoa! I know where that is! That must have been awesome!" exclaimed Conch.

"Sure, well anyway, after that, I met this boy and-"

"Oooh! That's your boyfriend isn't it! You are totally in love with him, right?" shouted Piper.

"What? No, no, no. You've got it all wrong. If you would have let me finish, I was going to tell you he is my guardian."

"Wow, a guardian! Gee, Varcia lady, you must be the real deal!" said Roke.

"My name is Scarlet, and no more interruptions!" I said slightly playful but I was still irritated.

"Do you guys want to hear the story or not?"

They all snickered but nodded silently.

"Okay. Now, what I was saying was that I met my guardian. Then he told me how I am the Last Varcia. Since then we have been training and I even met another guy named Omi. Now the whole reason I am even out here is because I wanted to find Omi a gift because he gave me one."

"Well did you find him a gift?" asked Conch.

"Yup, want to see?"

They all nodded and stood closer to me. I fished out the old necklace from my pocket. As I lifted it high, all three of them were wide eyed and mouth opened.

I chuckled. "Like it?"

"Gosh, that's pretty!" exclaimed Piper.

I placed it back. "Well it's for him. He's a water flair"

"No way! Those things moved to a different realm!" exclaimed Conch.

"No! They became extinct like…uh…a hundred billion years ago!" interjected Roke.

"Give it a rest geniuses! Everyone knows they just don't exist!" Piper said loudly and rather obnoxiously.

"Yes they do," I finally said. "Omi is the very last one."

"Okay, so you're in love with *him*." said Piper more to herself than to me.

"No, no, no; I'm not in love with anybody! Plus, Omi is like, twenty something."

"Sick! How old are *you*?"

"Me? Well, I'm seventeen."

"Wow, you're old, too!" said Roke.

"Yeah and you're pretty!" added Conch.

"Will you be quiet, Conch! You are such a loser!" Roke said with his eyebrows scrunched.

"No I'm not! I just have a working pair of eyes!"

"Well, me, too, but I wasn't going to be all uncool and announce how I think she is totally pretty...oops."

"Guys! You both are losers so be quiet!" said Piper as she hit them both on the head.

"Okay, okay, let's settle down. We really need to go home now." I said as motherly as I could.

"Alright, but can we stay up all night?" asked Conch.

"No, I have to train in the morning," I said firmly.

"But we're not tired yet!" Piper yawned.

"Yes you are" I said with a smile.

"Okay, but can you carry me?"

"Yea, me, too!'

"Me three!"

I raised one eyebrow. "You guys want me to carry *all* of you?"

"Please!" they all said in unison.

"With a cherry on top," added Piper in desperation that could only be said from a child.

I sighed and bent down. "Get on," my tone was flat and unwilling.

They all cheered! Piper climbed on my back as Conch and Roke climbed up on my left and right side. Even now, I have no clue how I did this, but somehow I managed to slowly carry them all back to the hut. These were some reckless kids, but I actually liked them. To tell the truth, they were actually pretty cute. I was exhausted but we finally made it back to the hut. I let them sleep in the bed and I sat in a corner. The chair I sat in was squeaky and uncomfortable but I was asleep in an instant.

# CHAPTER 22

## INFECTED AGAIN

The next morning, I woke up to see Tamaku and Omi talking to the kids. They were laughing and giggling. I longed to go back to sleep, but the noises were too loud to ignore. After a few yawns, I stood to my feet drowsily, rubbing my eyes.

"Hey Scarlet, you are up early," said Tamaku gazing my way.

"Yeah, I'm guessing you and the kids are getting off on the right foot."

"Yeah, Scarlet! You missed it! Omi told us that he is twenty four, but he looks eleven!"

"Well it looks like you guys are getting off to a good start. I guess I won't have to introduce you guys, huh?"

"Nope! Omi and Tamaku are way cool!" said Conch.

"I had woken up to see these kids lying in your spot. I started to panic but then I saw you fast asleep in the corner. It looks like you really out did yourself this time, Scarlet," said Omi.

"Yeah, she saved our lives yesterday! She even got you a gift!" Piper said to Omi.

"Really?" Omi said as his eyes widened. I had forgotten all about it.

"Well I was out walking last night and I just happened to save them," I said modestly.
"But Piper helped; and I did find you a gift, Omi."

"You should see it, Omi! The Varcia got you a great gift!" said Roke in his loud, high pitched voice.

"Okay, you can really call me Scarlet, and I'm going to show him in a second."

Omi looked as if he wanted to see it quickly but he tried to stay indifferent. "Uh, you don't have to do it now if you don't want to, Scarlet."

"Oh, sorry Omi, I kind of forgot about it. Well anyway, I just got you a little something for the bracelet you gave me."

He smiled at this. I quickly grabbed the long necklace from my pocket. I placed the relic in his open palm. He stared at it in amazement as he lifted it into the light.

"This is really nice. I have never seen anything in such good shape that has to do with water flairs. No one really talks about us anymore."

He smiled wide and turned my way. "Thanks," he said motioning for a hug.

"It's the least I could do." I then wrapped my arms around his small body. But before I could pull away, it was happening again...those thoughts. The sickness was here again.

Suddenly, I felt as if I needed to inflict pain. I needed to get away from Omi. These feelings were getting stronger by the second. I pulled back abruptly. Everyone gave looks of puzzlement upon my obviously shuddered expression.

"Alright, I'm tired of it. What is wrong?" asked Tamaku.

"Uh, no I was just...I"

"She's in love with Omi!" exclaimed Conch and Roke.

Omi laughed. "I don't know about that, but *I* have a secret" said Omi in a playful tone.

"A secret! Tell us! Tell us, Omi!" said Conch as he tugged at Omi's shirt.

"Okay, but we have to go outside so no one will hear it."

"Okay, let's go, guys!" shouted Piper as she darted out the door with Roke and Conch close behind.

"I'll be back. It looks like you and Scarlet need to talk," he said on his way out. "I'm coming guys!"

As the door shut, Tamaku did not waste any time.

"Those kids are a handful, aren't they?" he said accompanied with a nervous chuckle.

"Whatever," I said shortly. I just wanted him to leave me alone. I wasn't trying to be mean, but I didn't want anyone to know about this problem I had been having. I just can't seem to get this under control...

# CHAPTER 23

## IN TAMAKU'S VIEW

I just can't seem to figure this out. I wish Scarlet would just tell me what's going on. I hate wondering. I just want to know. I really care about Scarlet...I thought she knew that.

"So, is everything alright with you?" I asked.

"Yes, I have just been a little out of it lately. Last night was pretty hectic," she said with a small smile. It seemed false to me...and forced.

"Yes, but I am proud of you. Piper told me how you fought that soldier."

"Oh, that was nothing" she said irritably.

"Yea, that Piper girl is very fond of you."

"I wouldn't know. She never gets my name right."

"She says she does that because it annoys you, you know. Actually, all three of those kids wouldn't stop talking about how cool you are." I smiled.

She was smiling. Sometimes I just have to stop and stare at her. My feelings for her are so strong. If only she loved me the way I love her then life would be a lot better. But I know that will never happen. I never will forget the time I told her about my late grandfather. She started to cry so I held her in my arms. She pulled away almost instantly. Even though I knew her, she barely knew me; I hated myself for that. What was I thinking? But I am just glad that she is here with me for a little longer. I still wonder what it would be like to have the girl of my dreams by my side for the rest of my life. I know I sound like a fool in love but I guess when you love someone you do silly things.

She doesn't have much longer to be here. I don't know what I will do when she leaves. I will be even more upset then I am anticipating. I already know it; misery loves me. Now I know for sure I have to tell her my real feelings. I know that in my heart I must. I will tell her. I have grown mentally a lot in the past few days. I now realize that I cannot let Scarlet slip away from me without knowing that I have fallen deeply in love with her. I will admit I am scared but I must tell her. I know that they say ignorance is bliss, but that cliché didn't make sense. This situation was different...very different.

All I want is for her to open up to me. I guess all I can do at this point is be as nice as possible.

"Listen Tamaku," she started, "I am just fine, okay? So please don't worry about me."

"Then why are you acting so weird?" I challenged. I noticed my tone of voice was more disrespectful then concerned. I composed a better tone. "You know you can tell me anything, right? That's why I'm here...to help you; I told you that since the beginning."

"I guess I'm just a little worried about my lightning ability. I guess I'm just really out of my element mentally...but I'll be fine."

I sighed. "If you say so, Scarlet."

# CHAPTER 24

## EVIL IS RELENTLESS

Today was pretty laid back. The twins had gone to sleep, and Omi and Tamaku were playing cards in the hut. I decided to go outside and practice my water manipulation. That did not last long because I had done all those techniques so many times already. It was pretty boring doing the same moves all the time. I wish Omi knew more so he could teach me new stuff. Tamaku had helped me with Raico training but I was very good at that as well.

Whenever I think about that night Toki died I get upset. I have grown a lot since then. I was so weak back then that it disgusts me. I couldn't even manage to get a scratch on either of them. I was so afraid, but now I could easily kill those two with only my Raico. I am actually happy I got this evil in me. If that woman had never arrived, I would still be nothing but a weak school girl. I love this new power. I am no longer afraid of Taurid. He is no threat to me.

No.

What am I saying? I shouldn't be glad to have this evil within my soul. My whole goal is to get rid of it! I can be strong but pure at the same time. I feel it again. It is running through my veins. I was just on my way of getting rid of it and now I am back to where I started. I began to think the thoughts again. There was no time for this. I had to think of something quick. I know Tamaku would notice and worry again. I do not want that to happen.

Images of me killing numerous people came to my mind. The pictures of blood flow and gushing were unable to leave me. I hate it! I absolutely hate it! I could barely take it! Too many thoughts bombarded my mind at once.

To kill; not to kill; no blood, please no blood. Stop it! No, continue! This was worse than ever before. I started to claw at my leg. I felt my finger dig deep into my skin. I saw blood from my

176

body. For some reason I liked it, but at the same time I despised it! Was I breaking down? No, I was going out of control. I watched as the blood flowed faster now. I absolutely loved it. Invigorating even, I felt no pain. The gashes I had created had no physical effect on me. I fell to the ground. I couldn't feel anything. My body felt numb as the thoughts over ruled me. I started to pull my hair from the torture going on within me. My thoughts were jumbling. I cannot stop. I had to do something. I heard the door open.

"Hey, Scarlet, what is wrong? Are you in pain?" Tamaku sounded frantic.

I couldn't look at him. My eyes were closed. I didn't want to open them either. I didn't even think I could. I was completely immobilized. I was in a stupor that left me fully conscious yet out of it completely. The murderous thoughts were roaring over Tamaku calling my name. *I need to kill...see the crimson liquid spill out of an open wound. No! I needed no such thing. I don't want to see anything. Of course I want to see, my body thirsts for bloodshed...if only I could kill, if only....Stop it! Evil, leave my mind! No, stay; it is you that has given me such power! No longer will I be weak, but strong!*

It was Tamaku. He had both of his hands on my shoulders. My mind calmed. I felt like a terrible load had been taken off my shoulders. It felt as if the evil itself had been extracted from my very being. Tamaku was talking, but I could not hear him. All I needed was to look in his eyes. That is what I did. My thoughts were clear again. I could feel the air brushing against my cheeks. My surroundings were acknowledgeable now. I was out of my stupor. I winced in pain as I felt the piercing sting of the incisions on my left leg.

I get it now. He was the way out of my wickedness and confusion. Just his eyes; that's all I needed. I could feel tears flowing from the joy that he brought me that I cannot describe. Without thinking, I wrapped my arms around him and embraced him. I did not want to let go. For once, I was not afraid to get close to him. I thought about the time he told my about how his grandfather died and how I began to cry. He tried to comfort me then, but I pulled away from his arms with no hesitation. Why did I do that? I do not know why.

No, I know why. It is because I know he could never feel the same way I do about him. So I told myself that I only "liked" him. That was a lie that I once believed to be true. The truth is...I have fallen in love with Tamaku. Though it has only been a few days, that is all it took for me. I know I might be a little too young for this, but that cannot stop the way I feel. That is why I don't know if I want to go back home or not. Then again, living with someone you love that doesn't know it...is pointless. Living with someone you love but doesn't feel the same way is also pointless. So there are two options here; I either don't tell him and have to live with the guilt all my life, or tell him and maybe get my heart broken. Is there any happy ending through all of this? Both options may hurt me in the long run.

As I am in his arms now, I know in my heart I must tell him how I feel. It is not something I want to do but it is something I must do. I can never expect to be happy if I never take risks. I said I wanted an adventure. This is my adventure.

"Scarlet, what happened?"

"I don't exactly know. I was fine then I just...well I don't know but somehow I calmed down when you came, Tamaku."

He smiled tucking in his lips. "I was inside and I heard you screaming and yelling. When I came out here, blood was everywhere. You really hurt your leg." He started to bandage my wound with a piece of cloth he tore from his shirt.

"I'm sorry, Tamaku. I don't know what is going on with me right now. But now I feel normal. I don't know why I embraced you like that. I'm sorry."

"You don't have to apologize. To tell the truth, I was very happy when you did."

My face grew warm. I knew I was blushing from this. "Well I guess what I should be saying is thank you."

"You're welcome, and I did it because I wanted to. I have gotten very close to you these past few days. I have come to realize that protecting you is no longer my duty at all. It is my absolute desire. Whenever you need me, just call on me. I will make my way to you. To tell the truth, all I want to do is be by your side...forever."

I was shocked by his statement. What did he mean by that? Does Tamaku actually like me? No, that cannot be true. I want to tell him the same thing but I am too nervous. I changed my mind. I can't tell him how I feel. I just don't have enough courage.

"I'm sorry," he said. He must have thought I was disturbed by his comment when I didn't reply.

"Oh, please, don't be sorry. You haven't done anything wrong. I just don't know what I want right now."

"What I am saying is true. All I want is to be by your side."

This was the perfect time to tell him my true feelings. But I knew he couldn't possibly mean all these things he was saying. No, I won't do it. "Yes, and together we will defeat Taurid." I gave a false smile; my inside was weeping.

He looked kind of sad but he gave what seemed to be a false smile, too. It is almost as if he was expecting something, but was deeply let down.

For the rest of the day I was angry at myself. I did not do what I wanted to do. That was my chance and I blew it.

Later, I found Piper sitting outside alone. I sat next to her and patted her back.

"Hey," I said.

"Hi, Varcia," she said in a dull tone.

"Is everything okay?" She looked like she had been crying.

"Yeah, but I have been thinking. You need to know how to use lightning manipulation, right?"

"Yeah, that's right."

"Well remember how I told you about my sister, Lawny?"

"Yeah, I remember that."

"Well I was thinking...maybe tomorrow we can try to find her."

"That sounds great Piper, but I thought your sister hated you guys."

"Yeah, but I can tell you really want to know lighting manipulation so I figured I could help. I don't want to be so unhelpful. I know I'm still little so I can't do a lot to help you out."

"Oh my goodness, you would do that for me?"

"Yeah...you're cool, Varcia"

"My name is—never mind. Okay, well I guess I should tell Tamaku then. It's almost nightfall."

That night I laid awake thinking. I have been diligently counting the days that I have been here. Today is day eight. This means I only have four more days left here. The battle with Taurid is approaching. I still have not learned any lighting techniques, which I may learn tomorrow if we find that Lawny girl but that is unlikely. It is abundantly clear that this evil that resides in me is not gone. That outburst I had today worries me. That time I was lucky that no one was outside with me or someone could have gotten seriously hurt...or worse. It is almost as if I had no control

180

whatsoever. My every thought in my mind was contradicted by another. The scratch on my leg is very painful but at the time it felt good. Maybe I should tell Tamaku and Omi about what is going on with me. I just fear that if I tell them they will fear me, though they should.

I am not evil. I do not want to become evil either. However, it is thanks to this evil that I have become so powerful. I fear this power though. I fear its magnitude. I fear my own abilities. I fear for my friends. I fear for myself… Maybe I am evil.

My father always told me that fear is full of torment but love casts out fear. Maybe I need love.

I woke up early that morning to see Piper awake as well.

"Good morning, Varcia! Get up! Get up!" she said as she whipped the light cover's off of my body, exposing me to the chill of the morning. I could barely open my eyes.

"Good morning, Piper," I said with a yawn. "You have a lot of energy today."

"I am so happy for today! It's going to be sweet! Just me and you hanging out! I made this for you, too. I really hope you like it." She pulled out small lavender notebook.

"Wow, thank you." I flipped through the pages to see colored blank paper.

"It's a friendship journal. You can right down all the good times you have had with your friends, like places you have went, funny things that have happened, your worries, all sorts of stuff!"

"This was very nice of you. When did you make this?"

"I made it last night when you went to sleep!"

"Thanks Piper, I think I'm gonna write about you in it."

"Really? Me? You're even cooler now!"

I giggled. "You know what? I want to make you something, too. That way, when I leave here, you will always remember me."

"You're leaving?"

Did she really not know? "Yes, didn't Tamaku tell you? I am a human. The longest I can stay here is twelve days. Today is the ninth day for me. I only have three more days left."

Her smile faded. "But I don't want you to leave, Varcia."

I wiped away her tears with my fingers. "To tell the truth, I don't really want to leave either, but I have people that love me back at home. If I stay here, I will never get to see them again."

"Will you ever come back one day?"

I knew that would be impossible. Once you leave this realm you can never come back... Tamaku told me that.

"Maybe I will come back one of these days. If I do, you will be the first person I will come to see." I smiled at her. I hated lying, but it was one of the many ways to tip toe around people's feelings.

"Okay...well at least your still here now."

"Yep. Don't worry, cutie, I still have more days with you guys" I said as I smoothed her hair lightly.

This talk made it even more difficult to leave. Even though I just met Piper, she really looks up to me. The gift she gave me I truly loved. I had met some amazing people here in Audren.

There was Toki. She was very kind hearted. She was almost always smiling. I wish she didn't have to leave us so quickly. She was such an optimistic person which was a great part of her personality. She always looked on the bright side of things. I really look up to her even now. I miss her so much. I know in my heart that she is truly happy where she is. She did not deserve to live such a life here in Audren. The men that killed her were nothing but scum. I wish almost every day to see Toki one last time. Just to see her smile would make my heart soar.

Then there was Serenity. Though she is not here in the flesh, she has been with me all my life. Through everything she was here and I had no idea. She is very wise and always helps me see things clearer than I ever would on my own. If I didn't have her, I wouldn't be able to use my powers. She seems to care a lot about my wellbeing which really touches my heart.

Then there was Omi. He is one of the most mature people I have ever known. He has no family whatsoever. The way he has coped with that is amazing. Omi has taught me many things. If it wasn't for him, I probably would have still been wondering in that forest. I never really thought about it till now, but it is amazing how I immediately trusted Omi after talking with him. I guess he is just a very loyal guy. Now, I almost never think of that dumb dream I had.

Then there was Tamaku. I hate him and at the same time I love him. I hate him because he is such a wonderful person. If he wasn't so wonderful I wouldn't love him like I do. It sickens me how much I love him. What sickens me more is that I can't even tell him. I used to think love was wonderful and exhilarating. I used to dream of the day that I fell in love with a guy. Now I know that falling in love is a curse. Love is when you think of someone non-stop. If you did miraculously get them out of your mind, they will quickly ease right back in. Tamaku is the first guy I have ever met that makes me feel like I am on top of the world. Every time I look at him my hearts begins to race. When he looks at me, he makes me feel like I am the most beautiful girl in the world to him. But I know that's not true. I can never truly believe that Tamaku has any feelings for me. I am nothing but a normal high school student from the human world. I'm probably not even his type. Does he even have a type? Of course not. Well...maybe.

I went to wake up Tamaku to tell him that Piper and I were leaving. I saw him on the floor with his face away from me. He was on his side using his arm as a pillow.

"Hey," I said as I shook him lightly.

"Yeah, I'm awake. So you two are setting off already to find that girl?"

"Just for a bit. We just want to see if we can find her somewhere. She's the only one I can learn lightning manipulation from."

"Okay, see you later for some sword handling I guess."

"That sounds great. Don't worry, I won't be long." I lowered my voice a bit, "I honestly just think Piper wants to hang out with me. She's so cute."

He laughed a little.

I could hear Piper yelling for me to speed it up outside. "Okay, I had better get going. See you later, Tamaku!" I said with a wave. Just as I turned, I felt his hand holding me back.

"Scarlet, wait, I think I need to tell you something."

"Well can this wait? Piper is getting restless."

"Well...yeah, it can wait."

"Sorry, Tamaku, I'll catch you later!"

~~~*~~~

### Tamaku's View

I did it again! I missed my chance again! I want to tell her. Why didn't I do it? I couldn't even say anything. "Jeez," I accidently said aloud.

"Tamaku, what happened?" asked Omi sleepily as if he had just awakened.

"Nothing happened, I am just an idiot."

"What do you mean?"

"Well...have you ever had to do something but you are just too much of a coward to do it?"

He sat up. "Well yeah, but I think everyone has felt that way before." He then widened his eyes a bit. "Wait, is this about Scarlet?"

I chose my words carefully. "Well, I guess so. Up till now, I always thought she trusted me. But something is definitely wrong with her and she won't tell me."

"I hate to agree, but I must. I think I have an idea about what is going on with her; when Scarlet told us about that woman she saw...I think that was true."

"Yes, I have thought the same thing! But why has a woman made her act like this. Ever since she has become so powerful, it seems as though she is different," I said.

"That woman must have given her power. But it was an evil power. I know it because while I am training with her, her once pure spirit energy has become dark but very powerful. It seems to me like it has taken over her body somehow."

"Wait, if this was going on, why wouldn't she tell us? We are her friends after all. I even tried to get her to tell me."

"I think she just doesn't want us to be concerned about her. But, if it turns out that evil is taking her over, we have to do something about it quickly. If we don't act soon, only time will tell us the results."

"Well, what should we do?"

"I'm not sure, but I can sense something else is wrong with you as well."

"Well, I am just kind of shaken up about this whole thing. I mean, I am happy that Scarlet is here but...she only has three more days left. I just don't know what will happen when she leaves." I said with a sigh.

"Can't she come back and visit?"

"No," I started, "As a human, once you exit this realm, you cannot return a second time."

"Well why don't you just ask if she can stay a little longer?"

"Omi, don't you know the rules? A Varcia can only stay in this realm for twelve days. If she stayed even a moment longer, she would never be able to return to the human world."

"You really want to stay with her, don't you?"

"More than anything," I admitted. "I know I am just her guardian but...I really care about her. I was so happy when she met *me* for the first time. I have known her for so long and when she said my name for the first time...I almost wanted to cry."

"Why don't you tell her this, instead of telling me?"

"I can't. She has wanted to return home from the day she set foot in this place. What kind of person would I be to try and hold her back from going to her real home? I just have to watch her go. No matter how hard I try, I still cannot find the courage to tell her. Plus, I already know she can never feel the same way."

"Tamaku, you truly don't get it," Omi said bluntly.

"What?"

"Tamaku, I am a little bit older than you so I am also a bit wiser. Can't you see that Scarlet feels the exact same way about you? Tamaku, open your eyes. You have to tell her. Like you said, her time here is almost over. Part of this is my fault. I should have spoken up sooner. Though I also thought you be able to see the obvious. Tamaku, I'm your friend and I am definitely here for you. I will not force you to do anything but I strongly urge you to tell her. Do it before it is too late. There is no guarantee that we will all make it out of Taurid's palace alive. Three days doesn't seem like a long time, but a lot can happen. You need to make a decision and soon."

He yawned and lay back down—nice.

I thought about what he said. Was he serious? Well, he was right about one thing. I do have to make a decision. I never thought about it before, but we will be going up against Taurid. There is no guarantee of survival. Omi is wise. I just wish I was, too.

# CHAPTER 25

## THE ENEMY

As Piper and I moved through the forest, I breathed in the cool, damp morning air. We had been looking for about an hour now and still no Lawny. All I could see were the dead trees and open skies. The only sound heard was of the crunching of dead grass under my feet.

"Varcia, can I ride on your back?" asked Piper whiningly.

I sighed. I guess she would be fatigued to have such short legs and a long way to go.

"Sure thing, Piper." I stooped down.

She started to giggle as I moved forward. This caused me to chuckle. "What's so funny?"

"Nothing really, I'm just really excited!"

"For what?" I asked as I continued to walk.

"It's a secret!"

"Oh, really? Gee, Piper, I sure wish I knew. That must be some secret of yours," I said jokingly.

"Well, okay. I am just really excited that I'm with you! I can't wait to see you fight something!"

"Who said I'm going to fight anyone?" I chuckled.

"Well, you just gotta, Varcia! When I grow up, I want to be just as cool as you!" She began punching the air as if she was fighting an imaginary opponent...cute.

"And how do you intend to do that?" I asked.

She thought for a second. "Well...I'm gonna practice every day at my fire manipulation! And...ummm...I'm gonna get a Raico sword just like you, Varcia!"

"Well, it takes more than just practice and a sword, you know?"

"Oh yeah, that's right! I also need pure determination!"

I laughed. "Well it seems like you are well on your way, my friend."

She gave a satisfied sigh. She then rested her head on my back and wrapped her arms around my neck.

"Yeah...but I'm nothing like you, Varcia...you're awesome," she said.

Little did she know, this power wasn't even mine. The power doesn't belong to me, I belong to it. I just wish I could go back and stop this from ever happening.

For another hour I walked in silence. I was absolutely exhausted and I had a feeling we were walking around in circles.

The wind was picking up. My dark hair swirled in the breeze lightly against my red cheeks. I bit my lip to thaw the cold. My bare arms had sprouted chill bumps from the frosty weather. Something was definitely wrong—it's never "this cold" in Audren. With every step I took, the temperature seemed to drop just a bit. Was this a trap?

I stopped in my tracks. It seemed like Piper had fallen asleep on my back. I looked to my right, then my left. Then, in the trees I saw I figure flash past.

"Piper," I said softly.

She didn't stir.

"Piper," I said louder this time.

She yawned. "Why is it so cold?"

"I don't know, but you need to wake up, sweetie." I slowly let her on her feet.

She immediately clung to my side for warmth. "Is something wrong?"

I peered around the trees. *What was that?* I thought.

Then again, like a flash of lighting, I saw the figure again. It was like a blur of white swishing through the trees escaping sight.

"Varcia, what's going on?"

I immediately placed my finger over my mouth to hush her. I reached for my Raico without looking down. The cold bit my cheeks as I stood still. I didn't dare move a muscle.

My heart began to race now, but I did not know why. My hands shook from the nerves my body had cultivated. I didn't dare show my fear...not when Piper was there. I felt obligated to be strong for her, but I could not promise I could live up to the hero she conjured me up to be.

She clenched to my side anxiously as though she was clinging on to dear life itself. I could feel my blouse dampen from her silent tears.

"I can feel it," she said edgily. "He's real close," she sniffed. "I think he's going to kill us."

Who was she talking about?

Though it was frigid, my palms were moist from sweat.

"Scarlet," she whispered, "I'm scared."

For the first time she actually said my name. I was going to comfort her but the wind mysteriously picked up wildly. From the shadows I heard eerie footsteps. My throat tightened and my legs felt as if my bones were made of rubber.

My heart dropped. I felt a presence behind me but when I turned I was greeted by vacant space.

I suddenly heard another crack of a branch and dragged my gaze to its direction. There he stood; a man with a crooked smile on his pale face. He stepped forward began to approach me.

He was dressed in a black cloak. He wore a black metal band that stretched across his forehead with jewels of all sorts imbedded in its surface. He had long, silver hair that was neatly tied back. It was not of old age because his face had youth. His perfect bone structure was jaw dropping. His face was beautiful?...but unnatural. He was beautiful in an eerie fake way. His eyes were a dark auburn making his facial structure even more intense.

His presence was almost impossible to withstand.

Piper's tears were more audible now.

I wanted to turn from the man but my eyes would not shift.

I could feel my body shudder at his presence. He was aware or my trepidation, and broadened his grin.

I felt my soul plummet to the soles of my feet as he still eased closer—he was still about 15 feet away.

"Hello, Scarlet," his tone was musical, almost as a joke.

What surprised me is that he knew my name. I could not understand why his mere presence left me in this state.

"So we meet at last, Varcia..." his tone was more frigid now.

My mind was still in a state of clear thinking. I had just enough logic to come up with a legitimate notion. *It was him...it had to be.*

"Oh don't be frightened by me, Scarlet," he said as if I were a small child. Then the grin immediately erased from his lips and his face stiffened. "After all...you're the one who is going to kill me...*right*?"

Piper submerged her face into my side, her tears still flowing. He snaked closer to me I felt the hair on my arms stand up high. I swiftly scanned the area for an opening. He didn't miss my frantic eyes. "There's nowhere to hide," he said stiffly. It was almost as if he had read my mind. But sadly he was right. I could not find any place to flee to.

Close, he lifted a pale white finger to my cheek as he stroked it gently. "You're definitely beautiful. You look just like Kiley. But you are just a mere child."

Kiley. Kiley was my mother's name. How did he know her? To have this man know her baffled me. I craved to ask him but it felt as if I spoke I could lose my life. It felt like he was peering into my very being with those eyes of his. I felt like my every move...every thought was carefully being analyzed.

His long nail, without warning, glided across my cheek as if he was cutting tissue paper with a box cutter. I could feel a trickle of blood but I felt no pain. My fear was too great. He then collected the blood in his palm with a smile. He locked eyes with mine. I could see him clenching his fist tight. Then, when he opened his palm, all that lay there was a small pile of crimson dust. He blew it out of his hand.

I felt like I was about to vomit from this horrific sight. I could feel my face twinge as he began to laugh. His laugh crackled in the air releasing a sound I have never heard. It was drenched in evil that made me sick to the stomach.

192

"My dear, I am anxious for our battle."

I could not take any more…I collapsed to my knees feeling the dry earth under me.  My body felt hollow, I was motionless.  I couldn't tell if I was breathing or not.

"Don't fret…I'm not going to do anything to you…*not yet.*" He crouched down to my level and drew close to my face.  "But I do want you to remember your place.  In this world, I am at the top…you are at the bottom.  To reach me, you will need a little more than 'pure determination'…you need power."  His tone was dark—demonic.  "It wouldn't be any fun to kill someone who doesn't have a chance…that's why I am willing to offer you more power."  He extracted a small glass bottle from his cloak—about as tall as a few inches—and laid it by my side.  He then drew his lips close to my ear.  "You wanted to learn lightning manipulation.  I'm giving it to you," he whispered.

I could not bear to hear his gruff voice.  This was my enemy… Taurid.  His demonic aura felt as if it was engulfing my entire body.  This was my soon to be opponent.  As I thought, I felt his frigid breath down my back chilling my soul as he hovered over me.  He had so much control over me by just being there.  I felt nauseous…almost as if I would shut down at any given moment.

~~~*~~~

"Scarlet! Scarlet, please!"

I fluttered my eyes in attempts to adjust my vision.  As I rubbed my eyes, I was greeted to an unwanted flood of light.  I did notice that it was warm.

"Scarlet!" exclaimed Piper as she wrapped her short arms around my torso.  She flashed a pearly white smile, missing the two teeth in the front.  She squeezed me tight but I sat idly still unable to completely open my eyes.

After a few seconds my mind flickered to the memory of the horrifying event I had prior.

"Where is he?" I asked.

She pulled away and looked at me sullenly. "He left about an hour ago…you passed out," she almost whispered.

I was guilt-ridden that my fear left Piper alone with Taurid, though I don't think I would have helped any more than I would if I had have been conscious. "Are you okay?" I asked sitting up, as I began to examine her arms and legs for so much as a cut or bruise.

"He left soon after you passed out. I don't even know if he noticed me. He seemed like he only cared about you."

This was a relief. I instantaneously shot my gaze to the side to find the small glass bottle exactly where he had placed it. Without thought, I grasped the bottle tucking it snugly into my skirt pocket. I had expected a shock or sting to come upon me as my flesh came in contact with the relic—my assumptions were pleasantly wrong. I looked back up to see Piper watching me.

I then reflected on the fear that had once consumed me. Taurid's piercing stare was enough to send my mind in a dreadful daze just by thinking on it.

I slid my hand upon my cheeks to feel the slit on its surface. *Still there,* I thought.

"You have never seen him before, have you?" asked Piper. I almost forgot she was with me for a moment.

"No."

"My mother used to tell me that it feels a lot better if you don't think about it. At least you know what you're up against now…"

She was right. This whole time I was fooling myself ignorantly. I knew my chances were slim but now I feel as though I don't have a dying wish.

"That bottle he gave you…" she said.

"Yeah, what about it?" I should have seen this coming.

She shot her crystal blue eyes into mine. Her usually bright, childlike eyes now appeared dark and vacant. "It's bad."

"Why do you say that?" I retorted.

"You don't need that to get stronger. He only gave it to you to…hurt you." her tone was solemn.

I knew what she was saying was true but I didn't have any other options. All power comes at a price; even I know that. This power may have happened to cost…my heart…and the merging of my pure soul with that of…evil—though my soul was already tainted with it. I needed that power…I find it selfish if I do not take it. If I saved my life, it would save thousands of lives in exchange. One against all…at least that's how I see it.

That fear I had of him angered me. I showed him my weakness and now he has the advantage. I never want to feel that feeble, vulnerable…again.

With Piper's hand in mine, we slowly traveled through the thicket of the woodland. She had not spoken a word and nor did I. My legs ached as we strode bare bushes and trees. The light of the day barely shinned through the tall, leafless hemlocks and oaks that shielded our route.

I had hoped that Piper wasn't actually mad at me for taking the bottle. I didn't want her upset, but she could never understand how I feel. At the same time, I hoped that she kept her mouth shut about our little encounter today; the last thing I need is people worrying—more. She seemed apprehensive, but I was hoping for the best. She kept her gaze straight ahead as her short, brown pigtails bounced with every step she took. It made me sad to see her like this but like everything else...I had no choice.

About another hour had passed before we had, at long last, reached the hut. Conch, Roke, and Omi had been playing some sort of card game outside. Piper's eyes brightened almost instantly. "Omi!" she shouted as she unleashed my hand and ran to hug Omi and the

twins. It made me a little more upset than I would ever expect for her to be so excited to depart from me and flock to them. I could tell she wouldn't tell them what happened. I have kept many secrets... so I just knew.

Omi waved to me and the twins followed suit. As I entered the hut I was surprised not to see Tamaku. I took advantage of this time alone by nearly collapsing on the small bed, rupturing the sheets that adorned its surface. I kicked off my shoes carelessly still lying vertically on the bumpy mattress.

I thought for a moment with my eyes shut. I knew the kids at school had to have taken notice to my abrupt absence. I was curious to know what they all were thinking. I know that my aunt and uncle have probably filed a missing person report by now. Little did they know, no search party could ever find me; I was no longer in the same realm.

For some reason, I felt an impulse to remove my locket. For just a moment I felt as though I wasn't in control of my hands. I had removed the locket throwing it to the ground. I felt a chill flow down my spine as my skin received a feeling of bareness. I didn't like this feeling but I had no energy to counter it.

I noticed a glimpse of light oozing into my peripheral vision. I inched to the edge of the bed, but drew back from what I saw. The locket was floating in midair, glowing in a marvelous, lush, gold color.

"Serenity?" I could hear my voice.

With a whoosh, the locket dangled its way into my, involuntarily, open palm. I was greatly mystified. My eyebrows knit together.

"There it was again," said Serenity.

"What?"

"You were being controlled again…I'm sure of it. I have told you before; you have to fight this if you ever wish to become normal again. If you keep allowing this to enter your mind, you will be given up to evil for sure. I have noticed that you have figured that out yourself, which is all the more reason not to give in," she protested. "I am here to help you, but my abilities are powerless if you continue to be overshadowed by evil. Receiving more power is not the way to defeat Taurid. Fighting evil with evil will get you nowhere. It will repel against itself. If you fight for the light, you will overcome the darkness. Power is not the answer…love is."

The light dimmed. I threw the locket down and balled my fists. She did not understand either. If love is the answer, how come all the other Varcia have failed? I would be different. I can't fail. Without this strength, I would be weaker than I am now. No one fully understands my position…I didn't even know if I did.

In the midst of my thoughts, the unwelcomed guest had reared its hideous form again. It was here again. Just as before, I felt it circulate in my body and spreading quickly. The grave feeling caused me to coil. I dug my nails into the rigid sheets in attempts to suppress my prolonged urges to tear innocent flesh. I grinded my teeth, holding back a screech that would be sure to draw unwanted attention. I hated this. I wish I could have power on my own.

My vision became obscure as I lay with eyes fastened tight. In a matter of minutes, (which felt like hours) my outbreak had finally come to an end. I didn't want to get up; not now. I wanted to lay there and not have any feelings or thoughts. I wanted my mind vacant and stable. My body felt drained of energy and drenched with paralysis.

The hut door creaked open. Then the familiar form of Tamaku came into view. For some reason, my desire to shut out everyone vanished.

"Hey. Do want to do some training? Your four step combo could use a little work," he said with a grin.

I most certainly was not in the mood for training but I did not want to pass up doing anything with Tamaku.

"Sure," I said with a little too much desperation.

He motioned for me to grab the Raico at the foot of the bed. I quickly did so as he held the door open. But before I could pass he stopped me. He studied my face which made me uncomfortable, but I then understood why. I knew I must have looked drained, and maybe a little sick. After that last break down I had, I probably looked even worse than I thought. He did not question me though, which was a relief.

In the large field, we sparred like always. He was right about my four step combo being a little flawed, but I effortlessly corrected my error. It turned out I had simply had my timing wrong. I blocked and dodged all his attacks with ease in which he had grown accustom to. Even at his full ability, he had no chance against my excellent precision and mobility skills.

Our session was clearly over leaving me a little upset but I dared not make it known.

"You did great today. I have to admit that you are out of my league," Tamaku said with his alluring voice as always—though he never did it on purpose.

"You weren't too bad yourself," I said trying to mirror his almost irresistible gaze (though I wouldn't call mine very appealing).

I had turned away, but soon I was halted.

"Wait," he said in a sheepish tone.

I turned around, "Yes?"

"Want to take a walk?" he asked with his hand outstretched and eyebrows raised. He noticed my nervousness and shot me a rather adorable crooked smile.

After a few moments of hesitation, I took his hand. "Where are we walking to?"

Without answering, he began to walk with my hand in his. I didn't want the entire trip to be silent so I decided to create some sort of small talk.

"How come I didn't seen the kids when we left?" I asked. It seemed like a pretty good conversation starter.

"Oh, them?" he said sounding a little surprised I would bring them up. "I think Omi took them to town."

"That sounds cool."

"No, it's actually pretty warm out," he said with a confused frown.

I almost laughed at his oblivious statement. "No, I didn't mean *cool* as in *cold*."

He leaned his head in confusion. Then we both laughed hysterically.

"Hey, do you want to see something?" I asked before an awkward silence could fill the air.

"Sure."

I then removed the small friendship journal from my pocket. I held it in front of him.

"Aw, this is really cute. I remember seeing Piper working on this last night. She asked me if she could borrow some markers. I was lucky to find a few that still worked. She was working on this for hours. I fell asleep while she was still making it. I didn't know it was for you though. A friendship journal, huh?"

He smoothed his finger across its surface. The small book had drawings of rainbows and stars adorning its lavender surface. It also had two stick figures holding hands. One looked like Piper and the other looked like me. He flipped through the blank pages as we walked.

"You haven't written in it yet," he pointed out.

"Yeah, I know. I think I'll work on it tonight."

"Wow, Piper really loves you, Scarlet. You should make something for her. She's going to be heartbroken when you leave."

"Yes, that is what I was thinking. I just don't know what to make for her."

He was silent for a moment. "Maybe you should give her that scarlet ribbon you have in your hair," he proposed.

As I thought about it, that actually was a pretty good option. I had forgotten all about that ribbon. I untied it and examined it. It was in pretty good shape. I then placed it in my pocket.

It was quiet for a moment. The only sound that filled the air was the scratchy sound of the dead grass beneath our feet. My body was still very sore. Tamaku apparently took notice.

"I have a better idea" he said with a hyper undertone.

"And what might that be?" I asked with one eye brow elevated.

"Let's fly!" he exclaimed. Without waiting for a response, he darted towards the front and out came those celestial wings that

200

glistened bright as before. I only witnessed them a few times, but I was just as awestruck as though it was my first.

"Are you going to get on or just stand there?" he asked jokingly.

I answered him with a smile as I climbed on his broad wingspan. Within seconds we were catapulted into the air at a tremendous speed. When I rode on his back, I always had a feeling I could fall off. The only thing that fastened me to his back were my fingers latching on to the feathers. It was a very open air feeling.

"So what happened this morning anyway?" he asked casually. The question couldn't have been worse.

"Nothing," I lied bluntly.

"You can tell me, you know," he said obviously not buying what I was putting on the table.

"I know."

"Then why don't you?" I could hear the agitation in his voice.

"There is nothing to tell," I said somewhat annoyed at myself for lying to him.

"You seemed shaken up about something earlier," his voice trailed off.

I didn't answer.

He took this opportunity to continue. "You're not going to tell me anything, are you?"

I stayed loyal to my silence.

# CHAPTER 26

## CONFESSIONS

As we continued to fly, it was silent.  The only sound that could be heard was the roar of the wind passing us at high-speed.  I looked at the many clouds that hovered in the sky.

"I have a secret," Tamaku murmured.

"Um," I didn't really want to respond.  I feared that if I said I wanted to hear what he was going to say, I would then be obligated to share my problems.

"I think it's something you would like to know."  His voice was apprehensive.

"You don't have to tell me...I'm not going to tell you mine," I admitted but kept my voice strong.

"That's fine, but I still *want* to tell you," his voice sounded ductile.  I was not going to show my burning interest.  But he proceeded anyhow.

"Well my secret—which isn't really much of a secret—is that... *I care about you...a lot.*"

I was astounded as I cupped my hand over my mouth.  He continued to speak giving me time to recuperate.

"That is why I need you to tell me what is going on.  I just want you to tell the truth," his tone was sincere.  "That's why I'm dying for you to tell me—I'm begging you," he said with a chuckle but he was very much serious.

I knew I would become obligated! But his words sent me in a haze of delight. I relinquished to him then and there. "Okay...I'll tell you."

He gracefully landed us down to a stop on the beach. He rushed in impatience as he led us to the very edge of shore on the beach. I glanced around seeing the many people around the busy city on the board walk. I then shifted my gaze to the place I had fallen when I first arrived here. As the crashing waters washed up on the dry sand, it nearly touched my toes. No one was actually on the beach. Back home, our beach was always crowded.

He sat next to me with his eyes glimmering and locked with mine. We were only a few inches away from each other which made me feel nervous but I hid my emotion...and quite well. I brought my knees close to my chest and wrapped my arms around my legs.

"Well," I began as I looked ahead towards the water and toyed with the dry sand. "I am just not wholly myself," I managed to force out.

After a small pause, (I suppose he was thinking) he began to speak.

"How so?"

"I am positive that you have detected my tremendous progress since my water cyclone incident," I said.

"Yes." I hated his short answers he kept releasing. I resisted rolling my eyes and continued.

"But I am afraid this power I have was never mine to begin with. It causes a lot of complications. I even fear that it is evil."

He frowned. "So you think you contain evil powers and it affects you greatly. You also think it can take over you," he stated more than asked.

My eyes locked with his more intensely. I didn't say that last part. "So you already know," I said trying to sound indifferent, but failed miserably.

"Of course I do...lest we forget that I *am* your guardian," he looked away. "Plus," he added, "I saw you acting weird in the hut before I came in."

"If you knew, then why did you put me through all of that to say it?" I said, struck with mild anger.

"I wanted *you* to tell me. I wanted you to trust me."

I was still fuming. Ignoring my evident anger, he drew closer to me and started asking more questions.

"But I am curious to know what it feels like," he prompted.

"I just get disturbing thoughts...a lot."

"Like what?" he asked curiously.

"I thought you would have known already," I said crossly.

"Yes, but I never said I could read your mind," he said.

I chose my words carefully. I didn't want to startle him too much. "I have thoughts like...hurting others, inflicting any kind of pain. I have the oddest urges to see blood." I knew in the back of my head that I couldn't sugar coat it.

"Do you have these thoughts about anyone in particular?" He asked seeming very calm, almost not understanding the magnitude of what I was telling him.

"No; I have these thoughts about anyone I seem to come in contact with. Most of the time I can tune them out when they are not that strong, but sometimes..."

"You feel like you might actually act on your urges," he finished.

"Yes."

"Do you think you will be able to control yourself like you have been doing lately?" He asked.

"I am not very sure. But I know with my power level, I can easily take out just about anyone."

"So this all started with that woman you saw?" he recalled.

"Yes, she is the one that gave me my power; I am sure of it. I haven't been the same since then."

"So that's why you didn't tell me? You thought I would be cautious of you?"

"You should be. If these feelings continue to get stronger, there is no telling what I could do. I can't fully explain it, but it feels as though the evil circulates through my body. I feel consumed by it...controlled by it...I feel almost..."

"Overtaken," his dark eyes penetrated in mine. I nodded in agreement and was very pleased that he seemed to understand me. He seemed to be about the only one...

"Yes, but I think that is exactly what I need to be strong."

"So you think that this evil power you have is the only way you have a chance at defeating Taurid. You also are willing to sacrifice yourself for the sake of Audren." He said this calmly but I could feel the disapproval in his voice.

"If you want to put it that way," I replied.

"But you are stronger than evil," he said.

"No, I'm not. No matter how hard I try I cannot suppress these urges. I have been able to ignore them at times, but I can't ignore them forever. I have the strangest feeling that I will not be able to hold back...and I think that time is coming soon," I could feel the frost in my voice. He drew closer to me, causing me to shudder. There were only millimeters between us.

"But I'm not afraid," he whispered.

"Why won't you listen to me?" I said as I pushed him away.

"Can't you see that I'm not the same as before? At any given time, I could hurt you".

"Do you want me to stay away from you?" he asked, both angry and confused as he pulled back a few inches as well.

"Evil will take over me fully soon."

"But when I look into your eyes, I can see the genuine Scarlet that I know."

"For now that's what you see. But soon the Scarlet you know will no longer be in existence. Even now I feel an urge merging and I can't stop it. Every moment I am going deeper into the line of fire but I cannot turn back. I don't ever want to see you hurt on my behalf."

He leaned closer again. "I won't stay away."

"Why do you care so much?" I breathed.

"You should know by now that you're special to me."

I immediately looked away from him. My heart pulsated. I didn't look back up at him but I could feel his stare. I flinched as I felt a warm hand pull loose strands of my brown hair behind my ear. I reluctantly managed to steal a glance at his face but regretted it after seeing his concerned glare.

"I could never let you go at this alone. We can work together to help you overcome this. Your beautiful spirit could never be engulfed with wickedness."

His enchanting gaze still left me speechless. I knew my expression showed my feelings, and for once, I didn't care.

"I still don't understand why you think that?" I almost shouted.

His hand eased its way on my cold hand. His touch made me stagger. "Because you agreed to this, because you still want to fight. You are going to risk your life to save people you don't even know..." He slid his hand away.

I almost felt a tear roll down when he did. I wanted to feel his touch again. I didn't want him to keep his distance from me but I also didn't want him to end up dead.

I clenched my scalp violently. *It was happening here? Now?* I felt my fingers begin to twitch. No part of my body was prone to this. I wanted to cut something, to grasp something.

I dropped to my knees clenching the sand underneath me. My back and neck were damp from perspiration. I tightly shut my eyes in efforts to fight it. I cried out leaving a ring in my ears. I felt someone touch me. I wanted to swipe them away but I did not. I felt my curled fingers loosen. I felt myself regain a normal posture.

I opened my eyes to see Tamaku. I knew my sudden anxiety had come to a close. It was his touch. His two hands were rested upon my tapered shoulders. His hands were shaking. I could see him attempting to hold back his fear, that's how I perceived it.

I wanted to shed tears but my body simply would not allow it. I was afraid that he might take my advice from earlier now.

"I warned you," I said, still tearing up.

"I am not afraid," he whispered matching my low tone.

I couldn't tell if he was frightened or not. His face just kept a blank vacant look now. This worried me. I could not read his expression and it made me angry.

"Then how do you feel?" I asked as I looked into his dark eyes.

"...Deeply in love with you."

# CHAPTER 27

## MOTHER

Light flooded the cold damp dungeon cellar as a guard stood in the doorway. "lord Taurid summons you," he said gruffly.

Kiley struggled to her sore feet as the guard roughly unlocked her chains letting them tumble to the ground with simultaneous clinks. Without a second to spare, the guard clutched her arm churlishly, leading her out the doorway. Her bruised arms still ached from the last beating she had received from another guard. Almost every week, she would get a beating for absolutely no reason—at least not for a reason she was aware of.

The entire walk was silent but her mind was filled with thoughts of Scarlet. She knew he had done something, but she had no idea what that "something" was. She cringed as many scenarios scrolled across her mind. In just 3 short days, Scarlet would be on the battle field with him. She believed in her daughter but in the back of her head, she felt uneasy.

But what could Taurid want this time? Hadn't he had enough of belittling her to the point of nothing? *Outrageous*, she thought. *Nothing is ever enough for that man. The audacity!*

In a few more minutes she was almost thrown into the spacey throne room, which was a total transformation from her tight, stuffy cell. She lifted her gaze at Taurid as he sat comfortably on his cushioned thrown. He stroked his chin as he examined her.

"What could you possibly want?" she asked, disgusted.

"You still cannot control that unruly tongue of yours, can you?"

She ignored his question, "What did you do to Scarlet?"

"Still concerned about that daughter of yours? I find it quite puzzling that you worry about her so much, but you were willing to leave her without a mother," he said with an edge to his tone.

"Stop it," she commanded cholerically.

"So many nights the child must have gone, crying because she had no mother to tuck her in at night and kiss her forehead," he taunted voluntarily. "So many times the child must have needed a mother to comfort her, but you were nowhere to be found. It is also pitiful that you allowed her and her father to believe that lie of you dying when you really neglected them both. Now look at your daughter, she has no one." He began to laugh.

She balled her fists, attempting to stand up.

"Guards," he commanded pompously. Not a moment too soon, two soldiers seized her perfidiously.

"I hate you," she wailed still striving to break free from the guards.

"She will be put to death tonight!" He shouted to one of them.

"Please," she immediately calmed her unruly efforts to break free. "Don't kill me yet, just let me see Scarlet first!" she abjured vigorously.

"Kiley, you helpless girl; your daughter does not even recognize you. I am putting you out of your misery."

"No! Please, I will do anything you say, please, just not yet!"

He laughed for a few seconds. That same hideous laugh she knew all too well.

"Unhand her," he commanded with left over chuckles.

They instantly dropped her to the ground like a rag doll.  She kept her gaze low giving him the most respect she could muster. Her thoughts flickered upon Scarlet.  She only hoped that Taurid would allow her to see her daughter once more.

"What happened to your disrespectful attitude, Kiley?"  He asked without expecting an answer.

"Are you repentant for your deeds?"

"Yes…" she said in a hushed tone.

# CHAPTER 28

## AFFECTION

I immediately felt as if I would collapse into his arms. He held my shoulders gazing into my eyes for a response. I would have answered him back quicker, but I was overwhelmed with joy. After all this time of wondering, I was finally happy, truly happy for the first time in all these nine days. He was still waiting for a response.

"I...I love you, too," I divulged as I stared back into his eyes with the same intensity he gave me. A small smile eased its way on his lips in response to me.

He glided the back of his hand across my now blushing cheeks. His touch was gentle and smooth, causing shivers to trail down my spine. But the way I felt was...invigorating. Then, he looked out into the ocean. He stood up, and began to run to the left.

I examined his movements. *What was he doing?*

He ran to a high pile of rocks and boulders. He climbed them; he reached the very top. It had to be at least twelve feet high.

He began to remove his shirt, and gestured me to come to him.

I stayed where I was. "Tamaku, what on earth are you doing?" I shouted out.

"Come over here and see!" he shouted back with a vibrant smile across his face.

Reluctantly, I stood up. He began to motion for me again. I sped up my walk; I had my arms crossed against my chest. When I reached the mound of sediment, I stood. I had never really climbed rocks before.

Tamaku laughed and stepped down a little and extended his arm for me to grab.

As I did, he effortlessly scooped me up into his arms and carried me to the very top. "What is this about?" I asked as he let me down. I was always a little scared of heights, so I stayed close to him.

"This!" he said as he leaped into the blue water. He popped his head above water laughing, and shaking his hair like a small puppy. "Come on, Scarlet! The water's not that cold."

"I'm not doing that," I told him.

He laughed again. "Why not? You're not scared of heights, are you?"

"No." I Lied.

"You're not scared of a little water, are you?"

"No."

"You're not scared of me, are you?"

"No." This was true.

"Then what's wrong, Miss Varcia?" he asked, wading in the water.

"I...I can't swim, okay," I admitted.

"What? I thought you lived near a beach! You're seventeen and you don't know how to swim?"

"No." I had never really been taught. Every time I was at the pool or the beach, I always stayed in the shallow end.

"Jump in," he said with his arms wide open.

"No! I'll drown!"

He laughed once more. "You're afraid of drowning when you have me right here?" he teased.

"Yes. Most people that can't swim are afraid of drowning, and I think that is a quite reasonable reaction," I replied.

"Aw, Scarlet's scared of a little challenge. That's okay, Scarlet. When you're a big girl, you can jump in with the big kids, okay?" He said in a teasing voice. He saw my glare and began to chuckle. "Oh, well. I guess I'll have to enjoy all this fun by myself." He began to hum a little tune as he back stroked closing his eyes.

"Fine!" I shouted. I inched to the edge of the rocks. My heart was pounding. I saw Tamaku perk up and have his arms open for me again. A large smile spread across his face. I sucked in a deep breath and closed my eyes. Before I knew it, I was falling in thin air.

I screamed, but not out of fear, but out of joy. I felt myself under the water. I didn't know what to do. I couldn't touch the bottom. But before I got frantic, I felt arms under my back and legs, lifting me to the surface. I gasped in air and wiped my eyes.

"Tamaku," I said as I wrapped my arms around his neck securely.

"I gotcha, I gotcha," he said softly as he held his hands against my back.

"See," I said as I laid my head against his shoulder, keeping myself as high above the water as I could. "I'm not scared."

"Sure," he chuckled.

"I feel...weightless," I said as laid back in the water, closing my eyes. I spread out my arms, letting water glide through my fingertips.

"You know, the water can carry you, too," he said as he removed one hand from my back. But before a fraction of a second passed, I screamed and wrapped my arms around him again tightly.

"Don't let me go," I said, my heart still recovering from that surprise.

He chuckled softly. "Scardy cat."

"Shut up," I giggled. I lay back again. I felt Tamaku swirling me in slow circles. "Don't let go," I whispered.

"Scarlet Lansing, I will never let you go," he said softly. I had the feeling that he didn't only mean physically…but emotionally.

I sat up and drew closer, never looking away from him. I placed both of my hands on the side of his face studying it. There was almost no space between us as I faced him and he faced me. Our smiles had faded.

"No more secrets, right?" he murmured.

"Yeah…no more secrets," I promised.

"Then I should tell you something." Our faces were so close, the slightest of movements would have had our heads bump.

"What's that?" I asked barely paying attention to what he was saying.

"I'm curious," he said in a velvety voice.

"About what?" I asked a little more interested now.

"About…what it would be like…when you leave."

My soaring heart plummeted down with an excruciating drop. I had completely forgotten about that. I was only in Audren for three more days. I felt the warm tears roll down my cheeks. The last thing I wanted to do now was leave Tamaku.

He then wiped away my tears with his thumbs. He gave a few *Shhh*'s before speaking. Once I had quieted down a bit, he began. "Scarlet, don't grieve this. One of the reasons I didn't want to confess to you, is because if you felt the same, you wouldn't want to return home. You have scores of people shedding tears hoping you will return. The human world is your true home." He sounded true, but I could never leave him.

"But I don't want to leave you," I argued, tears welting.

"I don't want you to go either. But if you stay here pass these last three days, you will never see you friends and family again."

I felt tears again. I knew he was right. I missed everyone...especially Matt, Ryan, Uncle Dan, and Aunt Danielle. I know they missed me. But I couldn't bear to leave Tamaku. I hated making decisions.

"And if you leave here, you can never return," he continued.

I went over both scenarios, but they both would make me upset in the end. I had to make a decision before my time here was up. I can truly say that my own future rests in my hands.

"I'm sorry Scarlet, but you must know what you are up against."

I was still crying. "What will you do if I leave?"

He stroked my arm smoothly in efforts to calm me—it was working. "I don't know," he whispered.

I wrapped my arms around him, laying my head against his chest again. I felt his arms around me, which made me whimper. The thought of never being with him again sickened me.

"What do you think I should do?" I asked sniffling.

"It hurts me to say this...but I would never get over the guilt of keeping you from your friends and family. I will miss you, but I know that it would be best for you to return home and savor the moments we share now."

He made sense but I didn't want to listen. He pulled me away to look at my tear shot eyes. Again, he wiped away my tears as tears glistened his eyes.

"I want you to be happy. I promise you that if you stay here, you will be miserable."

The wind began to pick up again, rattling my loose hair. I stared in Tamaku's face. He looked upset as his eyebrows scrunched together. I was nervous now. I could almost hear my heart thumping wildly in my ears. This secret didn't sound like a pleasant one.

"How much are you willing to defeat Taurid?" He asked with the same expression casing his face.

"More than anything," I said truthfully. I still did not contemplate what he was getting at.

"How much do you love me?" he asked.

"More than anything," I repeated, this time with a smile.

His expression was still unchanging.

I pursed my lips. He still sat silent. His eyes grew even darker than before.

"Is there something wrong?" I asked apprehensively. I reached my hand towards his.

He then immediately flickered on a smile. "No, nothing you need to worry about," he said as he lightly tapped my nose. I wasn't convinced; I didn't want to question him either. Maybe it was better if he didn't tell me.

"Omi and the kids are probably back by now," he said sullenly.

"Are you sure you're okay?" I asked referring to his morose tone. He then shot me the same smile he had before.

"Yes," he said taking my hand. "If you're happy…I'm even happier," he said.

I chortled at his suddenly playful behavior. Looking up into his face again, I saw him staring right back at me. He was smiling but his eyes were unreadable.

"You are really beautiful," he whispered appealingly.

I could feel my cheeks flush on his every word.

"Even more beautiful when you blush," he added.

I could feel my face get even redder. I had never been so content and worry free. For once, I couldn't hear a single evil thought. My mind was at peace and my soul soaring in the heavens. My body felt light and free as he carried me effortlessly. I actually found myself smiling wide. I almost never wanted to return home…never.

# Chapter 29

## THE ERADICATION

After returning to the hut, Tamaku decided to head into town and find something for dinner. Omi and the kids were back already.

"Scarlet!" they all exclaimed as I entered—even Piper. I embraced them all with a smile but the only one I craved to embrace was Tamaku.

"We only have two more days after tonight, Scarlet," said Piper as she climbed into my lap. I thought upon her words. She was right. In just two more days I would be going head to head with Taurid.

"You're right. I can't wait," I lied. I am frightened out of my mind.

"You're so strong, Scarlet," she said twisting around to hug me. Just then Conch and Roke surrounded me wrapping their small arms around my waist together.

"Listen," I said. Their eyes glimmered as they lingered on my next words. "You guys are strong, too, okay?"

They nodded attentively. I continued looking at each one of them. "That's why, no matter what happens you'll stay strong."

They nodded again. Three sets of bright blue eyes stared back into mine. Piper then spoke up. "Scarlet, will you be our sister?"

That took me by surprise; I think my face displayed it, too. "Of course," I said as I kissed each one on their rosy little cheeks.

"But how can you be our sister if you have to leave?" asked Conch glumly.

"Just because I'm not with you guys doesn't mean I don't love you," I said in a motherly tone. I liked talking motherly to them. It just felt natural.

Roke began to cry. The tears flowed like little steams down a valley of redness.

"B-but I'm going to miss you, Scarlet."

I wanted to tell them I may not even leave, but I still hadn't fully made up my mind.

"That's why you have to be strong, sweetheart." I then lifted him up in my lap.

I casually glanced up at Omi to see him staring at me disturbingly. His light eyes were piercing. He attempted to lighten them up as he noticed I was looking. He then gave a false smile. I didn't respond.

I then continued to comfort Roke as the other two children began to tear up.

Omi broke the silence. "I guess we don't have much time left." He looked normal again.

"I guess that means I really need to get to work."

"Yes, and that's why I will now challenge you to a friendly match!" he smiled widely.

"Wait, you want me to fight *you*?" I asked incredulously.

"Even though you have learned many skills you still have not really fought anyone yet—at least not anyone of high level. Sense I am higher skilled, you should fight me to help you practice for Taurid."

"Oh, that sounds like a great idea!" I said enthusiastically but my mind felt the sting of ambivalent thoughts.

"Okay, but we won't actually hurt each other badly. Remember this is just for practice," his tone was even but I could sense a bit of rightly deserved apprehension.

I smiled but in the back of my mind I began to think. *What if I receive evil thoughts while I'm battling Omi? Maybe I shouldn't do this*, I thought. There was no guarantee that I would be able to control myself. I didn't want to hurt Omi, but he was right...I needed practice.

We went outside into the beaming sun. Omi had already assumed his battle position. I grasped my Raico. I decided that I will try to refrain from using any water techniques. It was the least I could do to not subdue him.

Without a word, Omi came dashing at me. He, too, had a sword. I quickly leaped up to dodge him. I figured I would try to just dodge so he could get tired from attacking. That way there was no way I could hurt him if I never attacked.

He swiped his sword and shouted out some kind of technique. All of a sudden boiling water started to shoot out from his sword.

What technique was this? He never showed me. I quickly flipped to dodge this attack as well. I needed to stay loyal to my plan of not attacking.

"What's wrong, Scarlet? Why are you holding back? It's very obvious," he informed disappointedly.

"Nothing is wrong," I said poorly attempting to hide my distress.

"Well, attack me!" He started laughing as he clenched his sword again. His childish side was showing. He came towards me once more with full force. He began swinging his sword wildly in attempts to lock me in a vulnerable position. I tried to dodge but he was too fast. With another swipe, he cut my left leg.

Then it happened. All I could think about was how I could slaughter Omi. I tried to fight back these thoughts but I could not. I clenched my head with my hands. I knew I needed to get away from him immediately before I did any damage. But I did not want to. I wanted to kill him. All of a sudden it felt like my body was moving on its own accord, out of range from my soul and mind.

I charged to him with my Raico in hand. I started swinging my sword towards him again and again. I was too fast for him. My movements were sharp and flawless but out of my own control. He could not dodge; he didn't even have a string of hope. One swipe after another I cut his flesh causing the blood to gush.

He started screaming from the agony that I inflicted upon his child-like form. But I ignored his pleas. I continued to stab him rapidly with my sword hearing the crunch and gushing of his body.

I was killing him...I liked it. The power running through my veins was enlivening. He kept trying to run but I was too quick. I saw tears streaming down his face. He was drenched in his own blood. He fell to the ground. His body was motionless like an empty carcass, coiled in a ball on his side. But I knew he was not dead yet. If I slashed him one more time it would be the end of him. I walked up to him and stomped my foot on his back. He moaned in agony. Just in a matter of seconds he was almost defeated. All that was left was one final blow.  I needed to kill him.  My compulsive urges I could no longer conceal.  So many thoughts raced through my conscious, both evil and good!  I do not want to kill Omi but I do.  This sickness is uncontrollable.

He still did not move.

I had an opening

I could kill him now.

I raised my sword that dripped with blood above my head.

His body began to shudder.

I will not do it.

I will not kill my friend.

Then again...we all must die someday.

Stop me...please.

# Chapter 30

## UNIDENTIFIED ME

This was it. This bloody brawl will now conclude. The worst part is...I have no control to stop it. My sword was still lifted. With that I quickly swung down but... My heart felt numb. My sword fell from my hand.

I felt his heart beat against my spine. Tamaku held me in his arms. His heart was beating so fast. My body grew cold. I looked around me to see the out pour of blood. My hands, my feet, and my chest...blood. I saw my friend on the ground. He lay in a pool of crimson liquid. Did I do this? No...I did not do all of this. But...I did.

He had his arms around me tight...Tamaku held on to me as if he had no choice. His heart beats on my spine still. I can feel it pulsating. I do not want him to let me go.

I am a murderer. I am evil. I am no longer good, though I long to be just that. I could have stopped myself; but, I did not. Now my friend is lying on the ground motionless. It all happened so quickly.

Omi. Forgive me.

No. This evil that possesses me is not the true me. Tamaku knows that. That is why he is embracing me now. He wanted to stop me. He knows I am not evil. I now know why he is the only one that can stop me. It is because I love him with all my heart. My heart is good simply coated with evil. Love shines through my evil layer. This evil has taken over me not by my own choice. I say that I have no control. I do not have control. All I have is love. But...I am overtaken.

I do not know how to use this love. Can love ward off evil? Only Tamaku knows about me. I allow him to embrace me because I love him. His heart has slowed down. He has calmed. His skin is soft and warm. I feel the sweat from his chest on my back. I can feel his breath on my neck. He has not said I word. He stopped me from making the last blow. He was not scared of me. I did not choose to have this evil take over. I was merely an empty vessel which was a simple target for evil. I was a blank canvas. Now I am drenched with darkness.

That's why I call it a sickness. You cannot control an illness that comes over your body. No one chooses to fall ill. You do not like illnesses. Illnesses have effects on you in which you cannot control. This evil is a sickness.

### ~~~Tamaku's View~~~

I watch her from the shadows as she transforms before my eyes. I can see Omi covered in blood. He is not fast enough. Now she chases him with the intent to kill. Her eyes are filled with evil. I cannot look into them for the evil is overwhelming. This is not her. This is not the true her.

Omi cannot hold her off much longer. He is going to die here. I cannot let that happen. *Too many people I hold dear to me have slipped out of my grasp.* I must stop her now. I must show her love to awaken her from this evil trance. The real her is merely asleep. Scarlet, I love you. I must stop you.

I ran from the shadows to her. Immediately, I wrapped my arms around her. I laid my head against her back.

She dropped her sword.

She did not speak.

I did not speak.

I close my eyes and stand here now. I do not want to let her go. I will not let her go. *Too many people I hold dear to me have slipped from my grasp.* The scent of blood on my clothes is overwhelming. It is the blood of Omi.

She has calmed. Her breathing has slowed. She has awoken from her trance. She is back to herself. I wish I could read her heart. I think I know why I can stop her. It is because I love her. This evil she has is only an outer shell. I think my love for her is able to shine through.

# Chapter 31

## WARRIOR WITHIN

We still stood in silence. Maybe a quiet time is what I need. Omi is still laying there. He has not moved for a while now. I cannot tell if he is dead or alive. It is all my fault. Though I was not in control, I cannot help but feel liable for the events that had just taken place. I wish Tamaku would just kill me. I feel as if I do not deserve to live though this fate was out of my hands...inevitable. But it was by my hand that Omi is lying there.

I will break the silence.

"Tamaku...I think I killed him," I stammered feeling the quivering of my lips.

He was silent.

He still stood silent.

"It's my entire fault, Tamaku! Don't you care?"

He did not respond.

I broke his hold on me. When I did, I felt a surge of pain in my heart. Being away from him was almost unbearable. But I didn't care. Omi needed me. I crouched down next to his body. He was lying face down. I was afraid to turn him over, for then I would see the real damage I had done. I did it anyway.

I slowly turned him over on his back. I expected the sight to be ghastly but the results were otherwise. His face had a couple of cuts but nothing major though I could not say that for the rest of his body. To my surprise, he opened his eyes slowly.

"Did...I do something wrong?" Omi said faintly. He winced instantaneously.

His words made tears stream down my cheeks. "No, Omi. You did nothing, it was me," my tone was wistful.

"Please do not cry, Scarlet," his tone was even more inaudible than before. "I don't like to see you cry."

I wiped my eyes. His face was so pale. His voice cracked as he spoke.

"Omi, forgive me," I whispered.

"Of course Scarlet; you had to have had a good reason. Please just tell me why."

I did not know what to say. The only thing I can say is the truth. "It is because of the sickness."

He was silent for a moment. "I do not understand."

"It is the evil that has taken over me. It causes me to do terrible things, think evil thoughts; it is trying to make me evil. The wickedness is dissolving my true self at this very moment. I do not know how to suppress this sickness."

"How long has this been going on?"

"It started the day you started training me. Up until now, I have kept it somewhat at bay."

"Why did you keep this to yourself all this time?"

"I did not want you and Tamaku to fear me. But now I know I should have told you."

He was silent. "But, you seem to be normal now. How are you so calm now?"

"It is because I love him."

"What do you mean?"

"It is because I am deeply in love with Tamaku.

"I knew you loved him. I also knew about your evil thoughts," he admitted. "But I just wanted to hear it from you," he tried to smile but quickly flinched from the pain. He grasped his chest where there was a gash.

"Omi, are you alright?" I asked inching closer to him.

He did not answer. He lay motionless. He had simply passed out from the blood loss. I turned behind me to see Tamaku was not there. I could not worry about that now. I needed to get Omi inside. I put Omi on my back. I was thankful to see the kids still playing cards. As I opened the door they looked up with horrified stares.

"S-Scarlet, what happened?" asked Roke.

I lied. I wasn't going to have them scared of me. "I don't know. But we need to help him quickly," I said. I glanced out the window as I laid him on the bed. The sun was already setting. This was bad. Only two more days till I fight Taurid, Omi is hurt, Tamaku is nowhere to be seen, and I feel worse than ever.

I managed to bandage a few of his major wounds. I watched him as he lay silently...still sleeping. After a few hours, the kids were asleep, too. I then cried silently when I was the only one left awake. I hated myself for this. I hated that I hurt my friend. At the time I knew I couldn't control it, but now I still felt like I could have tried harder. There had to be some way out of this evil.

I wasn't sure how long Omi could hold out. He had many deep wounds...he lost so much blood. I knew I had to go find Tamaku. I couldn't lose him either. I walked in the night with the crescent moon shining upon me. I had to look everywhere for him. I wasn't exactly sure why he left. He did so quickly.

The air was cool but refreshing. I couldn't keep my mind off of Omi. I never realized how much I cared about him until now. All I wanted to do was see him, smiling, happy. At the moment, I couldn't promise his life to continue. It was just like the dream I had. The dream I had days ago manifested to life right before my eyes. I knew this would happen. I knew I shouldn't have fought him anyway.

Then, I heard the all too proverbial tune of the Airos Pipe. The music filled the night air vividly. I knew it was him. I knew where it was coming from. It was the valley where Toki was buried. The tune was none other than the lullaby my mother sang to me so many years ago. The song of the Midnight Airos twirled upon the billows of the forest.

I made my way to the almost celestial sound. I could spot him in the distance; his back was to me, unaware of my presence. I stepped closer, caution filling each step as I placed one foot in front of the other. My mind filled with wry thoughts. I then stood only feet away from him. His lungs still circulating air into the pipe. The sound of it put me in a pleasant daze. Suddenly, it felt like things mattered a little less.

With the sound still penetrating my ears, I sat beside him. He stopped playing, his eyes still staring ahead.

230

"Why did you leave?" I asked holding back the grief I felt from his absence.

"I couldn't bear to be there..."

"I'm sorry," I whispered, feeling a small tear escape my eyes. I looked away.

"That's not what I meant. I meant that I couldn't bear to see you that way. I finally understand what you wanted to tell me all along. But...my opinion of you still resides." He placed his hand on mine. I could feel his stare.

"Is that why you stepped in...just in time."

"Like I told you before...you can't do this alone. That's why we need to work through this together. When I saw you today, I was scared," he looked down, his tone was a little below a whisper. "But I couldn't sit back and watch...you needed my help."

He placed his hands on my shoulders and turned me to face him. His eyes were gentle but firm. "We are going to Taurid tomorrow. We need to finish this once and for all. If this evil power you have came from him, he should be able to take it away." His view sounded rational. Taurid should be able to take the power away. I just wasn't sure if he would.

"But this whole time I have been relying on this evil power," I objected. "I don't know if I have any power that is my own."

"Scarlet," his voice was hard. "Don't you remember when you first got here? You and I had begun training you with your own power."

"But it was so low...I can't defeat him with that."

He was silent for a moment. "I have a plan."

"What?"

"I will tell you at the right time...you have to trust me. It won't work until I tell you tomorrow." He stared into my eyes with truth. I trusted him, I trusted him more than I trusted myself.

"When are we going to be there?" I asked.

"We should get there early...sometime in the morning." He seemed to be talking to himself more than to me, but I listened carefully.

"Then they wouldn't be expecting us," he added. He transferred his penetrating gaze back to me. "Everything will be okay, Scarlet. I will make sure you never feel like that again. Don't worry about tomorrow. I know you can vanquish him. You and I will see him tomorrow. I will help you all the way," he promised. His eyes were warm and accompanied with a smile.

I stared at him again. He stared at me with hot intensity in his dark eyes. I could feel the soft wind toy with my hair flowing around my face. I still had not made a decision on returning home or not. Every time I heard his voice, the difficulty in choosing became more bewildering. I couldn't even imagine going a day without hearing his voice or looking into his eyes.

"I'm curious about something," his tone was soothing. He began to run his fingers through my loose hair. His eyes zeroed in on my face.

"What is it this time?" I asked with a small grin.

"I am very curious."

"Mhm," I prompted.

"Well I'm curious…about what it would be like to kiss you."

My heart immediately shuddered. I couldn't even begin to contemplate what he had just said. I was so overwhelmed with happiness I could barely breathe. It felt like my heart had stopped right in the middle of a beat. My stomach filled with fluttering butterflies that battered it. I deliberated what I would say next but I came up with nothing. I could feel my lips quiver still unable to move my body. But before I could utter another thought, his soft lips pressed against mine. He pulled me closer to him. But then as soon as it happened it was over. When he pulled away, I felt as though my heart miraculously restarted. I could breathe, but I wanted him to take my breath away again. He stared back into my eyes just as he had before. I couldn't hold back a smile.

"Well I hope that made you feel a little better. I hate to see you so upset," he said stroking my arm with the knuckles of his fingers. "And just think, by this time tomorrow Taurid will be dead."

"Yeah," I said sullenly. I hoped so. He sensed the distress in my tone.

"What's the matter?"

"I'm just a little nervous," I admitted.

"It's about the evil, isn't it?" He had a hint of irritation color his tone.

I nodded sheepishly at his reaction. His eyes lightened a bit. "I told you Scarlet, I'm here to help you. I told you that from the day we met…I will always protect you."

"I know, I know, I just don't know how I will do it..."

"I told you, I have a plan." He smiled wide pulling me into his arms. His kissed the top of my head and stroked my back gently. I loved being close to him. I couldn't ask for anything I wanted more. I honestly couldn't picture me without him. I think I made a decision. I want to stay in Audren, even if that meant I would never see my family or friends again. I would miss them, I know. But I had to make a decision...and this was it.

When Tamaku and I returned, we were greeted by darkness and thick sleep. Omi was still where I had placed him. I was relieved to see his chest rise up and ease down with steady breaths. Tranquility had finally settled in the face of the more than eventful day. As I laid on the bumpy floor, I could think of nothing but sleep. I knew I wouldn't be kept awake with thoughts. All I could hear was the light breeze brushing against the straw hut with a howling sound. I could feel my eyes gaining weight with the exhaustion. Without another moment passing, I was asleep.

I woke up feeling completely refreshed. It still wasn't daylight. It was early in the morning. The whole hut was still ridden with quaint slumber. I grabbed a match, lighting a small lamp on the side table. I slowly stood to my feet remembering Omi. I knew he must be parched. I grabbed a match, lighting a small lamp on the side table. I took a small mug and filled it with water I had conjured up. Filling it a centimeter away from the rim, I slowly made my way towards Omi making sure not to spill. As I came closer to the bed, I noticed he was aberrantly still. Stepping a little faster now, I noticed his pale complexion. Oh, no. I set the mug down running to his side. He looked so peaceful but I knew what had happened. I placed my palm on his arm.

Cold. I then proceeded to touch his cheek, forehead. Cold. I shuttered at the sight. I placed my hand over my mouth on the verge to breaking down in tears. I went on my knees next to him, holding his small hand in mine. He had been dead for hours. I couldn't help but releasing a horrific screech in agony. It was my entire fault.

There were flies beginning to gather around him. I shooed them away angrily with warm tears ambling down my face. I then noticed something on his chest. It was a small piece of paper accompanied with a small pen. I reached over his cold body seeing my name at the top. It said:

*Scarlet, I wanted to say thank you for all your help with my wounds. Without you, the bleeding would have never stopped. Even though you have done an excellent job, I am drawing closer and closer to my last breath. My guess is that I will be gone before sunrise tomorrow. I am fine with this, for a true warrior isn't afraid of death. Do you remember the time I told you the story about my family's death? Do you also remember how I told you about the look Taurid had in his eyes that day? You had that exact same look in your eyes. That's how I know this had nothing to do with you. This whole situation has Taurid written all over it. Let my death be a motivation. When you face Taurid, think of me and you will find strength. However, do not act on revenge but instead avenge this loss! I wanted you to know all my true feelings in this letter because I am sure this will be my last chance. I hold you and Tamaku as my best friends. Piper, Roke, and Conch were the best children I have ever known as well. Tell everyone that I love them, and most importantly, tell them not to mourn my death. Tell them to stay strong...for me. I love you Scarlet. Do a great job...make me proud.*

It ended there. His last words were to me…his murderer. The one who killed him was the one he wrote the words "Thank you" to. That's a true friend. Where did that leave me? I don't know. But I did decide to make a decision. Looking at him, motionless, breathless… *lifeless.* I deserved to be in his place. I deserved to be laying there without another breath. I looked at the note again. I wasn't reading it; I just looked at the handwriting…Omi's handwriting. The last essence of his life being in existence was addressed to me. I could never live with that. That's why I have to risk my life for him.

I then reflected back on the bracelet that was on my right wrist. It was the bracelet Omi gave me. The tears dripped from my eyes. I had come to realize that everything that has happened to me in Audren is what has given me more drive to complete my ultimate goal…to kill Taurid …more than ever now.

When I first arrived at Audren, I was nowhere near prepared to fight or protect anyone. I had no idea who I really was back then. I don't mean just when I arrived, I didn't know who I was my whole life. I thought I knew, but I didn't. It was at that moment, I figured it out. I discovered who I was. I was more than I would have ever expected. I was more than I would have ever thought of. I was not a normal girl. I wasn't a normal teenager, or student. To be honest, I was nowhere near the banks of normality; I was wading in the waters of a true warrior. I, then, understood that I was the one that would kill Taurid. I would fight for Audren once and for all.

Omi's death would not be in vain. I did not kill him…the evil did. Today was the day that I would assume battle. I knew I had to make it count…for Omi.

When the light of the morning crept into the hut after what felt like days, everyone was greeted to same horror I was. Piper, Roke, and Conch were heartbroken one by one. I had never seen them cry so much. Even Tamaku was in tears. But I had shed my tears already.

After a while, we decided to bury him in the forest. The warm sun did not feel very warm. The sky was colored pink and purplish lighting on our funeral spot. My body felt cold and stiff. Tamaku dug a five foot hole and we lowered Omi's body into the pit. The children were still deeply in tears.

When we returned to the hut, the kids had fallen asleep, for it was still early morning.

"How are you feeling?" Tamaku asked in a morose tone. He must have assumed I felt even guiltier than before.

"It's hard to explain. I just know that I have to defeat him, more than anything now."

"Aren't you upset?" he asked taken aback by my serious tone.

"Of course I am. But I can't focus on that. Now is the time for avenging." He knew what I was referring to, and then glanced at the sleeping children.

"What are we going to do with them?" he said.

I knew this may have become a problem. "We will leave them here," I said firmly.

"Do you realize how long we will be gone? If we never come back, what will happen to them?" He asked frowning.

I glared in response. "If we take them they will surely be killed. Piper isn't that immature. She can use her fire element abilities if things were to go...*differently than anticipated.*"

"I guess that is our best plan. At any rate, we must leave now. The journey to the palace is a long walk away. Even by sky, it will be a prolonged crossing." I nodded.

"But one more thing," he said. "Aren't you going to give Piper your gift? I can't promise that you will be able to do it later."

I then remembered the Scarlet ribbon in my pocket. Tamaku was right. I may never be able to do it later. I extracted it, placing it lightly in her open palm. After that, we set out.

I didn't know for sure of what I was going to do. It was just a matter of my own skill against Taurid. With my Raico at my side, I climbed onto Tamaku's back. Then, without another breath to spare, we were catapulted into the still early morning sky. This time, I was not able to enjoy the clouds, and vivid colors of the sky. My mind was fixed on one thing and one thing only: the blood curdling, ghastly, horrific demise of the dictator, Taurid.

Tamaku was right. The journey was extensive. The agonizing anxiousness of my heart and mind were inadmissible. With each second that passed by, my aghast-ridden soul would rile even more. But I was put out of my misery when I saw three black flags through the clouds. There was indeed the palace. It looked as capacious as a city but as gruesome as a place filled with demons. The aura it gave off, even from a distance, was almost unbearable to withstand. I could sense Tamaku loosing energy from the aura as well.

"I'm going to land," he shouted looking at me from the corner of his eyes.

I didn't respond. For some reason I could not stop gaping at the palace. As we got closer, I became less afraid. Finally, we landed behind some trees, meters away from the palace walls. Even being this close, I could barely fathom that we were actually there. After all these days of training and anticipating this day, it was finally here.

"We must not waste any time. We need all the time that we can get. Are you ready?"

"Yes."

With that, he took my hand and led me swiftly towards the back of the castle. There was a small crawl space that only elevated about a foot above the ground. He eyed it as if deciphering who should enter first. But in seconds he mentally elected himself as he crouched down, and then finished on his stomach. He carefully slithered his way in, disappearing into the tight, dark space. I didn't want to prolong this any further, so I quickly followed suit. It was a bit more effort filled for me but I did successfully make it in. I barely landed on my feet, for the ground was deeper then I had expected. But I could not see a single thing. It was pitch black. I carefully listened to hear Tamaku's breathing not very far away. I then felt a hand, which startled me, until I heard Tamaku's soothing voice.

"Scarlet?" he said, basically a whisper.

"Yeah," I assured him. "Where are we?" I noticed the terrible stench that filled the stuffy air.

"You will see in a moment. I have to make a fire."

"What do you mean?"

"Piper isn't the only one with the fire element," I could tell he was smiling, but still quite serious. "But when I do make the fire, you must promise not to scream, no matter what you see. The slightest screech can send us plummeting into a trough of trouble," he warned.

I didn't like the sound of this. But with one deep breath, I decided I could handle whatever was coming. "Okay, go ahead."

I heard a snap of his fingers then I could see his face. His eyes twinkled in the orange light of the fire. A small flame danced on his index finger.

"Okay, we have to move on. Do not make a sound," he reminded me. He grasped my hand firmly. "I will be right here with you."

He then turned forward lighting on a large hallway. It seemed normal at first, but as we continued the stench got stronger. I almost wanted to gag from the hideous smell. But then I realized what Tamaku was referring to. I felt my eyes widen and my mouth open, ready to wail in terror.

# Chapter 32

## APPROACH

I could feel Tamaku's warm hand whip over my mouth to silence me. I could feel my limbs shaking at the sight. There, on the low ceiling, were numerous corpses dangling inches from us. Also on the ground were dead bodies embellishing the stone floor. I couldn't bear to look. I dug my face in Tamaku's shirt as he whispered comforting things to me.

"*Shhh.* It will be alright. I'm right here, Scarlet." I felt him peck his lips on the top of my head. "We won't be in here long. This is the only way to enter the castle without being seen."

It felt like an eternity while we walked through the dirt less graveyard. The smell was inadmissible and I was frightened to open my eyes even the slightest bit. I still could not erase the nauseating images I had seen. I had not lifted my face from his chest.

But then I felt that harrowing pulsation in my heart I knew all too well. I was being overtaken again. I knew this would happen. All of a sudden I felt as if I would not be able to control my next move. I had a terrible incentive to grab something, or cut something.

"Tamaku?"

"I know. Fight it." His tone was placid.

I began to grind my teeth, clenching tighter to him. "I...I can't. It is getting stronger," I breathed.

"Fight it," he repeated with a little more force.

I squeezed my eyes closed, tighter now. Then I felt a tad bit woozy as we walked. I then began to feel physical pain on every inch of my body. I knew this was a defect from the evil. Then, I saw a woman in my mind. She was absolutely beautiful. She wore a long white gown. Her hair was long, blonde and draped over her shoulders. She was in a fetal position with her eyes gracefully closed. She seemed to be floating in midair. Everything around her was black and she gave off a radiant white glow. Then she opened her eyes and glided to her feet.

"Scarlet," she said in a delicate, almost harmonious tone. I knew that velvety voice from anywhere.

"Serenity?" I said softly.

"Yes, 'tis I. I am here to help."

I then remembered how I had removed the locket and tossed it to the ground.

"What's going on?"

"Scarlet, I have always lived inside of you. Like I told you, that locket is not my true form; I am an energy being. When you took off the locket, I was still connected to you in spirit.

Now, I have revealed to you my true form."

I was mesmerized by her appearance. Everything about her was the true essence of beauty. Every curl of her hair was mended flawlessly. Her piercing eyes were the color of the ocean. Her bare feet were perfectly sculpted. She seemed as though she was only the size of my palm.

"There is a reason I have revealed myself to you. I must tell you something very important. It is about your mother. She is in this castle. Taurid will most likely use her to his advantage. I am giving you fair warning in case you have to make a difficult decision."

"Wait, what do you mean?"

"What I want you to know, is do not be afraid of him. The good hidden in your soul can submerge his evil incredibly. Do not be tied down by a decision...instead fight without cowering."

Before I could make a sound in response, the image of her had faded and I was only greeted by the darkness of my closed eyes. My mind returned to reality. I could smell the sweet scent of Tamaku as I still had my face buried in his chest. He had one arm around me still guiding the way. I hadn't even noticed that I was shedding tears.

"We are almost out," he comforted.

Then Serenity's words rang in my ear from when I first met her: *do not be afraid.* I now understand that those words don't only apply to Taurid; they also applied to the small things. I then knew that I should not be afraid of the dead bodies around us.

I slowly lifted my head from Tamaku. He stopped before I opened my eyes. I could feel his hands on the sides of my face.

"Hey, you don't have to look. I will keep guiding you," he reminded.

I bit my lip. "I know. But I can't be afraid." I was still a bit reluctant to open my eyes.

I then felt his warm hand. "I admire your courage, in fact I love it." His voice was as smooth and charming as always. At that moment, I fluttered my eyes open. The light from the fire was too bright at first but my eyes quickly adjusted. Then I looked at Tamaku who was looking at me. I then deported my gaze to the front. I cringed at the sight on contact, but I reminded myself over and over about what Serenity said. I clenched my fists and opened my eyes. The bodies were still disturbing but I was able to look. Tamaku was right. I could see a light at the end of the hall. With a small glance at him we continued. I did not look anywhere but straight ahead.

Soon we were closer than ever to the end of the hall. We stopped again and Tamaku turned me to face him.

"Okay, this is where it gets a little more challenging. This is the only route we can go to get to the throne room undetected. If you have not noticed, the place we just passed is where they keep dead servants...servants with Audrenian blood."

I nodded attentively.

He pointed to the light ahead. "Now, we are about to pass through the Water chamber which leads to the boiler room. This is where all the water is stored. This place is flooded with guards."

I felt my eyebrows knit together. "Then how are we going to pass?"

"I have a special tune on my Airos Pipe that I can use to make us invisible to them."

I sighed in relief.

"But," he added, "once I play the tune you must not blink."

"I can't blink?" I asked, surprised.

"No. If you blink, so much as one time, the tune will lose its affect and we will be visible to everyone. If that happens, they will know we are intruders and kill us for sure."

My heart began to race. How could I not blink for so long? I felt the nerves bombard me a mile a minute. I didn't want to join the dead that we just passed.

"Listen, it won't be that hard. Just don't think about it and it will be very easy. You just have to stick with me on this one." Without another word, he grabbed me by the hand as we walked to the edge of the door way.

"Okay, I am about to play the tune. When it is done, do not blink."

I nodded, still on edge from the doubt.

He looked at me one more time before slowly pulling out his pipe. Then he placed his lips on it, blowing lightly playing the halcyon tune. I took as many flutters and blinks of my eyes as I could in preparation. But then I heard the deadly stop of the music. In an instant, Tamaku took my hand again and whipped out into the guard filled chamber. I could barely keep up with his fleeting pace. I did, however, get to gaze at the chamber. It was a wide open space with high ceilings. It was intriguing to watch the soldiers' hustle and bustle around busily. It appeared that none of them had the slightest clue we were there. The walls were white and felt very airy and fresh compared to the pungent hall. There were glass columns everywhere that were filled with water.

But the infringement didn't last long. For in a short time, the urge to blink reared its way into my mind. As I looked head, we still had a long way to go before reaching the next corridor to the boiler room.

My eyes began to burn from the dryness. I looked at Tamaku who was focusing straight for the exit. He didn't seem too much in pain. I, on the other hand, was the exact opposite. It had been 47 seconds, I counted. The urge yearning to blink was becoming horribly insufferable. I felt as if my lids would lower themselves at any given moment.

I looked at the soldiers again. A few of them we passed right by without them having the slightest clue. It actually would have been quite amusing if I wasn't struggling to keep my stubborn eyelids from closing. The doorway to the boiler room was incredibly close now. Only a few more steps left. I looked at Tamaku again. I was greeted to the same stiff look on his face.

But in almost an instant, I tripped over the leg of a table, surrounded by guards. I felt myself, not only fall flat on my face, but also close my eye lids and open again.

Before I could stand, I heard a large commotion of guards ringing in my ears. I looked to see Tamaku all the way across the large arena-like room. He was being seized by two guards on his left and his right.

"Tamaku!" I shouted almost instinctively.

"Scarlet, the boiler room is right down the hall. Whatever you do, do not look back. You will have to find your way from there. I will find you soon, don't be afraid," he shouted while he was being hauled off with the soldiers.

I wanted to say something but I could not speak. I watched as he disappeared into the confluence of soldiers. I then turned to see three guards running my way. I then whipped my gaze to the door, now only feet away. But before I could move a muscle, I felt a pair of big rough hands on my back. Without turning, I grasped my Raico and jabbed my blade into the being behind me, hearing his agonizing yelp. I felt blood squirt from him, but I did not turn back. I yanked my sword from him and continued to run. More guards were coming. My sore legs were throbbing but I ran with speed. The door was there. I opened it. The door was light weight and very convenient for one in a hurry.

I knew the guards were gaining on me, closer by the second. I then rushed over the threshold and closed the door behind me, latching it with the lock from the inside. I stood back examining my work. The guards were helplessly banging on the door hoping for entrance. It was very possible that they could break the door down. I decided to waste no time.

I quickly turned to see a large furnace blazing with internal flames. *The boiler room.* I saw another door way. I began to run to it but I quickly changed pace. I had no idea what would greet me on the other side of the door. But then I remembered a more guaranteed enemy behind the opposite door.

# Chapter 33

## KILYEY...TAMAKU'S VIEW

"So what should we do with him?" Asked a guard.

"If we take him to lord Taurid, he will make *us* prepare the gallows," said the other.

"We could always kill him ourselves," suggested the first. It disgusted me how they were deciding my own demise right in front of me.

"No, Taurid would not approve."

"Let's just throw him in a cell," said the other pointing his thumb behind him.

The other nodded. With a few tugs and shoves, we made our way down the halls of the palace. My arms were sore from their hard grasp. I had to keep up with their speed, though my feet and legs ached.

One of the guards swore and mumbled something else but I couldn't understand him.

"What's wrong Kio?" asked one.

"I don't have my keys on me. All I got is the key to Kiley's cell."

"Well, I guess now she'll have a new roommate."

I didn't like the sound of this. Scarlet was somewhere, but I had no clue as to where. I just hoped that she was doing okay by herself.

"Alright, speed it up," commanded one of the soldiers impatiently.

I didn't respond. I stared at the dark stone of the palace. The guards were not letting their cruelty die down, that was for sure. But with one last shove, I found myself on my stomach in a small, stuffy room. I then heard a door crash behind and there was absolutely no string of light anywhere. I could not see a thing. I let out a small sigh as I slowly traced the air to find a solid wall to lie against. I had no success. All I could feel was the thick, stuffy air that surrounded me. I guessed that this small room wasn't so small after all.

"You're trying to find something to lean against, right?"

I had thought I was the only one in the cell.

"Just follow my voice," it said. It was a woman's voice.

"Um, okay. Can you sing or something for a moment then?" I asked still a little apprehensive about this. It could be a trap.

She then began to sing. Her voice was smooth and graceful. It sounded like her voice was intertwined with the entity of beauty itself. It was so lovely; I almost failed to notice what she was singing. The song was Midnight Airos.

I paused before beginning to inch towards the sound of her voice. I was almost entranced by its velvety smoothness. But I did manage to find the wall. I then leaned my back on the cold stone. I could feel the presence of the woman a few feet from me. "Thank you," I had almost forgot to say it.

"It was nothing. I know every part of this wretched cell," she said stiffly but her voice was still lovely sounding.

"Oh, uh, well, thanks anyway." I paused for a moment still a little nervous; after all, she was a complete stranger.

"What are you in for?" she asked with boredom coloring her tone.

"Me and my friend broke in here, and we unfortunately got caught by guards," I could feel the grimness in my voice from recalling how I had no idea where Scarlet was.

"Why did you guys do that?"

"Isn't it obvious?" I then realized my disrespectful tone and continued more lightly, "My friend is the last Varcia."

"You mean, Scarlet is here already?" she said almost instantly.

"Wait, you know Scarlet?" I asked in the darkness.

"Well, I guess you could put it that way."

"What?" I was still confused.

"My name is Kiley. She does not remember me, but I am her mother."

"She said that her mother was dead," I argued softly.

"It's a long story," she said with a hint of grief.

"Well, I'm Tamaku, and I have time," I pressed.

She was silent.

"Please?"

Her silence was screaming me the answer *no*.

250

"I am her guardian. Please, may I know?"

She sighed. "It started about 400 years ago," she began.

I was taken aback by this time span, but I stayed silent.

"I was just a mere maid servant. I lived with my mother but my father had died when I was born. I grew up in this palace. I had warm clothes, and three meals a day just like all the other servants. I always did my job and I often had to tend to King Taress. I was only 22 when I was first was appointed to serve at a dinner party hosted here. It was the biggest job I had ever had and I had to do it perfectly. That night, the ballroom was filled with people from all over the region. Other lords and ladies, duchesses, and squires were all having a dinner for the king's birthday. I was awestruck to see the marvelous ball gowns and the exquisite lights of chandeliers and the shining of jewels. I was to serve the desert, the most important part of the entire meal—at least that's what King Taress always said.

"It was that night, in midst of all the commotion that I saw him. I had always heard great things about King Taress' wise adviser Taurid, but I had never actually seen the man. He was nothing like I had pictured. I expected Taurid to be old, almost like an elder, but instead, he was a very handsome young man and didn't seem too much older than me. I was captivated when I saw his prefect physique, stunning auburn eyes, and his wispy graven black hair dancing on his collar bone."

"I remember laying the saucer of cake in front of him. When King Taress noticed me, he stopped me before I could rush away. I remember it almost perfectly..."

~~~*~~~

"Wait a minute, I know you; aren't you Kiley, Karline's daughter?" asked the king taking a sip from his cup.

"Uh, yes, my lord," I said barely croaking out my words. I had never spoken to the king before. The thought of it made me tremble.

The king gave a warm chuckle as he wiped his napkin across his smiling lips. "You look just like her," he said wiggling his index finger. After a few chuckles, he looked up as if he was remembering something. "Ah, yes. Karline was my top maid when I was still young. When she had you, it was the talk of the palace. Your mother was quite a gem back then. I even remember when I first saw you wrapped all tight in her arms. I have not seen her around lately. How is she now, Kiley?"

I was still taken aback by the king speaking to me directly, but there was no time to freeze up. "Uh, she is very well, your majesty." My mother always told me to never ramble to royalty so I was determined to keep my answers short. I could feel my heart pounding; I only hoped it wasn't audible.

"Good, good; are you hungry Miss Kiley?"

My mother also taught me to never refuse royalty. "Oh, um, yes, King Taress." I was awestruck to see the long table filled with all sorts of food. There had to be at least one hundred people at the table.

He gave a wide grin as he pointed to a chair next to Taurid. "You may sit next to my adviser, Taurid. I think he will be very pleased to have your company." He chuckled again. I could feel my cheeks flushing with redness. I had to admit that the king was just as kind as I had expected, but sitting next to his top adviser was a little much.

I slowly walked my way over to the empty seat next to him. I was careful not to look too ungraceful. Since my mother failed to teach me how to eat with royalty, I wasn't enthused to join them in such an event.

"Martin! Please bring the lady some tart and cider," the king called to the servant nearby. I had never had such nice treatment before. No one has ever served *me* anything. The only time I had ever got anything sweet to eat was when I was a child. I looked down to keep from making any eye contact. I did not want to seem disrespectful. I wasn't sure if gawking at royalty was politically correct.

"Kiley, is it?" asked Taurid suddenly with a pinch of interest in his tone.

I did not lift my eyes, "Yes, Sir."

"That is a very lovely name," he complimented. I could feel him looking at me but I didn't dare lift my gaze.

"Oh, thank you, Sir."

"You can just call me Taurid." He gave a chuckle. "Did I mention you have a lovely face as well? I noticed those stunning green eyes of yours from across the room," his tone was charming…too charming not to look at him.

"Thank you, err…. Taurid." I looked down again.

I then felt a warm hand engulfing my own. I then felt warm lips on my hand. I turned my gaze immediately at him.

"Pleased to meet you, Miss Kiley." His penetrating auburn eyes pierced into mine. His face was so lovely.

"The same to you, Taurid," I replied still shaken by his touch.

Then the servant appeared with a small platter in his hand. He set the delicacy in front of me. The over baked piece of bread had a small glop of icing on top. The cider looked like the apples they were made from were not grinded down all the way. Mother always told me that royalty eat strange delicacies.

"Thank you, Martin. You may turn in for the night. You have worked very well," the king grinned.

"Thank you, your majesty. Have a good night," said the servant with a smile accompanied with a bow.

The king then turned his gaze to me still stained with that grand smile of his. "How do you like the tart, Miss Kiley?" His tone was so endearing.

"It is quite delicious, your majesty." I lied. It was disgusting. My mother always told me to compliment anything royalty offers. For about another twenty minutes, I struggled to remember which fork was for which kind of food. Royalty dining was very confusing. So many eyes were on me as I ate. I couldn't tell if I was using the right posture either.

"Wonderful," the king clapped joyfully and giggled, too. "It is quite a lovely night! A marvelous night for these festivities; do you agree, Taurid?" Said the king as he took a sip of his drink.

"Why, of course, your majesty. The stars are adorning the sky superbly tonight and the chirps of the cicadas truly are invigorating. The weather is quite comfortable as well. I think it may even call for a dance…the orchestra is here, after all," Taurid pointed out, shooting a glance in my direction then back at the king.

The very chubby king scanned the rest of the guests at the table. They all seemed eager to do some dancing. "I agree with Taurid! We shall have some dancing immediately!" He then motioned for the orchestra to raise their instruments. The scores of guests flocked to the floor grabbing partners one by one.

I had no idea what to do. I figured I could use this chance to run back to my quarters in the kitchen, but I was stopped.

"Miss Kiley, wait," it was the dashing Taurid. He then took my hand gently staring into my eyes. "Please, may I have this dance?"

Mother had never taught me dancing. She always told me I had two left feet. I had to refuse before I embarrass the king in front of all these guests. "Oh, I am hardly dressed for the occasion and it is rather late, maybe-"

"You look beautiful." He shot an irresistible crooked smile.

I was speechless. My thoughts were jumbling. I peered down at my ragged dress I worked in. It had to be at least 4 years old with stains that have been there from the start. The only thing that was not torn or patched was the neckline. I looked horrid. "Thank you, but-"

Before I could utter another word, I was swung into his arms. He quickly placed his hand on my waist as he took my hand. He was smiling as he twirled me around the dance floor.

"I must warn you that I have never danced before," I rushed my words in hopes not to be cut off.

255

"Oh, really?" He said in a playful disbelief. "I am surprised. You seem as though you would do quite well at dancing."

"I am only a mere maid servant." I could feel the shame in my voice.

"You are the most lovely maid servant I have ever seen. Fair lady, you could pass as an angel."

I couldn't hold back a smile. I barely noticed us dancing almost perfectly to the upbeat tune of the orchestra.

"It seems as though you have been dancing for years," he said glancing at my rhythmic feet.

"This is my first time," I said looking down.

"My dear, you are quite wonderful. The king can barely keep up," he said casting his gaze to the struggling king. He was dancing quite awkwardly with a lady that was half his size. He seemed to not notice because he was grinning wide and laughing.

We both laughed at this. He stopped for a second and studied my face.

"Is something wrong?" I asked.

"No...it's just that your laugh is very adorable."

I looked down again. "Why are you like this to me?" I asked still smiling.

"Like what?" He chuckled, twirling me around once more, "Charming?"

"So you do know what I mean?"

"Of course. You are very charming as well. "

"What?" I said. "Look at me. I am ragged and nowhere near royal. You are King Taress' adviser. How can you find me charming?"

"You know, not everyone considers riches or the outward appearance attractive."

"Yes, but...I'm a nobody."

His eyebrows knit together. "Nothing of the sort; you are indeed... *somebody.*"

"We just met," I pointed out.

"That is true, but I can see your eyes. Don't you know that the eyes have a language all of its own?"

"A language?" I snickered.

He leaned in closer to my face, it took me by surprise. "Yes. The eyes tell everything about a person that they may not voice. I can see how lovely you are on the inside just by gazing right into them...it is rather simple."

"So what are my eyes saying if I may ask?"

He paused for a moment studying them. "They say that you love all those close to you and that you also have an emptiness that you feel but...you don't know how to fill it." After that was said, he seemed to awaken out of a trance and back to normal. "Am I correct?"

"Hmm. Yes, I guess so."

"What do my eyes say?" he asked with a smile.

"They say... you are missing a certain person. I can see the pain of the memory. This person hasn't been in your life for a long while though. Is that right?" I tried to match his tone from before but his still sounded better.

"Hmm. Yes, I guess you could say that," he chuckled.

We were silent still dancing to the music.

He broke the silence. "So tell me more about yourself."

"Well, what would you like to know?"

"Well...everything! What is your favorite color? What do you do for fun? Anything..."

"Well...my life is not very interesting. The only thing I really do is work," I admitted.

"That is alright; what kind of things do you do?" his tone was grand.

"You are actually *interested* in what kind of work I do?" I asked incredulously.

"Why, yes, I am. Something about you makes me interested..."

"Well I mostly wash dishes and clean up in the gardens and clean most of the bedrooms."

"But you were serving today," he replied.

"Yes, but that has never happened before. I normally just stay in the background."

"Do you ever have fun? Surely you don't work *all* day."

"Well I do have fun, just not a lot. I read for fun. I love books; all kinds, but Romantic ones are my favorite." I was actually enjoying myself. It is not every day that someone wants to know more about me than my name.

"I love books as well! I also love Romantic novels. I do like to get in touch with my sensitive side every now and then," he chuckled. "But honestly, I love books. I am not sure that you have heard of it, but have you ever read the novel *Mirror on the Staircase*? It is one of my favorites."

"I just finished that a week ago! Oh, don't you just love the main character, Myrna?"

His eyes brightened. "Yes! She is so different from Charles but they still end up together! Remember the time when she finally told off the Mayor? She said-"

"'*Love is not a charity, Sir, it is the true manifestation of beauty',*" we both quoted in unison.

"Truly a good quote," I said approvingly.

"Yes, truly grand. I had no idea someone else loved that book as much as I did," he said.

"Well, I do. Molly Partridge is my favorite author. I also like her book called *Legislature of Departure*," I said.

"Oh, my word, of course! I loved the poetic language they used, especially Benjamin. I loved how he always compared things to nature. Remember when they were in the garden, and he told Bethany-"

*"'The way I feel around you is like the chirp of the Blue Jay when the child he has waited so long for finally hatches. When life is new, my love for you replenishes along with it!'"* we both quoted again in unison.

"We are two peas in a pod, I must say," he said with his beautiful white teeth exposed in a smile.

"I must agree!"

The orchestra's song then ended and flowing into a slower song. We, too, began to slow down our dancing.

"I think I have something you may like…" his voice trailed off as he reached into his pocket. In a few seconds he pulled out a beautiful lavender flower…the Midnight Airos. I felt my eyes widen at the sight. I wanted to scream in joy.

"It's…it's beautiful!" I said, "I have read about them in books, but never before have I even seen one in person. I always wanted one."

"It was very difficult to find around the palace, but I do have my sources…" he then gave a mischievous wink.

We both laughed.

I decided to change the subject. "So about that tart from before…how did you like it?"

He placed the flower in my hair as he spoke. "The king does have a heart of gold, but I swear he was trying to kill me with such a wretched pastry. Truly atrocious, I must say."

I threw my head back in laughter. "You had me fooled; it seemed as though you enjoyed every morsel," I giggled.

"You know what Mother always says, unless you are willing to get decapitated, always compliment the king's baker," he joked.

I had never laughed so much in my life...nor smiled. I had to admit Taurid was quite charming and his pearly white smile was contagious.

"I must admit, I have never met someone so compatible with me as you," he said.

"Yes, I would have to agree. I have always been best friends with my mother, but she is more extraverted than I."

"I have always preferred quieter women anyway, but I also like a women that can put me in my place when I am in the wrong," he said smiling.

"I could do that."

"What are you inferring?" he joked.

We laughed once again.

"So, what kind of gossip has been happening in the servants' living quarters?" he asked with a hint of interest.

"It appeared that Bessie, the king's favorite boar, has gotten loose again. She has just had her child and the only trace of her whereabouts is the pungent gifts she has left in the halls and food particles missing from the kitchen."

He chuckled, "Well, I have not heard about that one, but I have smelled some rather revolting scents in the halls."

I continued, "But I am curious as to what is happening in your neck of the woods..."

"Well, Duke Perabaldo's twin sons decided to play a practical joke on Martin, the king's favorite servant."

"Oh, do tell," I said attentively.

"While Martin was taking a nap in the kitchen, the mischievous duo decided to stir up some trouble. Their father was out hunting and they were left unattended. They then decided to feed freshly grinded boysenberries to him in his sleep. Turns out the poor chap was allergic and his cheeks blew up like a horse's behind. He was in such agonizing pain, he was immediately hauled off to the infirmary. Luckily we have the best physicians in the region."

"Well that is quite awful. I'm glad he is back to normal now."

And again, we laughed.

I was going to tell the story of the rabbits and moles eating away our gardens, but instead I said. "Taurid, why in all of Audren are you so kind to me? I am only a maid servant after all," I noted.

"It is because it is you I have fallen for."

I felt my heart dive. "I don't know what to say," I was astonished by his words.

"Like I said, you seem more like an angel. You are so breathtakingly gorgeous, and your voice makes me want to melt. I have seen you before around the palace. I have wanted to talk to you but you always seemed so busy. But now I want to make you mine like I have intended to." His eyes were stunning that I could not look away. I had fallen for him as well...just like that.

"Yes, I will be yours." I said this without thinking but I couldn't help it. I meant what I said.

"Thank you, Kiley. Now, you will never have to lift a finger around this palace again," he promised.

I then found myself staring back into his eyes with more intensity. I couldn't stop. There was no space between us for we had stopped dancing; the whole world was moving but we were still.

~~~*~~~

"So you mean, you and Taurid are...together?" I asked, astonished.

"Oh, that is where you are wrong, Mr. Tamaku. You see, things weren't always like a fairy tale. Sure, the first few months were grand, but once my mother found out about this, it was not exactly smooth from there. I even remember the day as if it occurred only hours ago..."

~~~*~~~

I was only minutes away from the fountain. My heart raced from the anxiety of seeing him like always. I hated going behind Mother's back but it was the only way. She would never approve of this. I even had to admit that a scruffy maid servant such as me had no business in any kind of romance with a royal adviser. But love is love and it can happen to anybody, anywhere. I also had to admit that such secrecy did give me a rush, if you will. I felt as though I had a double life.

Finally, I made my way through the tall grass, seeing the old fountain in the distance. The light of the moon was selfish, so it was barely light enough to see him. He was already running my way with his arms wide open. I couldn't run very fast due to my long skirt. After a few clumsy trips, I was finally tight in his arms.

He gave out a pleased sigh squeezing me tightly. "Oh, my precious Kiley, I missed you so much."

"Taurid, it has only been a day," I said sweetly.

"Yes, but with so much work and difficulties with the king, a day feels like weeks," he then kissed my cheek softly.

"And with all the cleaning and serving that has to be done, it feels like months!" I chuckled.

"But I finally have you all my own now," he said in a more romantic tone.

"So how was your day?" I asked pulling away a bit facing him.

"Dreadful, I'm afraid. Besides missing you more than life itself…" his voice trailed off and we laughed at this. He continued, "The king was deeply distressed and very irritable."

"Oh, that is dreadful," I agreed. "He always has such a joyful soul. What was wrong with him?"

"It was that old dog of his, Edgar. It had been sick for a while you know?"

"Ah, that's right. Don't tell me the poor thing passed on," I said in a desperate tone.

"Oh no, quite the opposite; in fact, the old thing is as alive as ever. So alive, he had a rather large accident right on the king's throne. It turns out no one has walked the poor animal since Tuesday." We both laughed again. After the last few giggles he recuperated and cleared his throat. "So how was your day, my love?"

I smiled at his term of endearment. "Nowhere near as exciting as the king's, but it was pretty dreadful as well."

"What happened to you?"

"Um, I would have to say the very large—and quite hard—stair case leading into the vineyard. I fell down the whole flight in seconds." I showed him the small cut on my arm.

He seemed much panicked. "Kiley, you are lucky to be alive!" Then his eyes narrowed in that handsome way I loved. "But then again, I do find your clumsiness very attractive."

"Oh, be quiet," I laughed.

He just smiled for a moment. "I like your hair today," he complimented. I then recalled how I had actually styled my hair. It was up (I never wear it up) and the hair that normally draped over my face was pulled back snugly.

"I only did this so I could clean the outhouse today," I informed.

"I like it. I can see your face much better." He kissed my forehead.

I knew in the back of my mind that I should head back home but my body would not obey.

"But I did pick something up for you when I went to town today. I really hope you like it, my dear." He then fished in his pocket, pulling out a small box with a satin, scarlet ribbon tied around it...my favorite color.

"Oh, you shouldn't have," I squealed.

"Open it, I am sure you will enjoy it," he urged.

I slowly untied the ribbon placing it in my skirt pocket. After glancing at him, I proceeded to lift the lid of the box. I felt my eyes widen at the sight. It was a beautiful silver locket. Its surface glimmered in the moonlight leaving me mesmerized. On its smooth surface, was a cursive *A*. I shot him a smile as he pulled me closer.

"I really do love it," I said softly.

"Well I really do love you...you're worth it."

"I love you, too."

He walked behind me and placed the necklace around my neck gently before he kissed my cheek. "There is something I want to show you."

"Not another gift," I said.

"Just come."

He then grabbed my hand, leading me to an open valley near the courtyard. His speed was swift but I could kept up. We stopped right in the middle of the scenic grassland. He then turned to me.

"What are you showing me?" I asked.

"Look up," he instructed.

The sky was beautiful. It seemed as though all the stars in the universe were gathered together brightly in our view. But the star that stood out was in the center of it all. It was the largest and brightest one of them all.

"It is beautiful, but I don't understand what you want me to see," I said.

He then pointed to the star I had noticed. "It is that star that is the most beautiful. That star reminds me of you. Every time I am away from you, I am reminded of your bright smile and I am comforted because you will be waiting for me when I return."

"I...I don't know what to say." I felt almost dazed by his compliment. Almost all his words had me dangling on his musical voice.

"You don't have to say anything," he said sweetly.

I smiled at him. Words could not describe how I felt towards him. Love was an understatement. Whenever he called me his, I felt like passing out. Whenever he touched me, I fell into a cold sweat. Whenever he kissed me, I felt like collapsing on the spot. Everything he did sent me on a wonderful journey. His words sent shivers down my spine. That is why I could never get enough of him.

I then returned back to reality. I had stayed too long. My mother would surely be looking for me now. I quickly removed myself from his arms. He knew why.

"Not already," he said with a sigh.

"I'm sorry. I wasn't keeping track of the time. I must go now." I said turning away towards the road.

I was stopped. I was immediately pulled into a kiss. "I'll miss you, Kiley." He said it the same, glum way he always does when I have to leave.

"I'll miss you, too.  But I must be on my way before my mother takes notice.  I'll see you tomorrow."

"Okay."

"Good bye!" I shouted as I began to run.

"Kiley," he called from a slight distance.

I was getting a little upset by his more clingy behavior today. I had to go!  "What is it?"

"I love you." I could see a tear role down his cheek.

I felt terrible now.  I wanted to stay with him but I knew I couldn't.  I always felt terrible leaving him.  He even said those special three words that always made my heart race. "I love you, too."

And with that I sprinted down the road without looking back. I had told my mother that I was going to clean the wash rags for the king.  I had been gone for almost an hour, and I was very nervous to face her.  My mother was not stupid...everyone knows it doesn't take an hour to wash rags.  My only hope was that she had fallen asleep.

I rushed home but on the inside I wanted to stay as far away as possible.  I finally reached the door of the small living quarters for me and my mother.  I wasted no time twisting the door knob.  I was greeted to darkness.  She had already fallen asleep.  I quickly tip toed over the threshold, and then walking towards my bed next to my mother's.  But before I could reach the middle of the room, a candle light flickered causing my heart to race.

There my mother stood, fully clothed in her day wear, glaring at me in a way I had never seen from her before. My normally, bright and cheerful mother was now giving me a stare that made me sick to the stomach.

"Where have you been, Kiley?" her tone was more than mortifying.

I didn't know what to say. If I told her that I had been with Taurid, she would forbid me to see him anymore. But I did hate lying to my mother, if I didn't tell her... I would have to hide it from her forever.

"I was...with Taurid." I admitted it.

"For what reason would you be with King Taress' adviser? What business do you have with him?" she demanded.

"Well...I met him a few months ago when I served at the king's dinner party. Oh, mother it was marvelous. He was so nice and-"

"Do not even tell me that you are involved with this man! And where did you get that locket? You know we are inferior to royalty!"

"But Mother, the way he looks at me is as an equal! He says he loves me and I know-"

"Listen to yourself! You don't honestly think he loves you, do you?"

"But he does, Mother! I know it!" I was pleading for her to listen to me but she was too firm on her stand.

"You are just a child, Kiley."

"I am not a child! I am 22 years old, Mother!"

"Don't you dare raise your voice at me," her tone caused a shiver to run down my spine.

"Now you listen to me. I do not want you to meet with him ever again. It is not proper to get involved with a superior. If I so much as hear of you even speaking to him, I will bring this to the king! He will deal with it one way or another."

Tears were flowing from my eyes now. I could feel my heart begin to thump painfully. My throat grew tight. I could feel my breathing grow unstable.

"Do you understand me, Kiley?"

"Yes, ma'am."

"Remember what I have told you. I have ways of knowing." She took in a deep breath and began to change into her night gown. "Now go to sleep. You have a lot of work ahead of you tomorrow."

I didn't answer.

~~~*~~~

"So what happened after that?" I asked.

"I ran away."

"How?"

"I don't really remember how, I just remember that was one of the last times I saw my mother. I regret it every day."

"So you ran away with Taurid, right?"

"Yes. But I didn't leave the palace."

"I'm lost," I admitted.

"It is quite alright, Tamaku. Actually, my mother died about 3-months later from pneumonia. The sad part is, we never really became friendly again before she died."

"I'm so sorry."

She continued. "But, after that, I started seeing Taurid again. We were happy together for a whole year. I was convinced that we were perfect for each other. Every moment of the day, I thought about him. I no longer had to work as a maid servant. I was given my own room down in the royal wing of the castle."

"Wow, Taurid doesn't seem evil at all."

"That's because he wasn't. But that all changed..."

~~~*~~~

"Isn't this flower beautiful?" I said as I ran over to him with a beautiful Day Lilly in hand.

He examined it with a smile "Yes, but your beauty makes it seem like a weed."

"Oh, stop it," I giggled. "But I am thinking of doing some flower arranging for the ball this Saturday. The princess of Fracica will be there and I want it to be perfect!" I exclaimed while twirling it in my hand.

"That will be nice. I heard the princess is a quite a snob though."

"Oh, that's alright. I just can't wait to hear the violinists. Mrs. Rudder even made me a dress for the occasion."

He placed his palm on my cheek. "That will be lovely. I also heard that the cooks have already started working on the meats."

"Already? There will only be about 200 people there. But I guess it will be grand anyway." I kneeled down examining a small pink rose. I began to ask him what he thought about it, but I noticed the serious look on his face. "What's wrong?"

The sound of my voice seemed to snap him out of his trance. "Oh, nothing is wrong. As a matter of fact, everything is quite perfect. But I am thinking of something."

I stood to my feet. "What is that?"

"I am not sure if I should tell you or not." He looked down glumly.

"Oh, you can tell me anything. You don't have to hide anything from me, my love."

"Well...what would you say if I told you I was planning something?" he asked

"It depends...what are you planning?"

"Well, a couple of months ago, I did a certain technique."

"What are you getting at, Taurid? You're not making sense." I was so confused.

"You know that my spirit energy is very high."

"Oh, yes because you used to be a soldier in the frontlines of the king's army at 16 years old. How could I forget?"

"Correct...but a while ago, I wondered what it would be like to further my power."

"Well, why would you want to do that? What do you need power for? You don't have to use any power around here. We haven't been to war in over 5 years." I didn't like that sound of this.

"Have you ever wondered what it would be like to live...*forever*?"

"Um, not particularly," I replied. I could feel my blood chill just a little.

"Well, would you want to live forever?"

"I have never really thought about it before."

"What would you say if I told you I will live forever?"

I took a few steps from him. "What?"

"I performed a technique for immortality...and I slipped some of the concoction in your drink yesterday, I want to be with you forever Kiley."

"No! Why would do such a thing?"

"I did it because I am planning something," his tone was ice cold.

"What are you talking about?" I could see a different tint in his eyes. They weren't warm and inviting anymore, they almost seemed...*evil.* He seemed possessed by something. Something not of this world. I had never seen him this way. Just being in his presence made my limbs weak and my throat tight.

"I am going to kill King Taress!"

"Stop it! Stop it right now! You're seriously scaring me, Taurid!"

"Kiley, I cannot stand in the back ground forever. Can't you see? If I kill him, I can become ruler of this kingdom, and you and I can rein forever! No longer will we have to live in mediocrity, but we can stand over everyone else! That fool, Taress, is ignorant to what being a ruler really means! I will no longer advise him, for I know I am the best man for the job, and I want no one to stand in my way! We can get rid of this old world, and write a genesis for a new one!"

I could feel the tears in my eyes while my heart was breaking. "I don't even know you anymore." My tone was a whisper. My lips barely moved.

"Kiley, please," he said softly as he reached for my arm.

"Get away from me! I don't know what has gotten into you, but I want nothing to do with it!"

He swore. "You will regret this Kiley!"

~~~*~~~

"And that night, I heard the word that the king was found dead in his room. They said he was stabbed to death. I remember how much I sobbed. Also that night, Taurid crowned himself dictator of the Audren Realm."

"What did you do after that?" I asked.

"Nothing; Taurid had me arrested and put in this very cell. He was the most evil man anyone in this realm has ever encountered. This cell has been my home for all these centuries.

Unlike most Audrenians, I wasn't born with any special abilities. I didn't have any element manipulation, I couldn't fly either. But I did keep that locket that Taurid gave me along with the scarlet ribbon. Little did I know, that locket had power all of its own. It was like immense spirit energy incased in the necklace. Most people call spirit energy like that, energy beings. Energy beings are pure manifestations of pure energy and can function on their own accord. It all happened like this..."

~~~*~~~

I was barely able to feel my limbs that were numbed by the chilling air. Winter had fallen upon Audren. I knew this not because I had seen snow quilted on the ground, or saw the days fall short. I have not been outside in centuries. I lost track of the years ages ago. I can barely remember how to speak. I haven't uttered anything meaningful in about a decade. It is amazing that I am not insane by now. The only contact I have with others is when I am getting beaten or sworn at.

I will never die, but that is all I wish to do. Knowing that I will be alive in this condition forever makes me feel sick. But I always feel sick. I used to try to break free from these chains that bind me. Now I barely have the strength to breathe in and out. I don't understand why he doesn't just kill me. That's the only way I can die, he has to be the one to kill me. He has no reason to keep me alive.

Maybe he knows I want to die and be put out of this never ending misery. This cell is freezing; that much I knew. My lip was trembling and my cheeks burned with the bite of the cold. The ragged dress I wore gave me no protecting against the frigid temperature.

I peered down at the locket around my neck. Every time I did, I remembered the man I once loved. I also swore every time because I knew I would never age and never die. I had named the locket Serenity. I named it Serenity because that name means stillness or peace, which was the exact opposite of what I feel.

My thoughts were interrupted. "Kiley," it was a woman's voice.

"Who is there?" I demanded, with a rasped whisper.

"It is Serenity of course," it said.

"But you can't be...lockets can't talk." I was bewildered and frightened.

"It is not the locket that is speaking to you. I am an energy being inside. I am here to help."

"I can't be helped. I have been here for hundreds of years and I have never once had help from anyone."

"Yes, you can. You just have to leave this realm...you must go to the human world."

"How can I get there?"

"That is why I am here. I will help you leave here, but you must believe."

I was speechless. The breath had been taken right from my lungs.

"I will open a portal for you. All you have to do is walk through. But once you get there, you will need to find out for yourself what to do."

~~~*~~~

"And that is exactly what happened. Serenity made me a portal and I passed through. It was very hard for me to grow accustom to the human world. There was so much technology and words I didn't understand. I had wondered in the human world for months before finding Jim. I truly loved that man and he loved me. I had almost forgotten what love felt like. But he showed me. I ended up marrying him. Soon after, I found out I was pregnant with Scarlet. When she was born, she was the love of my life. I gave her Serenity and almost every night she cried. The only lullaby I knew was the Midnight Airos It always quieted her and gave her peace. I loved her so much and all I wanted was for her to be happy. I also was always paranoid that Taurid would come searching for me. I never wanted to put Scarlet in danger…"

<p style="text-align:center">~~~*~~~</p>

Jim is upstairs watching the football game. I have just put Scarlet to sleep. Oh, how beautiful she looks when she is asleep. She lays the same way every time. Her chubby little fingers serve as a pillow for her sweet head as her legs scrunch and her mouth opens just a little. I love her so much. I continued to rock her bassinette as she slept soundly.

I have not been able to stop thinking of Taurid this week. I am so afraid that all my nightmares of him coming after me would come true. I would die if anything were to happen to Scarlet. I knew what I had to do. I had return to Audren. She needs no ties with Taurid or Audren. I didn't even want her to know about my origins.

I would have to get away.

"Serenity," I called lightly for the locket was around my child's neck.

"Yes, Kiley?"

"Make another portal to Audren."

"Why would you want to do that?"

"Soon enough, Jim will notice that I do not age."

"What is the real reason, child?"

I bit my lip. "You know why."

"Scarlet is not in any danger, Kiley."

"What are you talking about? You know he can come after me any day now!"

"You are wrong, but I will let you go. The portal will be outside in the back yard. But I am curious to how you will make your escape."

I already made a plan for this. "I will pretend to die," I said shortly.

"I will not stop you, Kiley."

"Thank you...but I want you to stay with Scarlet...she needs some kind of protection."

"As you wish," she said.

I could feel my eyes flooding with tears as I gazed at my infant angel. I knew I would never see her again...that enough made me want to die but I had to be strong. I would miss Jim, too. I loved him just like Scarlet.

And with those last silent goodbyes, I ran out the door and entered the shed on the side of our house. I had found exactly what I wanted. I poured a bit of motor oil on the ground. I grabbed the matches from the top shelf. *It would seem like I burned to death. My remains would seem to vanish into ashes…perfect.*

Without another thought, I lit the small match. Stepping closer to the doorway, I tossed down the match that set the entire shed in blazing flames. I saw the portal…and I entered it.

~~~*~~~

"So you faked your own death?"

"It was the only way I knew back then…but now I regret it deeply. I still love Scarlet. I had only found out about this Varcia stuff when I returned to Audren. Apparently while I was imprisoned, four Varcia had already come here from the human world in efforts to defeat Taurid but all have failed. I also had no idea that he had murdered so many people. Is it true that it has not rained in all these years?"

"Well, yes," I said.

"So all the pressure is put on my daughter to defeat him… Words cannot describe how much I fear for her. I even gave her some of Taurid's power."

"It was you?"

"Yes… Taurid told me that the power had a grave effect on her. When I gave her the power I only meant it for her to become stronger."

279

"So you are the woman she was speaking about. Ever since then, she has not quite been herself. She has occasional break downs when the evil takes too much control over her. She killed one of our friends yesterday...the evil took over her." I could feel a tear in my eye. I should hate this woman. I should hate her with all my heart for the corruption of Scarlet. Though it was not her power, she acted without thinking of the consequences for her reckless actions. But...I don't hate her. Not in the least.

"What have I done? I never wanted anything like that to happen." She began to cry a bit.

"But she is not evil! It hasn't fully taken over her yet. We planned on asking Taurid to take the power back. We still have time!"

"You love her...don't you?"

"Well, yes, but how did you know that?"

"I can just tell...but what will you do when she has to leave here?"

I was tired of that question. "I don't know. I want to be with her, but I know she needs to go home...it's where she belongs. I love her more than anything," I paused for a moment.

"That is why I must get out of here and find her. You can come, too, Kiley. You do want to see Scarlet, right?"

"Well, yes, but how do we get out of here?"

"We'll break out...."

# Chapter 34

## SHORTLY

I knew what I had to do. I would have to muster up courage to open the other door. I had my Raico, which was all I needed. As I began to reach for the door, I saw a small shadow from the corner of my eye. I quickly turned to my left to see what was there. The fire of the furnace created three shadows.

I raised my sword. "Who is there?"

Then, three children I knew too well, hopped from behind the furnace. They all wore pots and pans as armor. They all had a different uniform.

"Piper, Conch, and Roke, what are you doing here? How did you even find this place?"

"We followed you! Duh!" said Roke.

"Yeah, but we flew here," I pointed out.

Piper stepped closer. "You *really* underestimate us, Scarlet."

"How did you get pass all those guards?"

"I took care of *that*," said Conch and winked.

"You know what? I don't even want to know. All I want you guys to do is hide in here until I get back."

"No way! We want to fight, too!" they all shouted in unison.

"You guys are lucky I am too busy to take you all back home! Now I can't risk you guys getting hurt. Do you hear all that pounding on the door? Those guards are after me! I have to get out of here!"

"Well in that case, we shouldn't be here alone, they could break down the door and get to us," said Piper, aware of her correct logic.

I sighed. "Fine; but you guys have to stay out of my way."

"Yes ma'am!" They saluted. They also had their fingers crossed as they snickered and exchanged looks.

"I saw that." I actually was getting annoyed.

They all laughed.

After shushing them, I turned back to the door I had intended to open before getting interrupted. I reached for the door knob, and with one twist I heard the click of the door unlatching.

As we entered, I saw a dark, stone hallway with torches on the walls for light. I grabbed one for more light to see the path. The hall was covered in dust and cob webs. The place looked 400 years old.

"What is this place, Scarlet?" asked one of the boys.

"Keep quiet; as if those pots and pans you're wearing weren't loud enough," I whispered.

"Did you hear that, Mitch?" said a gruff voice from around the corner.

"Sure did," said another man.

My heart fell. I could already hear steady footsteps. I knew we would have to fight. In a matter of seconds, I saw two large men standing only feet away. "Who goes there," the tallest commanded.

All of a sudden, Conch and Roke stood in front of me. "What are you guys doing? Get back here!"

They didn't answer. They both lifted their arms. Without a sound from their mouths, the stone walls detached with a roar. The stone was moving at every wave of their hands. They quickly extended their arms towards the men and the large stone followed hurdling at top speed. I could barely keep up; it was happening so fast. With another crash, all I heard was the crushing of bones.

"All clear," they said with a grin.

I grabbed them both by the arm. "Why didn't you guys tell me you had earth manipulation?"

They both shrugged. "I dunno," they said in unison.

"Well, I guess what I should be saying is thank you. We have to continue. This way," I instructed.

They all followed close behind. As I thought about it, having them tag along did do some good. I just knew that Taurid would be a different story. The bad part was, I had no idea where exactly I had to go. But the worst part was that I was away from Tamaku. To be honest, I hadn't stopped thinking about him once. I wondered what he was up to.

*~~Tamaku's View~~*

I had been brainstorming for a while now, but nothing has come to mind. We had no way to get out of here. I knew there were soldiers standing guard somewhere nearby. This whole journey was turning into a complete failure.

"I don't think we will be able to leave here, Tamaku."

"I'm thinking, I'm thinking," I mumbled. I took a few minutes scrolling through plans, but nothing seemed right. Then I remembered! I still had my Airos Pipe! I could use the invisibility tune again! I could also use my fire to light the way!

I quickly explained the plan to Kiley. She seemed to understand quite well.

"But wont the guards see the fire if we use it?" she said.

"That is the point!"

"I don't know where you're going with this, but for an odd reason, I trust you." I could tell she was smiling when she spoke.

"Good; now the only catch to this is that once the tune is over, you cannot blink."

"Is that feasible?"

"Just don't think about it. If my plan goes as I think it will, it will only take a short time. I also noticed that the guard didn't lock the door all the way on his way out."

"Well, light the fire," she said.

"Yes, ma'am," I said as I snapped my fingers, allowing a flame to engulf my thumb and forefinger. My eyes took a moment to adjust to the light. I then looked to my side and saw Kiley. I could feel my eyes widen at the shocking resemblance her and Scarlet had. They looked almost exactly the same. Kiley was very beautiful just like Scarlet. They both had the same striking green eyes and the exact same brunette hair, except Kiley's was longer. Scarlet's only touched her shoulders. Kiley's was all the way to the middle of her back. She did appear 22 years of age just as she said. They were even very close in height; Kiley was just a bit taller. I had been studying her for a while now, but I couldn't stop.

"Is something wrong, Tamaku?" she asked with confusion.

"Oh, uh, no, but I am just shocked at how much Scarlet looks like you. But I guess I will play the tune now. Remember, when it is done, don't blink."

She nodded.

With that, I pulled out my pipe. Playing the Airos Pipe wasn't as easy as it seems. Just like any other power, doing special abilities requires spirit energy. The last time I did this technique with Scarlet, it really took a lot out of me. I only hoped I had enough spirit energy left to hold the technique. Using fire and the pipe at the same time wasn't exactly simple.

I began to play the melody and it seemed to be over a lot faster than before, but I did not blink.

"Alright, we should hurry," I said.

I grabbed her hand and headed for the door. I opened it quickly and I then saw 6 guards in the hall. It worked; they did not notice our presence whatsoever. But I knew they would notice the fire.

One casually turned around. "Good scot! There is a floating fire," he called. One by one they all turned to look, and they wore the same worried expression.   I knew I had to do it now. "This is not a floating fire; it is I, King Taress!"

"Oh, no! He has come to make his revenge!" said another as he used his arm as a shield.

"That is correct! I have waited 400 years to get back at Taurid for my murder, and now, I shall have my revenge! All his soldiers shall feel my wrath as well!" I felt like bursting out into laughter, but I kept my eyes wide open and my tone serious. I only hoped that Kiley would not blink.

"Let's get out of here!" shouted another guard.  They all did just that.  They all sprinted into the darkness in hopes that "King Taress' spirit" wouldn't come after them.  The coast was clear.

"Alright Miss Kiley, you may blink now," I said with a chuckle.

She turned to me with a smile.  "You are too much, Mr. Tamaku.  I just cannot fathom that they actually fell for such foolishness.  But I did get quite a good laugh out of it."

"Well now the fun is over.  We should probably try and find a way to the boiler room.  That is probably where Scarlet is.  We can't waste any time."

"I just hope she is alright," she said morosely.

"Don't worry, Kiley. I know Scarlet can handle herself. We just need to find her."

"Do you know the way there?"

"Not from here, but all we can do is try our best."

She nodded. I began to walk holding the fire out to see the path. The stillness of the stone walls was eerie and the chill of the halls was uncomfortable. I occasionally glanced at Kiley. She kept the same sad look of years of dread and sorrows. Unlike Scarlet's, her eyes were filled with pain and agony. I really felt bad for her. She lost her mother, fell in love but got betrayed, and she lost her daughter. I had begun to appreciate my life that much more. Her body seemed weak and brittle. I also noticed various bruises on her arms and legs. Has she gotten beaten or something?

The person she once loved was the one that imprisoned her for so long. It seemed as though craving power is what leads to a person's downfall. Power causes people to want more; and in that want, they seemed to do anything to fulfill it. It seemed as though Kiley and Taurid's love would have made a wonderful story in the many pages of romance in history. I know that their love was true, but power abolished all its potential. It is truly upsetting...more than upsetting.

Love is complicated, but it is real all the same. The way I feel about Scarlet is real, but difficult because she will be gone. I know I say it a lot, but I love her. Sometimes I wish she didn't have friends or family...that way she could stay with me forever. It is quite selfish but true. But love isn't selfish...that is why I can't be. I hated the Varcia rule of the twelve day stay. Why can't it be longer? Why can't humans return? Why can't I go to the human world and stay there? Love is difficult...but real. As I stare ahead, I can see a mound of stone piled high. It appeared as though some earth manipulation had occurred.

"She has been here." Kiley said abruptly.

"What? How can you be sure?"

"I can smell her scent. She and three others have been here."

"Do you know how far she is?" I asked hopefully.

"No. I can only tell that she has been here. I can also sense that she went this way," she said pointing to the right.

I could feel my heart rate go up. Finally we had a clue to where Scarlet was. Even though it had been only hours, it felt like days. We both sped up. I could tell we were both eager to see Scarlet. I couldn't tell whose eagerness was strongest. I could only imagine how happy I will be to see her beautiful smile again. All I wanted to do was have her safe in my arms and forget about all this Taurid business.

# Chapter 35

## WHISPERS

"Are you sure we are going the right way, Scarlet? We've been walking for hours!"

"Conch, please just keep quiet. I can't concentrate if you all are babbling on to me." I scolded.

I could hear three little sighs behind me, but I ignored them. I hated not being prepared for things. This place could use a major make over as well. Even in these halls, there was dirt and dust. I hated how dark it was, too. I couldn't see why they didn't paint the place white, or blue, or even hot pink—okay, maybe not hot pink, but anything would look more inviting than gray.

I could feel myself rambling in my thoughts. For once the kids actually obeyed and stayed quiet. I even wished that there were some guards to fight. It was really boring just walking. There wasn't a door way or gate or anything...Just plain, gray, stone walls.

My thoughts were disturbed.

"Are you picking up anything?" said a voice.

I couldn't believe it! I knew that voice from anywhere! It was Tamaku, but he seemed to be talking to someone else.

"Yes, I am,"

It was a woman's voice. A voice that was not very familiar.

"That's Tamaku!" said Roke.

"Tamaku! It's me, Scarlet!" I called.

He immediately sprinted from around the corner, coming my way. I could feel my teeth showing from the enormous smile I displayed.

"Scarlet, you're alright!" he said as he squeezed me tight.

"Yeah, I missed you," I said taking in his sweet scent that I had been craving. I know I say his scent is sweet, but I don't know how else to describe it. It smells like spring I think. Just imagine being in a stuffy room for a full day, then finally going outside and breathing in entirely fresh air. A fresh spring breeze, if you will. It had to be one of the best smells I have ever encountered.

He pulled away placing my face between his hands, his eyes staring into mine. "I missed you, too. I was going to go crazy if I didn't see you soon. I'm so sorry I left you all by yourself."

I shook my head, "It wasn't your fault. It was these darn eye lids of mine that made you get hauled away like that."

"At any rate, you're safe." He then kissed me lightly on my forehead. My grin widened.

"EWWW!" shrieked the children I had forgotten even existed.

"So you do love him!" Said Piper making a gagging face.

"Scarlet and Tamaku sitting in a tree, K-I-S-S-I-N-G!" they chanted. (I didn't even know kids from other realms knew that immature little song.)

We laughed. "So how did you get out, Tamaku?" I asked.

He seemed to remember something. He then turned around looking at something. I followed his gaze and my eyes widened at the sight. It was her! It was that woman that gave me the evil! "How did she get here?" I screamed.

"Scarlet, calm down," said Tamaku as he placed his hand on my shoulder.

"That is the woman from before!" I shouted pointing her way.

"Scarlet-"

"No, Tamaku. I can explain," said the woman as she walked closer to me. It took all that was in me not to lash out my sword on the spot.

"Tamaku, what is going on?"

"Scarlet, you don't understand," she said. "I am not your enemy...I was just not thinking when I gave you that wretched power. I had no idea it would have such a grave result on you."

"Wait, what?" I lowered my sword

"Scarlet, I am Kiley, your mother."

"You mean...you're not dead?" I said.

"No...but I did make a terrible mistake."

"But, how did you get here? I mean, are you a Varcia, too?"

"No, I am an Audrenian. The mistake I made was posing as dead while I returned to this realm. Many years ago this place was my home. But when Taurid became ruler, I was imprisoned for centuries."

"But...you look so young," I said softly reaching one hand toward her. She took my hand in her own, keeping her eyes fixed on me.

"That is because Taurid made it so that I live forever without aging just as he. When I got to the human world, I fell in love with your father...after we got married...I gave birth to you." Her face seemed deep with sorrow.

"Then why are you here?"

"I didn't want Taurid to come after me...I wanted you to have nothing to do with this world or any of its people. That is why I left before you could learn to love me the way I loved you. But now

I realize that was a terrible mistake. I know I should have stayed with you... You needed a mother, and I should have been there to give you one...but instead I was a coward and left you with only a locket...I love you, Scarlet. I'm sorry for not being there to love you." She had begun to weep heavily.

I couldn't believe what was happening. My mother that I had always thought to be dead was standing right in front of me. She looked so much like me...it felt like I was staring into a mirror. When I saw here before, I didn't even notice the resemblance. All these years, I thought I was an orphan...now I have come to find out that Audrenian blood flows through my veins. My mother was never there all those years, but she wanted to be. I barely know her, but my heart beats for her. I had not seen her since I was an infant, but I felt for her. She was like a shadow to me my whole life...but I loved her. She was so beautiful...she looked as young as I did...maybe a little older. A woman that looked to be in her 20's was my long last mother. Seventeen years without her, now my soul yearns for her.

I wrapped my arms around her, holding on tightly. "Mom," I whispered.

"Scarlet... You are so big now...I missed all your childhood...I'm sorry."

"Mother, I love you...don't be sad. I'm not sad...I'm happy."

"I love you, too, honey."

It is hard to explain how I felt. It felt like I had known her my whole life...maybe even longer. Hugging her felt right. I still can't fully explain how I felt.

We let go. I studied her face as she studied mine. "You're so beautiful," we both said in unison. It made us chuckle just a little.

"I can barely tell the difference," said Roke, basically abolishing the moment; but my mom laughed.

292

"Jeez, Roke! Put a lid on it! Do you always have to say something?" scolded Conch as he crossed his arms.

"Are you kidding? You were totally staring at her mom! You're sick!" said Roke.

"You both need to knock it off! Your annoying Scarlet's mom!" Said Piper loudly.

"Wait, Scarlet, how did they get here?" asked Tamaku, finally realizing they were there.

"Um...I'm still trying to figure that out," I said raising my eyebrows. I turned, "Oh, Mom, I guess I should introduce you to our precious little angels," I said sarcastically.

"Those are *your* kids?" she asked in a shocked tone, glancing at me then Tamaku.

"Oh, no, no no! They are just my friends," I was a little shocked by my own emotion that backed up that resistance to that question.

"But their names are Piper, Conch, and Roke," said Tamaku pointing each one out.

"Oh, they are very adorable children," she complimented.

"Sure, well anyway, I don't think we should waste any more time here," started Tamaku.

"I know exactly where to go from here."

Thank goodness; finally someone actually knows what they are doing. I could not resist holding Tamaku's hand. He looked down at me with a warm smile. With him and me leading, the rest followed close behind. But I couldn't get my mind off my mother. I knew I should be paying more attention to her, but I missed Tamaku so much. I knew my heart was stolen by Tamaku for the time being...just for a while longer.

I felt that wonderful feeling of happiness again. I know I shouldn't be happy right now, sense we might be walking to our deaths, but I am. I found my mom, we are all in one piece, and I am with Tamaku. I was almost grateful he and I were in the front. No one could see how wide I was smiling.

We suddenly approached a rather large staircase. It was so dark I could only see a few stairs up. This place seemed to be a tad bit colder than where we were before.

"This is it," my mother said with worry coloring her tone.

"So after all this time...we finally made it," I said softly. I gripped my sword. I then thought. Toki...she died. Omi...he died. Taurid ...will die. The pain and sorrow was now piling on pound by pound. The true entity of evil would soon feel the wrath of 400 years. All the tears of the ages will no longer be in vain. I grasped my sword tighter. The words of Omi the water flair returned to my memory. *Do not act on revenge but instead avenge.* I would avenge the Audrenian people...

I was the one who took the first step on the staircase. The others seemed to ease behind me silently. I could hear my footsteps clack on the stone. Each one caused another bead of sweat to shed. One by one, my steps continued. My heart felt empty, motionless, and vacant. It was not racing as I had expected. I was at ease. My soul was not troubled.

But my thoughts were interrupted as I felt a presence at my side. Without looking, I knew it was Tamaku. He held my hand tightly. He then raised it, kissing it lightly.

There, we walked the stairs together, hand and hand. Finally, we arrived at a large door. It was too dark to see exactly how far it extended upwards. I then felt another presence at my other side. It was Piper. Her small hand held mine.

"Scarlet," she whispered. "I love you."

"I love you too, all of you."

With that, the door opened with a roar. The creek it created seemed as though it had not been opened in years. The doors opening slowly revealed what lay inside. I saw a large throne, with the enemy sitting right on it.

# Chapter 36

## EVERLASTING

I was mesmerized by the sight. The confidence I had was gone in an instant. He was just the same as he was before. The evil was just as strong as before. I could see my breath from the chill. I felt that same paralyzed feeling just like before.

The room was as big as four gymnasiums—maybe even bigger. The whole room was empty except for a black throne in the very center. It had dusty rubies imbedded in the surface. It was a very grim looking room.

He stood from the throne. I could feel his icy stare penetrating my helpless form.

"Oh my, I wasn't expecting you until tomorrow. But if you are ready to fight, please, count me in." His voice was smooth but blood chilling. He shot a crooked smile as he stepped closer. I could hear his terrible footsteps one by one and then he stopped.

"How did you get out?" He was looking in my mother's direction.

"Does it matter? I am not the one you will be fighting," said Mother in a challenging tone.

I was deeply astonished at the confidence she displayed when she spoke to him. It seemed almost effortless. I, on the other hand, didn't even have enough courage to speak.

"Do not use that tone with me!" He commanded having his smile completely vanish. His voice eerily became deeper...almost like it was some else's voice for a split second.

I could feel Piper hiding her face on my side.

"So it seems as though the mother and daughter found one another," he said softer this time. "It sure is a pity that you will both have to die on such an occasion."

It all happened too fast. He suddenly transported himself only inches away from me. He had been meters away before. His movements were so quick my eyes couldn't pick it up.

He must have notice me shudder when he did. He began to smile exposing his perfect white teeth. He then quickly whipped out a sword...my eyes were too slow to catch that as well.

"So did you ever 'learn' to use that lightning manipulation I offered you?"

I backed up. "Taurid," I could feel the cracks in my voice. "I do not want this power any longer. I will now ask you to take it back." I couldn't believe I was actually speaking...I must admit that my mother's courage inspired me.

He then began to chuckle. The chuckle turned into a crackling laugh that was ear splitting. It was a terrible laugh. "You stupid girl; do you not know that you are trying to give up all chances you have of even placing a scratch on me? Don't you know that you are nothing without that power?"

"Please, Taurid, take back the power that belongs to you. I have no use of it." I had to admit that I doubted this decision.

He then placed his hand on my chest. This kind of shocked me until I felt an excruciating pain. It felt like my very soul was getting extracted from my body. I couldn't help but cringe at the hurting sensation. I could see a dark light coming from me. Was it the evil? The longer it went the more painful it became.

"You're hurting her!" it was Tamaku's voice.

The pain still continued. But then I felt myself being forced to the ground.

"Scarlet, are you okay?"

I could hear my mother speaking. I moaned. It felt like all my energy had been drained to nothing.

~~~Tamaku's View~~~

"You're hurting her!" I shouted.

My words were ignored. I could barely watch as her body shook and her eyes scrunched together. She was striving not to make a sound. I longed to tell her that it was alright and she didn't have to be strong for this. It seemed as though she was not conscious. The darkness that was coming from her body was abundant. I assumed that it was the evil being taken out. There was so much. Then, Taurid threw her to the ground roughly once it was over. I began to run to her but Kiley beat me to it.

"Scarlet, are you okay?" she asked in a shuddered voice.

Scarlet seemed to be in pain. Kiley then turned to Taurid. "What did do to her?"

"I did exactly as she asked. Her main power was the evil, and now that it's gone, I wouldn't be surprised if she has no strength left." He began to chuckle at his own comment.

"Scarlet, I'm here, sweetie," said Kiley as she stroked Scarlet's cheek.

Miraculously, Scarlet gently shrugged off her mother's touch and began to stand to her feet. Her legs trembled as she tried, but she soon stood casting her gaze downwards.

"Now, Scarlet, why do put up a fight? I wanted to make it easy for you."

Scarlet didn't say a word, but then she breathed.

"I have been a student, a teacher, a friend, an enemy, I have been lied to, a liar, angry, excited, misunderstood, understood completely, a hero, a villain, sweet, bitter, relaxed, uneasy, clever, obtuse, right, wrong, loved, in love then finally...overtaken. I have been put through endless sorrows these past few days. I am not going to go down that easily. Yeah, I'm scared but I won't act on it. I will not die without a fight. With my own power, and this sword...I will overtake *you*."

Her tone was so fierce it sent shivers down my spine. I finally understood the full reason why I loved her. She then turned to face him but her long tumbling brown hair covered one eye and left the other glaring directly at him. Her stare had the intensity to pierce through any normal person's very being...but then again, Taurid was far from normal.

He kept the same expression. His eyes narrowed in her direction and a smile formed on his lips. He then began to clap as he paced around her. "Bravo!" he shouted grandly. "Truly a lovely speech! Please, if you have anything more to say, carry on. I have been quite bored lately and I have been dying for a good show." He then widened his grin. His joking manner started to irritate me. "Fools put on the best shows, you know?"

She was silent.

"What is this? You were so wonderfully boisterous just then. Isn't there anything else you wish to voice? Please choose your words carefully, for I promise they will be your last." His tone was dark. Just his presence alone made me feel like collapsing.

"Stop it!" Kiley cried. I could see the tears streaming from her eyes. She then stood in between Taurid and Scarlet. "I can't stand to see the only thing I have left being tortured by you! You have taken away everything I had to live for! You can take my life but not my daughter!"

He began to shake his head as he eased his long finger under Kiley's chin. He studied her for a moment. "Still the same, sorry maid servant from all those years ago...I cannot lie, Kiley...I always hated you. I honestly was just sorry for you at first. I cannot even count all the lies I told you...and just like a stupid servant, you *actually* believed that someone of my status would love such a lowly nobody like you. I fantasized about the moment that I would watch you lose all the blood in your body. I was just waiting for the right time."

And with that, he stabbed his sword right into her stomach. I watched as the blood poured from her petite form. With the sword still in place, she fell to the ground. Her body began to shudder as her hands twitched. Her face was stained in her own blood that was still pouring. I could see her fading green eyes locked on her daughter. She mouthed 3 words. *I love you.* Then her body stopped all movement. Her lifeless eyes remained open and her breath was no more.

I transferred my gaze to Scarlet. Her mouth was open and her body was still. She then looked up at her mother's murderer. She slowly paced to her body. She crouched down and slid her hand on her mother's. With her other hand, she closed Kiley's eye lids and stroked her face gently. "I barely knew you," she whispered. "But I love you more than my own life. I will never forget watching you trying to save me."

I couldn't help but shed tears. Though I only knew Kiley for a few hours, I felt like I knew her for years. The one she used to love turned out to never love her in the first place. To die with a thought like that must be one of the worst ways to go out. I think Taurid knew that, too.

"Aw, your dear mother is dead without even being in my presence for 5 minutes. Let me guess, your drive to kill me has skyrocketed to an even higher degree than before."

"What is wrong with you? How do you go on killing the innocent with no remorse? I'm not afraid of you, I hate you!" she shouted.

I was thwarted and motionless. I wanted to say something but was there anything really left to say? I watched silently but soon was awakened to a surprise. I had never seen her this way. In a matter of seconds, Scarlet darted at Taurid with her sword's blade targeted at his torso. But I cringed as he quickly dodged. But again, she swung her sword in his direction only to be blocked. He held the blade calmly against his fingertip. Was that even possible?

"Ah, now you have come into the fighting spirit, Scarlet." His tone was low and jeering.

I watched as her eyebrows tensed and she moved her sword and swung again. She missed but she recuperated by launching into the air flipping into another missing strike.

She needed help...but what could I do? All I had was my pipe and a small dagger. I transferred my gaze to the children. I noticed one was missing. I shot my gaze back to the battle scene to see Conch moving, what he thought to be discretely, to Taurid. That foolish kid! Taurid would see his movements for sure!

Scarlet did not notice.

Conch, at a slight distance, pulled apart a portion of the stone ground and lifted it. "I'm gonna help you, Scarlet!"

Scarlet then glanced in his direction holding up her palm for him to stop, but she was too late.

Taurid then snapped his finger towards Conch and he was set into flames instantly. The stone he had lifted fell with a boom. His small form then seemed to collapse without another movement. All I could hear was a faint cry coming from his fire engulfed body.

301

I then looked at Scarlet. She turned back to Taurid with tears in her eyes. I could not believe that two people had already been killed...one just a child.

Taurid then tipped his head back and let out the terrible crackling laugh.

What is wrong with me? Why do I just stand here? Scarlet began to lift her sword again, shooting at him full force. With a swing, I heard the clank of two swords colliding.

She was no match for him. I knew it would all be over soon. She leaped into the air again, coming down with her sword pointing down. With a swift movement, he easily dodged.

"Is this honestly all you have in you? How many of your friends do I have to kill before you can give a fair fight? I am growing tired of this battle. All these years I have waited for the Last Varcia. It turns out that you are not even worth killing. You are just as weak as the ones before you...maybe even weaker. You are a disappointment, Scarlet."

He then swiped his sword across her stomach. His movements were so fast, I barely saw it. I then saw her bend over holding her wound that was leaking blood. As if it was child's play, he ran his sword across her back which caused her to screech. The blood was dripping on the ground around her.

I felt as if I had no control over my body. It almost felt as if I was watching myself from another place. Without a thought, I sprinted to him and stabbed my small dagger into his arm. He swore as he tried to shake me off violently. I struggled to keep the sword in his flesh. My legs were dangling because he was much taller than I. I turned my head towards Scarlet. "Try to aim for his heart!" I instructed.

She seemed hesitant. She picked up her sword, still holding the gash on her stomach. I felt myself being thrown in midair. I then felt my skull being inflamed.  The sensation was too much.  My eyes were getting heavy...

# Chapter 37

## REMEMBERANCE

Everything was going wrong. I cringed as I saw Tamaku being bolted against the stone wall head first. He seemed unconscious.

I was feeling lightheaded with every second that eased past. My heart felt like it would burst and scatter to the ground. I had never felt such pain before. I could feel my blood tumbling to the ground. I am also hurting inside. I can still see my mother lying there dead. In the corner of my eye, I can also see Conch's body surrounded by fire. I knew things were only going to get worse.

"Now that is what I love to see," he said approving my agony. "So much blood!" he said as he crouched down and slid his finger across the crimson liquid. I don't want to finish you off just like that. I want you to die very slowly."

I glanced back at Tamaku to see him slumped over still unconscious. I was feeling so weak. My vision was getting clouded. I strived to raise my sword. It felt twice as heavy.

I wasn't sure if I could do any water manipulation. I didn't have the evil power or my locket. I knew I could at least try. But just as I raised my arms, his fist was against my jaw. I felt myself fall to the ground. As I hit, I felt his fist again, this time on the other side of my head. I felt queasy.

Suddenly, I felt his foot kicking my side with the force that caused me to cry out in pain and bolt against the wall. The blood was coming from my nose. I was also spitting some out. I just wanted him to stop. I could taste the salty, rusty taste of blood. I knew I was just a few steps away from really dying. But before I could rear another thought, I lost consciousness...

~~~Tamaku's view~~~

As my eyes eased open, the pain seared again. I winced. My head felt like it was hit by a boulder. I raised my hand to touch it but it was forced back down.

I looked down to see my wrists in chains and the same with my ankles. It was so cold. My memory then recapped. I looked to my left and was shocked. I saw Piper and Roke also in chains. They looked completely unharmed but they looked so still...almost as if dead. I began to panic but then I was relieved to see their small chests rise up and deflate down steadily. That was a good sign.

I then looked to right. I saw Scarlet. She was awake. But she was covered in cuts and bruises. I could see the large gash in her stomach. I could barely stand to look at her. I felt as if I would break down in tears. I felt like it was all my fault that this happened to her. *If only I had been strong enough to protect her.* How could I claim that I love her and not have acted earlier? She doesn't seem to notice that I am conscious again.

What happened? Everything went by so rapidly. Why were we all bound in chains? Taurid could have finished us off. I am so confused. My head is spinning. I casted my gaze upwards; I saw that we were still in the throne room. The two bodies had not been moved. But where was Taurid?

"Tamaku?" I heard her whisper.

"Scarlet, what happened here?"

She looked down again. A tear rolled from her eye and off the tip of her nose. "I blacked out. He just kept beating me...I tried to stay conscious but I was just too weak." She glanced at Piper and Roke. "At least the kids are okay," she whispered.

I reached my hand to her face and whipped her tear away and began stroking the side of her face. "Yeah, but you're not...and it's my entire fault."

She then placed her hand on my face. "No its not, Tamaku; I wasn't mad at you when you stood there and watched me fight. Remember that time when you had me jump off that cliff?"

I nodded. I wasn't quite sure where she was going with this.

"That was when you told me that I need to be my own hero. By jumping off the cliff, I had to depend on my *own* power. Tamaku, you were just supposed to teach me things...I am the Last Varcia...you don't have to be." She smiled.

I then recalled that conversation.

*"What? You said earlier you would always-"*

*"Yes I know, but the whole point of this is sudden danger. Like I told you before, there will not always be someone to protect you each and every time danger is afoot. Do not be confused; I will try to be there for you as much as I can but I can't promise that you won't get hurt or worse. Now with this, sudden danger is the key. If you knew you had someone to save you right now, it wouldn't be that dangerous now would it?"*

*She shook her head.*

*"That's why I cannot help. If I did I would be doing you a disservice."*

She really has grown a lot since then. She remembered one of the most important lessons I taught her. I never knew how true that really was until now. I looked at her again. She was smiling. To me, even with the cuts and bruises, she looked as beautiful as ever.

Her stare intensified. "That is also when I began to fall in love with you. You were so kind, sweet, innocent, and I looked up to you. You were everything I ever wanted to be. It would be my honor to protect you. You are Audrenian, too."

We shared a smile. I continued to stroke her face gently. Though she was in pain, her eyes remained soft. I still felt terrible for how things ended up.  I jumped as I heard a door open. My heart fell as I saw him enter.  Both Scarlet and I dropped our hands.

"I'm so sorry to leave you alone like that.  I have just been thinking of the way I want to kill you all I have decided you will each have a different style of death." His voice was sinister which made my heart quake as he exited the door contemplating his next move. Suddenly remembered something...

~~~*~~~

"Tamaku, stop fidgeting and sit quietly," whispered Mother angrily.  I hate acting bad for her, but whenever the elder's spoke it was so boring!

"Mom, when is it over?" I asked whiningly.

She shushed me.  "Tamaku, listen to what Elder Corley has to say!  It is very important.  If you talk one more time, I will give Toki your birthday gift."

I glanced at Toki to see her sticking her tongue out at me jeeringly.  "Shut up, Toki," I said under my breath.

"Mom, Tamaku told me to shut up!" Toki whispered to her.

"Both of you need to hush!  I won't warn you again."

I sat back in the chair and let out a deep breath.  I looked at my dad who had been listening the whole time.  I then transferred my gaze to the elders.  There were only three of them still alive. They all wore gray hair and their faces were engulfed in wrinkles. They meet every week which means my dad drags our whole family to see.

All they do is talk about the same stories over and over.  I never thought anyone could die of boredom but I feel a little lightheaded every time I am here.  Even now, I am striving to keep my eyes open.  My mom gets so mad when I fall asleep.  This had to be my worst birthday ever.

"Have any of you heard of her... Audrenia?" asked elder Corley scanning the small audience. It seemed as though no one had heard it before.

"Ah, I guess you all are just too young of a generation. That means you all still think it will be the Last Varcia that will kill Taurid." I looked around to see everyone exchanging looks and wearing the same confused look.

"I was expecting that," he chuckled. For once, I was actually interested in what he was going to say next. "It will be Audrenia, the Midnight Warrior that will take the breath from Taurid's lungs. She will be very beautiful. Her hair shall be long and flowing and the color of oak's wood and her eyes the color of emerald. Her body shall be "tall" and slender and the crown she will wear will be made of 7 Midnight Airos flowers. She will have immense spirit energy made of pure light. *She* will rise up and kill him."

Everyone was awestruck.

"I will also tell you all that there is one person in this very room that will encounter the princess." His tone became lower and colder.

Everyone immediately gawked at my father. I knew it was going to be him, too. He was the strongest Audrenian out of us all. He was the head of the Audrenian Council and by far the most hopeful in efforts to defeat Taurid.

~~~*~~~

That was it! I knew how to defeat Taurid once and for all! I had to conceal my joy. I knew it! Why have I been so blind all this time! Yes!

# Chapter 38

## SPIRIT ENERGY

Tamaku stroked my face gently. He looked at me as if I was beautiful even with so many bruises on my face. I couldn't hold back a smile. I could tell he was really stressing over what happened.

I then heard the door open again. We stopped immediately. He looked just as evil as before as he walked in the room.

"I'm so sorry to leave you alone like that again. I have just been thinking of the way I want to kill you all. I have decided you will each have a different style of death," he chortled. I was so enraged just by his presence.

"But I must leave once more. I need to talk it over with my soldiers," he acted as if our deaths were nothing. I noticed that Piper and Roke were awake. I had never seen them look so drained of life. I felt like bursting into tears just looking at them.

I watched as Taurid stepped towards the score of guards. His speech was muffled and it was hard to hear.

"Scarlet! I get it!" whispered Tamaku.

"Wait, what are you talking about?"

"Don't count us out just yet. I have a plan, but I am not completely sure how it will work"

"Tamaku, we don't have time for plans. He's gonna kill us," I pointed out. I watched the kids' facial expressions twist.

He then shot his gaze at them. "Piper, Roke, do you know how to assemble spirit energy?" he asked urgently.

"Yes, but I am not that good at it," said Piper in a rasped voice.

"Me neither," admitted Roke.

He thought for a moment. "Just try! Try to rile up as much spirit energy as you can!"

"Tamaku, where are you going with this?" I finally asked.

His dark eyes seared into mine. "It's you. She's you. Look, just get some spirit energy. As much as you can get! We can't go down without a fight!" his eyes were pleading.

I didn't argue. Tamaku seemed to be on to something. I strived to gain as much spirit energy as possible but it wasn't easy. When assembling too much at a time, it gets painful.

I saw Tamaku doing it as well. I was shocked to see Piper. Her spirit energy was actually visible! It was the color of radiant white light. Then, Roke's spirit energy was visible as well.

I focused on my own energy. It was so difficult to rile it up all on my own. But then I felt a warm hand on mine. I looked to the side to see Tamaku's head down and eyes closed. Then, his spirit energy began to shine. What was wrong with me? My energy was just not strong enough. But at that moment, I felt an unordinary pulsation on my heart. I could feel it. It was happening. I was being overtaken...but this time...

## Chapter 39

### UNDER THE INFLUENCE:  TAMAKU'S VIEW

When our hands touched, the spirit energy from Piper, Roke, and I began to transfer to her. I feel such pain on my body. I peered up to see her focusing. She will feel it in a moment. I really hope this works. If this plan fails, we are dead. That fool, Taurid, has no idea what is happening while his back is turned.

Then it happened. She began to grind her teeth but her eyes remained closed. I knew it! By giving her more spirit energy, she would begin to transform.

She then began to bite her lip. I longed to tell her it would all be okay. I hated to see her in such pain, but I am so sure that it would all come to a close soon.

The light she gave off shined even more than before. I motioned for the kids to stop the flow. We couldn't overload Scarlet with power. I then stopped as well. I stared at her in awe as she glowed magnificently. The energy increased by the second. She then opened her eyes looking straight ahead.

Taurid turned and his face was covered in shock.

"Guards!" he commanded, still gawking at the sight.

Scarlet was covered in light. I could just barely see her physical appearance change. She was taller than before. She also was no longer wearing her tattered clothes. Instead, she wore a long, flowing white dress. Her hair was perfectly curled and her eyes were as bright as pure emeralds. On her head was a wreath made of seven Midnight Airos flowers and in her hand was a sword that seemed to be made out of pure light. I was overjoyed that my assumptions were correct. *Scarlet is Audrenia, the Midnight Warrior.*

There were no longer any cuts and bruises on her skin. The Raico she once wielded was gone and replaced with a blade of light.

I was awestruck as she gaped straight ahead walking gracefully, yet strongly to Taurid. The guards did as commanded approaching her with their weapons outstretched. But it was no use. With just the presence of light, each and every one was immediately forced down. Audrenia had finally come to do what we could only wish for. The hero of the ages has risen to defeat the essence of evil. The moment my people have waited for is now here.

Then, in an instant, every guard was on the ground staring at her as she stepped closer to Taurid. He seemed as if he was frozen in fear.

"Taurid," her voice was different; no longer Scarlet's. "Your rein is now over. The force of good has come upon you and you shall not be spared. The Audrenians have suffered for 400 years, and now you shall experience their suffering tenfold. You will die by the hand of Audrenia and this land shall be restored. Your dark heart will now be seized with my blade of light. Your fate has been eternally sealed and will work in what you deserve. In the honor of everything good, your evil time is no more."

Then with that, she effortlessly speared her blade right into his chest. The light was too bright; I had shielded my eyes with my arms. The clash of good and evil was too much to bear but in my heart I knew that the light had subdued the darkness and Taurid would be no more. All I could hear was a blood curdling scream and a cyclone of wind which made my hair swirl in the gust and my clothes shift violently. I placed my arm over my eyes. But then, the wind died down and darkness fell once again in the throne room. I slowly removed my arms to see Scarlet. Her back was to me. She was not glowing any longer, but she still wore the same white dress. I peered down to notice that my chains were broken. I looked up again. I immediately stood up. I suddenly felt no pain. I felt completely energized.

I then watched as she fell to the ground. This was only a side effect to the immense power that had overtaken her. I quickly rushed her way, kneeling down on my knees; I placed her head in my lap. She looked as peaceful as an angel as I stroked her hair gently.

It was all over. Tears fell from my eyes on to her cheeks. She had done what my people have only dreamed about. She was finally in my arms. She saved us. This little angel was my love. I kissed my angel gently and she did not stir.

Then I was taken aback as I witnessed something incredible. The large, dreary castle was being swept with light. Also, the walls began to sprout Midnight Airos flowers making the room filled with shimmering lavender florescence. I gaped at the sight in awe as the fate of my world was now sealed in contentment instead of oppression. I then felt warm little hands on my back. I turned to see Roke and Piper smiling at me. They knew what I knew: *no longer obliged to wickedness.*

The castle was filled with light as we walked through the halls. I had placed Scarlet on my back as she still slumbered. The kids walked close behind staring at the wonders around them. After a while of walking, we finally met the exit. I slowly opened the door and was astounded by the sight.

The crashing and splashing of precipitation excited me. For the first time in my life, I had seen rain. The kids ran out before me and danced in the water. Sticking out their little tongues in hopes to catch the drips, they twirled and spun with their arms outstretched.

I couldn't hold back a smile as I saw Midnight Airos flowers carpeting the ground. These were signs that the struggle was over.

As we traveled through town, the normally lifeless and apathetic people were now smiling and laughing. I saw many children splashing in puddles. Many of them were holding plants of all kinds! Vegetables, flowers, and fruit!

People waved to me knowing that I had helped in the cause. But they knew that it was the Midnight Warrior that had finished the job.

# Chapter 40

## DECISION

As I opened my eyes, I felt different. I wasn't in pain but the complete opposite. I sat up to see myself in Tamaku's hut. Wait, where was Taurid? Was it all a dream? I noticed Tamaku sitting about a few feet away. He seemed to be asleep. I scanned the room to see Piper and Roke asleep as well. What time was it?

I slowly stood to my feet and noticed I did not have my school uniform on. Instead, I had a long white dress. It seemed like a lot happened that I missed. I did notice that my once aching body felt well rested and painless. It seemed as though all my wounds were healed as well.

I then eased my way to Tamaku. He was still sleeping peacefully. I looked at him for a while. He looked so cute when he was asleep. It seemed as though all his wounds had vanished, too.

I lightly shook him to awake his slumber. He soon fluttered his eyes open, adjusting them to the light. He didn't really seem to notice what was going on as he yawned drowsily.

"Tamaku," I whispered. He seemed to snap out of his unawareness and eased out a smile.

"Scarlet...you did it," he said in a low, still sleepy voice.

"Wait, what do you mean?"

"You finally killed him, silly" he chuckled.

"But...why can't I remember anything? All I remember is being bound in chains."

"It doesn't matter. All that matters is that you saved this land and its people from their demise."

I still wanted to know what happened but if Tamaku says it doesn't matter, I don't really care that much. I sat in his lap and laid my head on his chest. He had his arms around me holding me close. He seemed as though he would fall asleep again. I didn't mind, I was just happy to be in his arms without a worry or care...

~~~*~~~

"Scarlet, wake up," said a voice.

My serene feeling was disturbed by fatigue. I kept my eyes closed as I felt my body being gently shaken.

"Scarlet, please wake up."

I turned my head escaping the light as I shooed away the hands that were disturbing me.

"Scarlet," the voice said more sternly now.

I could hear myself groan but barely. I strived to sit up and fluttered my eyes open. My clouded vision depicted Tamaku. I rubbed my eyelids and squinted them open. "Tamaku?" I said hazily.

"Scarlet, you have to wake up. You know what day it is, don't you?" he said almost in a whisper.

My tired mind tried to reflect on what he was speaking about. Then I remembered. Today was the last day; the last day to breathe Audren air. I felt myself gain attention, leaving behind the desire to fall back asleep; just the thought itself manifested into a queasy feeling in the pit of my stomach.

"Tamaku, I already made my decision. I want to stay with you," I said in a pleading tone as tears and tears dripped from my eyes.

I could see the pain in his dark eyes. "Scarlet, you have to go," tears fell from his eyes now. "There are too many people waiting at home for you."

"But what about you, Tamaku? You love me, right?" I said in a desperate voice.

"That's just it...that's why I have to let you go. Scarlet, I love you, but I'm also not the only one that does. I couldn't live with myself if I took you away from everyone that cares about you."

I didn't say a word. I just felt the horrible feeling of my heart being stabbed over and over with the tormenting feeling of leaving him. I couldn't rear a worse thought. Didn't he know I would give up all those people for him? I knew it was probably wrong for me to feel that way, but I couldn't help it. I stood up and clenched his shirt digging my face into his chest. I couldn't stop crying.

"Scarlet, I...I'm sorry I just...can't let you stay here. I can't act on such selfishness."

In the back of my mind, I knew what he was saying was the right thing.

"Listen, we have a few more hours until the portal closes. In that time, I figured me and you could spend some time together. The kids are still sleeping so I will wake them when it is time to say their goodbyes. I want mine to be special." His voice was smooth and gentle.

I was excited to finally spend one on one time with him without worrying about Taurid. For the first day in the whole twelve days I have been here, I can finally take a day to relax.

I glanced at the sleeping children. It saddened me to see one missing. But I knew that Conch was in a better place. I couldn't stand thinking about everyone that was sacrificed in the effort to defeat Taurid.  What saddened me the most is that they never got to see this day.

I looked at Tamaku again.  He was smiling at me now.  I wiped away my tears and smiled back.  I figured I would make the most of the time I had left.  Then again, it is me that makes the final decision.

We then walked outside to be greeted by the cool, moist air of the morning.  The dew was still fresh on the scenic, green grass.  He held my hand in his as we walked.  The sun was still rising and the sky was painted blue.  We were silent for a long time.  I took that time to gape at the marvelous land that was before me.  I couldn't believe that this beautiful landscape was once a barren wasteland.

I gazed at the tall vegetation and flowers of all sorts. Various times, Tamaku and I stood just admiring the beauty.  I couldn't believe the complete transformation.  Hours passed by as we adored the reformed world around us.

"So do you believe me when I said that this place was just as beautiful before Taurid ever reined?" he chuckled.

"It doesn't even matter," I giggled.  "All that matters is that we are together right now."

"Yeah," he said casting his gaze upwards.  He then shot his gaze straight ahead in a sudden blast of emotion.  "I forgot! I wanted to give this back to you."  He then fished in his pocket and pulled out my locket.  "I found this under the bed.  I figured you would want it back."  He held it out on his palm.

I thanked him as I reached for it.  I then drew my hand back.  "Actually, I want you to have it.  I want you to have something to remember me by."  I closed his palm for him to grasp the relic.

He smiled and gazed at it.  "Thank you.  I really am happy you are letting me have it."

"You're welcome," I said sweetly.

"I want you to have something of mine." He sat under a tree nearby motioning for me to follow suit. I did so, feeling my dress (I had cut to my knees) flow in the warm breeze. I knelt next to him.

"I want you to have this," he said as he pulled his Airos Pipe from his pocket.

"Oh, Tamaku, I couldn't. That was your dad's," I said as I shook my head.

"Yeah, but..." he placed the pipe in my hands, "I want you to have it now. I don't want you to forget me...I have a terrible feeling that you will." He looked down as he said that last sentence.

I couldn't believe he would say such a thing. How could I ever forget Tamaku? He knew that...right? It almost angered me. "Tamaku, I wouldn't forget you. Why did you say that?"

"Are you mad?" he said sheepishly.

"No, but I want to know why you would say that."

"I just know that forever is a long time. You won't ever see me or talk to me again...with so much war, gossip, and people in your world, there is no telling how long it will be until your memory of me will fade."

"Tamaku, how could I ever forget? I have never had an experience like this one before! Before this, I was just a normal kid that was scared of college and leaving friends. But now I found a place that I saved...and I found love."

"Well, you know what they say: nobody ever forgets their first love." He locked eyes with mine as he reached for my hand. "Why do all good things come to an end?" he complained more than asked.

"I think it's because where there is love there is opposition; where there is light there is a shadow; and where there is kindness there is hate. With opposition, we appreciate the positive more."

"You mean, it's like a balance. The greater the conflict...the greater the love." He then ran his fingers through my hair never once looking away from my eyes.

"Yeah...a balance." I smiled a very small smile. I doubt he even noticed. By my surprise, he quickly scooped me up and on his back. I screamed out of joy as he did.

"What are you doing," I giggled.

"I want to show you something!" he shouted as his sprouted his wings and darted into the air. The adrenalin pumped the higher we went. I couldn't control my laughing and giggling. I had never been so happy and excited.

"Where are we going?" I shouted over the roar of the wind passing by.

"You'll see, soon" he said blissfully.

After flying for a few minutes, I was dying to know what it was. Then I noticed his speed slow and his altitude descend. Before I knew it, we were on the ground. We landed on a large field that had the greenest grass I had ever seen. It seemed musical, the way the blue of the sky and the green of the ground blended. There were no trees or flowers in sight. Just miles and miles of grass spread into the horizon. The wind was blowing, causing ripples to form on the grass.

I turned to Tamaku who was lingering behind me. "Tamaku, this is gorgeous!"

"Yes, but what I wanted to show you is just beyond these plains."

I gave him a confused glare. "What do you mean? It seems like there is no end to these plains!"

He leaned down closer to me and kissed my cheek and tapped my nose. He stood behind me with his hands on my shoulders. "You barely looked at the beauty in front of you. Look closer," he said gently.

I did as he said. I peered all around but saw nothing but grass. I didn't get it. I decided to glance it over one last time. That is when I saw it in the distance. It was a piece of paper that was folded in half and had a Scarlet ribbon tied around it. I paced towards it. It was a miracle that the wind didn't blow it away. I looked back at Tamaku before opening it. He was smiling small and nodded his head once. I returned my gaze back to the paper. As I opened it, I noticed it was a letter addressed to me.

Dear Scarlet,

It's Tamaku! If you're reading this, odds are you have already killed Taurid and I brought you to this field☺. Okay, you are probably wondering what this is all about but you will love it! But before your actual surprise, I told everybody to write down whatever they wanted to say to you. It's everyone's own personal letter to you. Enjoy it!

Hey Scarlet, it's me, Toki! Okay, I just wanted to tell you that I am so proud that you defeated Taurid! From the moment I first saw you, I knew Audren's fate was sealed in our favor. Tamaku is such a loser for making me write this letter, right? Don't worry, I am just joking. I'm glad that I get to tell you that I love you and that I only wish the best for you and wherever the future takes you. Always remember Audren and its entire people. I love you, Scarlet.

Scarlet! It's Omi! Congratulations! I knew you could do it! I am proud to know that the warrior you have grown into has finally come alive! Thanks to you, every curse Taurid has bestowed is now lifted! You know what that means, right? I NO LONGER HAVE TO

STAY LOOKING LIKE AN ELEVEN YEAR OLD! Yes, I will finally look my age! I can't thank you enough for all your help! This place desperately needed you, and now we have smelled the sweet scent of freedom!

Hi, Scarlet! It's Roke, and I wanted to tell you that you're the older sister I never really had (Piper's such a pain). I am super happy that you won. You are so cool. I think you're really pretty, too.

Scarlet, you are so cool! It's Piper, and I love you! You are my best friend and I'm really happy! I knew all along you would do it, and now, I'm going to be just like you! I'm going to beat up bad guys and still be really cute! Thanks, Varcia.

Great Job, Scarlet! It's Conch! I knew you had it in you! You re my ultimate hero! I think I'm going to start practicing all those amazing moves you do! Villains, here I come!

I felt tears streaming down my cheeks. I had no idea how Tamaku put this all together. It was so nice. I had no idea everyone thought so highly of me. Even though some were no longer alive, it felt as if I could feel their love. But then I noticed one more thing at the very bottom of the paper.

Look up.

I didn't understand. How *did* Tamaku put this all together? But I did as the note said. I looked up...

As I did, the tears poured from my eyes harder than ever. I immediately ran as fast I could. There they were in the distance! Everyone was there waving. They all had smiles on their faces as I got closer. The first one I hugged was Toki. She was absolutely beautiful! She no longer had any cuts or bruises, she looked perfect! As I hugged her, she embraced me tightly and she had the sweet smell of lilac. She wore a pink sundress and her hair shined as it flowed in the warm breeze.

I then hugged Conch. He looked just as he did before; not a burn in sight. I hugged him tightly and he laughed. I then moved on to Piper and Roke. They were smiling wide and my tears still flowed. But I was not crying out of sorrow, but out of joy! I squeezed them tight.

Then, finally, I hugged Omi. I hugged him the tightest. But as I looked at him, he was no longer the small water flair I had met. He was now taller. I had to look up at him as he looked down toward me with a handsome, strong face. His physique was no longer lanky and child-like. It was now toned and mature.

I then backed up a little still with a smile. "But...how are you guys all here? I thought..."

"It's because you killed him," said Toki as she walked closer.

"Yes," added Omi in a booming low voice. He had really matured. "Since his life has been destroyed, our lives have been renewed." He then looked up into the sky smiled. The innocent blood that was shed in this lifetime are no longer lost memories, but are instead here again."

I smiled but then I thought of something. Where was my mother then? It was because of Taurid that she is dead. "Where is Kiley, my mom?" I asked.

"She was born over four hundred years ago. Only those that would still be alive today are here again. It is all based on time and time only. Unfortunately for Kiley, she was lost in time itself," he replied.

"I'm so sorry, Scarlet," said Toki sympathetically.

"No, I'm okay." I fell silent for a second. "But I am so glad to see you all here! Words can't explain how hard I took your loss. And I'm glad to see Roke and Piper, too."

Piper then ran to me and jumped in my arms. Her force caused me to fall back into the grass. We both laughed. But then I thought. *This just made it that much harder to leave...but I knew I had to.*

Piper laid her head on my chest. "I'm going to really miss you, Scarlet."

"Scarlet, we all will," added Toki.

I sat up and turned to look at Tamaku. He was looking down obviously disturbed by the conversation. I wanted to stay and he knew that. I looked back at everyone else. They just stared back at me with the same longing for me to stay with them.

Then I felt a hand on my shoulder. "Scarlet, it's about time to leave now." It was Tamaku. I let down Piper gently. I held back the tears that were fighting to escape. I knew I had to be strong.

"Okay," I said to him. I then turned back to everyone. It was Omi that I approached. I needed to make sure I made some sort of restitution for his death.

"Omi, I am really-"

"It's alright, Scarlet." His eyes were soft and gentle as he looked down at me. Then, he wrapped his large arms around me and squeezed tightly. "Take care," his words were shaky. It seemed as though he was crying.

Then, one after another, everyone joined in one last hug. I couldn't fight back tears now. I didn't care either. *Nothing is worse than leaving friends...nothing.*

Then after everyone said their final good-byes, Tamaku took hold of my hand and I climbed on his back one last time. I turned to look at everyone once more, then, we took off.

The ride was silent. I didn't know what to say. Was there anything *to* say? I gazed down at Tamaku's wings, stroking them gently admiring their beauty. I looked up at the sky. It was still painted blue and the clouds were white as snow. My hair flowed in the wind loosely. I closed my eyes just to capture the feeling of open flight. Never again would I experience it.

When I opened my eyes, I noticed we were hovering over the beach's crystal blue water. Then, we landed onto the sandy shore. The sun beamed down causing the sediment to sparkle. Hearing the waves crashing behind me and the squawking of seagulls made me want to burst in tears again but...I was afraid I had no more tears left.

I walked the edge of the shore, staring at the water. I then sat down in a fetal position; I took my shoes off and placed my toes at the edge of the low tide. I set my chin on my knees and just watched. It wasn't too long until Tamaku joined me having one arm around me, placing my jacket and smartphone next me. I looked at him without turning my head, still silent. I just studied his perfect face. I studied every inch carefully scoping his jaw line and cheek bones. His black hair was just barely moving in the wind. He continued staring at the ocean.

"So what will you do now?" I asked.

"What do you mean?"

"Well...you're bound to find another girl you will fall in love with..."

"Remember what we said earlier today...you can never forget your first love. And I think...no one will ever surpass your first love either, especially when it is a beautiful, smart, and funny girl." He pinched my nose playfully. We laughed half-heartedly and he looked ahead again. "You have to remember...I'm always going to miss you...no matter who comes into my life."

"You know I want to beg for you to stay, right?" he continued, holding my hand against his chest.

I inched closer to him. I was sitting with my legs in Indian style and he was as well. We faced each other with barely any space in between us. Our knees were already touching.

"This is my first time ever being in love," he said. "I have never had a girl steal my heart. I always thought my heart belonged to one thing; Audren. Never did I think I would fall in love. Every time I'm around you my heart races...but it's the best feeling in the world.

"I always thought it was silly when Toki would come home talking about love and the many feelings that come along with it. I always thought that love had no place for me. I always felt as if I was on the outside and would never find anyone to give my heart to." He looked down but didn't seem to be looking at anything. He seemed to just be smiling dimly. "But now I know that there are people in the world that I will want to talk about all the time. There is a person that I want to dance around just thinking of them. I want to give this person all my attention and all my heart. A person I would never get tired of, no matter how much I see them. Love is so amazing.

"Scarlet, that's how I feel about you. Just the sound of your voice makes me want to just smile and laugh. Whenever we touch, I feel like shouting to the heavens about how much I love you. Every time I hear your name, I feel myself sweat just a little. I have never lost those butterflies in my stomach from the moment I saw you in person. You are all I think about, every night when I go to bed, and the next morning when I rise. You are in my dreams, in my mind, just everywhere! When we are apart, I feel like my internal self is gone as well. You are a part of me. I don't think you understand how I really feel. I want you to know that this is so hard for me. I feel as though you were created just for me and I for you; but now that you are leaving..."

He was crying. Yet not the same as I had seen him cry before. I held his head and placed it against my chest as I laid my head on top of his. I could feel the dampness of his tears. I was speechless. I didn't know what to say. All that I could hear was the crashing of waves.

"Tamaku, I...wish..."

He then lifted his head revealing his tears. He placed his forehead against mine and closed his eyes. "If you listen closely, you can hear my heart beating." He lifted my hand and placed it on his chest. I could feel and hear his heart thumping rapidly.

Could he hear mine?

But then I realized the whole point of why he was doing this is so that I could see that our hearts were beating at the exact same pace. It took a moment to take it all in. I breathed in his sweet scent. I felt his heart beat.

"I feel desolate for falling in love with someone that was never promised to stay," he whispered. "But...I don't regret a thing. I couldn't help but fall in love with you." He smiled but just barely. I couldn't hold back a small grin...accompanied with tears.

Then, we stared at each other. Studying each other's every feature. My guess is that we wanted to memorize them. I never wanted to forget his face. I loved him so much. Though I couldn't put it into words the way he did...but in a way, the way he described his love for me is exactly how I would describe my love for him. I know we sound like obsessive teens, but that's just the way love is sometimes. It's the best feeling in the world.

Without looking away, he slowly lifted his hand. I then lifted mine slowly. Our palms then were against each other, steadily intertwining our fingers lightly. We did the same with our opposite hands. Then we placed our hands lower, still together. I felt my heart rate skyrocket. We shared a kiss. I don't even think I have all the words to fully explain it. It was gentle...soft...placid...and...it was our last. I pulled him into a hug. I embraced him tightly as he did the same. It would be the last time I would smell his scent, the last time our lips would collide. I didn't want to pull away. I could no longer hear the sound of the ocean. If I could have stayed like that forever, I wouldn't mind.

But that is when it happened. Behind me, I heard a booming sound and wind picking up violently.

Tamaku stood up and held his hand out for me. I stood up feeling my throat tighten just by his touch. I looked at the door that was floating in midair. It was surrounded by gusts of wind.

"You have to hurry, Scarlet. The portal won't stay open very long," Tamaku warned as we rushed to the door that was slowly opening.

I could feel the tears again. Then, there formed five stone stairs leading to the now fully opened door. A beautiful white light shined brilliantly lighting on everything in its path. Tamaku walked me to the edge of the stairs then prompted me to walk up them. I did so until I reached the top stair. I didn't move at first. I was having second thoughts.

"Scarlet, you must not hesitate, you have to go," he shouted over the whistling and roaring of the wind.

The tears were streaming. His were, too. I didn't move and neither did he. We saw each other's tears and we both started wiping them away with the backs of our hands. I could hear the door beginning to close. I knew I had to go at that moment.

# Chapter 41

## BACK AGAIN

"Scarlet, wake up!" I heard a loud voice.

I gave out a yawn and slowly squinted my eyes open. "Wha..." I could barely speak.

"Dude, wake up already! We're going to be late for Science! You heard what Mr. Kowalski said yesterday, if anyone of us is late to his class again, we will have detention while all the other seniors go to the beach!"

I could still barely see. "Ryan?"

"Of course it's me, who else would it be? Come on! This is the third time I tried to wake you up!"

"Dude, Scarlet, you're still in your uniform. Did you even shower last night?" asked Matt as he walked to my bed running a comb through his wet hair. "That's gross, man."

"Wait, you mean, I was here yesterday?" I asked as I sat up. I had been gone for twelve days. They weren't even concerned about where I was?

"Scarlet, stop kidding around," Ryan scolded as he shoved a tooth brush in my mouth and tossed fresh clothes on my lap. "We only have 10 minutes and you still need to pack your bag. And don't even think about spending forever on your hair."

What happened? Why does everything seem so normal? I noticed that I still had my uniform on. Where was the white dress I was wearing? My laptop is exactly where I left it when I left. Was my whole Audren adventure just a dream?

"What are you waiting for, Scarlet? Get dressed!" snapped Ryan as he took the toothbrush from my mouth.

"Can you guys at least turn your heads or something?" I said, gurgling toothpaste.

They both exchanged wide eyed looks and immediately covered their faces. I changed quickly. I stood up and told them it was okay to look again. I was still a little shaken that my whole journey seemed so real but turned out to only be a dream.

"Okay, so are we ready?" Matt asked me as he tossed me my book bag.

Before I could open my mouth, "Yes! Now can we please go?" Ryan said.

"Alright," Matt said as they headed out the door. "Scarlet, kill those lights, would ya?" he said from the hall.

I stood there for a moment. I still could not contemplate how this was all a dream. I casually looked down and noticed that my locket was gone. That was creepy, but I wasn't fully convinced. I turned off the lights and walked out the door. I reached in my pocket for my spare key, but I found something else....

I pulled it out immediately, and my heart raced at the sight. In my hand, I held Tamaku's Airos Pipe. I knew it wasn't a dream! I started to feel happy, but then I remembered that I would never see Tamaku or anyone else from Audren again.

I locked the dorm room door and walked down the hall to catch up with Matt and Ryan. I placed the pipe in my bag and vowed myself that I would never speak of anything having to do with Audren until I was older and wiser. I figured I would just live my life as if my fairy tale simply never took place.

Chapter 42

PRESENTLY SPEAKING

It's been eight years since I've seen Audren. Talking about an adventure! That was one for sure; and it all happened in twelve days. Even as I share it with you it seems really surreal. Not only did life as I knew it change drastically, but I don't even know if I really expect you to believe it.

I do still keep in contact with all my friends from the academy. Ryan is married and currently working as the C.E.O of a major international software company (who knew) and Matt, well he just proposed to his girlfriend of 2 years. In fact, he developed a cure for a rare autoimmune disease about 3 years ago. The pharmaceutical trails were astounding. He is making national and international news as young Nobel Peace Prize winner. I am so proud of both of them.

As for me, I am well. I make it my business to remain busy and trust me graduate school is definitely ensuring that I maintain my "busy" goal. I do still think about my adventure in Audren. It's not every day, but what I have learned is that every time I look at that Airos Pipe, the memories return vividly. Even now I can see and hear the day Tamaku discovered my smartphone. I can barely hear that rap song and not think of him.

Tamaku said all those years ago...*you never forget your first love.* Sometimes I wonder if I will ever see him again. I know that humans cannot go back and forth between the human and the Audrenian realm, but then again, I am half Audrenian...

THE END

Tiana E. Williams

Winky Publishing

winkypublishing@yahoo.com

Made in the USA
Lexington, KY
13 September 2016